## Also by Simon Brett

A SHOCK TO THE SYSTEM
DEAD ROMANTIC
SINGLED OUT

## Mrs. Pargeter Novels

A NICE CLASS OF CORPSE
MRS. PRESUMED DEAD
MRS. PARGETER'S PACKAGE
MRS. PARGETER'S POUND OF FLESH
MRS. PARGETER'S PLOT
MRS. PARGETER'S POINT OF HONOUR

## Short Stories

A BOX OF TRICKS
CRIME WRITERS AND OTHER ANIMALS

## Charles Paris Novels

CAST, IN ORDER OF DISAPPEARANCE
SO MUCH BLOOD
STAR TRAP
AN AMATEUR CORPSE
A COMEDIAN DIES
THE DEAD SIDE OF THE MIKE
SITUATION TRAGEDY
MURDER UNPROMPTED
MURDER IN THE TITLE
NOT DEAD, ONLY RESTING
DEAD GIVEAWAY
WHAT BLOODY MAN IS THAT?
A SERIES OF MURDERS
CORPORATE BODIES
A RECONSTRUCTED CORPSE
SICKEN AND SO DIE
DEAD ROOM FARCE

# The Body on
# the Beach

—— *A Fethering Mystery* ——

## SIMON BRETT

BERKLEY PRIME CRIME, NEW YORK

THE BODY ON THE BEACH

A Berkley Prime Crime Book
Published by The Berkley Publishing Group,
a division of Penguin Putnam Inc.,
375 Hudson Street
New York, New York 10014

PRINTING HISTORY
Macmillan hardcover edition / 2000
Berkley Prime Crime hardcover edition / August 2000

ISBN 0-425-17500-6

Printed in the United States of America

**TO KEITH**
who knows this
part of the world
(and many others)

# The Body on
# the Beach

# 1

FETHERING IS ON the South Coast, not far from Tarring. Though calling itself a village, Fethering isn't what that word immediately brings to the minds of people nostalgic for an idealized, simpler England. Despite the presence of many components of a village—one church, one shop, one pub, one petrol station and a whole bunch of people who reckon they're the squire— Fethering is in fact quite a large residential conurbation.

The core is its High Street, some of whose flint-faced cottages date back to the early eighteenth century. The peasant simplicities of these buildings, sufficient for their original fishermen owners, have been enhanced by mains drainage, gas central heating, sealed-unit leaded windows, and very high price tags.

Out from the High Street, during the last century and a half, have spread, in a semicircle whose diameter is the sea, wave after wave of new developments. The late Victorians and Edwardians added a ring of solid, respectable family homes. Beyond these, in the 1930s, an arc of large, unimaginative slabs sprang up, soon to be surrounded by an infestation of bungalows. In the post-war period some regimented blocks of council housing were built in an area to the north of the village and named, by planners devoid of irony, Downside. Then in the late 1950s there burgeoned an expensive, private estate of vast houses backing on to the sea. This compound, called Shorelands, was circumscribed by stern walls and sterner regulations. From that time on, stricter planning laws and a growing sense of its own exclusivity had virtually stopped any further development in Fethering.

The roads into the village are all regularly interrupted by speed humps. Though tourism plays a significant part in the local economy, strangers to the area are never quite allowed to feel welcome.

Because of its seaside location, the village boasts a Yacht Club, a cluster of seafront cafés and a small but tasteful amusements arcade. During the winter, of these the Yacht Club alone remains open, and to members only. But open all the year round along the front are the rectangles of glass-sided shelters, havens by day to swaddled pensioners killing a little time, and by night to amorous local teenagers. In spite of the overpowering gentility of the area, and ferociously deterrent notices about vandalism, the glass of the shelters gets broken on a regular basis.

Fethering is set at the mouth of the Fether. Though called a "river," it would be little more than a stream but for the effects of the tides, which twice a day turn a lethargic trickle into a torrent of surprising malevolence. A sea wall, stretching out beyond the low-water mark, protects the beach from the Fether's turbulence. This wall abuts the Fethering Yacht Club, which controls access to the promenade on top. Only Yacht Club members, and some local fishermen who keep their blue-painted equipment boxes there, are allowed the precious keys which give access to this area. Against the wall, on the beachward side, is the cement ramp down which the boats of the Fethering Yacht Club flotilla reach the water.

The sea goes out a long way at Fethering, revealing a vast, flat expanse of sludge-coloured sand. When the tide is high, only pebbles show, piled high against the footpath and the wooden breakwaters that stretch out from it like the teeth of a comb. Between the path and the start of the houses, lower than the highest part of the beach, is a strip of tough, short grass. At spring tides, or after heavy rain, pools of water break up the green. The road which separates this grass from the start of the houses is rather imaginatively called Seaview Road.

At regular intervals along the beach are signs reading:

NO CYCLING AT ANY TIME

POOP SCOOP AREA

CLEAN IT UP.

Though hardly separated from the coastline sprawl of Worthing, Fethering believes very strongly in its own identity. People from adjacent areas even as close as Tarring, Ferring or Goring-on-Sea are reckoned to be, in some imprecise but unarguable way, different.

Fethering is its own little world of double-glazed windows and double-glazed minds.

Carole Seddon had always planned to retire there.

The cottage had been bought as a weekend retreat when she had both a job and a husband and, though now she had neither, she never regretted the investment.

Carole had enjoyed working for the Home Office. The feeling of having done something useful with her life fitted the values with which she had grown up, values which at times verged on the puritanical. Her parents had lived a life without frills; perhaps the only indulgence they had shown her was the slightly frivolous "e" at the end of her first name. So Carole felt she had earned a virtuous retirement—even though, she could never quite forget, it had come a little earlier than anticipated.

Ahead of her, she imagined, until time finally distressed her body beyond repair, lay perhaps thirty years of low-profile life. Her Civil Service pension was at the generous end of adequate; the mortgage was paid off; there would be no money worries. She would look after herself sensibly, eat sensibly, take plenty of long sensible walks on the beach, perform a few unheralded acts of local charity for such organizations as the Canine Trust and be, if not happy, then at least content with her lot.

Carole Seddon did not expect any changes in the rest of her life. She had had her steel grey hair cut sensibly short and protected her pale-blue eyes with rimless glasses which she hoped were insufficiently fashionable ever to look dated.

She bought a sensible new Renault, which was kept immaculately clean and regularly serviced, and in which she did a very low mileage. She had also acquired a dog called Gulliver, who was as sensible as a Labrador is capable of being, and she had kitted herself out with a sensible wardrobe, mostly from Marks & Spencer. Her only indulgence was a Burberry raincoat, which was well enough cut not to look ostentatious.

If her clothes were older than those usually worn by a woman in her early fifties, they represented sensible planning for the future. Carole was happy to look older than her age; that accorded with the image of benign anonymity she sought.

And someone who wished to slip imperceptibly into old age could not have chosen a better environment than Fethering in which to complete the process.

As she took her regular walk on the beach before it was properly light that Tuesday morning in early November, these were not, however, the thoughts going through Carole Seddon's brain. They were old thoughts, conclusions she had long ago reached and fixed in her mind; they never required reassessment.

But new, disturbing thoughts cut through the early-morning sounds, through the hiss of the gunmetal sea, the wheeze of the wind, the resigned complaint of the gulls, the crunch of sand and shingle on which Carole's sensible gumboots trod. The new thoughts centred round the woman who, the previous day, had arrived to take possession of the house next door. It was called Woodside Cottage, though there wasn't a wood in sight. But then Carole's own house was called High Tor and it was a good two hundred miles to the nearest one of those. That, however, was the way houses were named in Fethering.

Despite its High Street location, Woodside Cottage had been empty for some time. Buyers were put off by the amount of modernization the property required. Its former owner, an old lady of universal misanthropy, had been dead for eighteen months. Carole's initial neighbourly overtures, when she first started weekending in the area, had been snubbed with such ferocity that no further approaches had been made. This lack of contact, and the old lady's natural reclusiveness, had meant it was like living next door to an empty house. Death, turning that illusion into reality, had therefore made no difference to Carole.

But the prospect of having a real, living neighbour did make a difference. A potential variable was introduced into a life from which Carole Seddon had worked hard to exclude the unexpected.

She hadn't spoken to the newcomer yet. She could have done quite easily. The woman had been very much up and down her front path the previous day, the Monday, volubly ushering in and directing furniture-laden removal men. She had even engaged hitherto-unmet passers-by in conversation, exchanging cheery words with Fethering residents who, Carole knew, were deliberately taking the long route back from the beach to check out the new arrival.

Her name, the woman readily volunteered to everyone she spoke to, was "Jude." Carole's lips shaped the monosyllable with slight distaste. "Jude" had about it an over-casual air, a studied informality. Carole Seddon had never before had a friend called Jude and she wasn't about to start now.

The woman's relentless casualness was the reason why her neighbour hadn't engaged her in conversation. Though, as she sat by her open kitchen window, Carole had heard Jude's exchanges with other residents, she'd had no wish to be identified with the communal local nosiness. Her early-morning walk with Gulliver completed before the new resident and the removal vans arrived, she had had no further need to leave the house that day except for a quick midafternoon dog-relieving visit to the waste ground behind. Carole would find a more appropriate, more formal occasion on which to introduce herself to her new neighbour.

But she didn't see theirs ever becoming a close relationship. The newcomer's casualness extended to her dress, an assemblage of long skirts and wafty scarves, and also to her hair, blonde—blond*ed*, surely—and coiled into a loose bird's-nest, precariously pinned in place. That could, of course, have been a temporary measure, the hair pushed untidily out of the way of the inevitable dust generated by moving house, but Carole had a feeling it was the regular style. Jude, she knew instinctively, wasn't her sort of person.

She felt the prickle of small resistances building up within her. Carole Seddon had spent considerable time and energy defining her own space and would defend it against all encroachments.

She was shaken out of these sour thoughts by Gulliver's bark. The dog was down near the water's scummy edge, running round a bulky figure who was walking across the flat grey sand towards his mistress. This was surprising, given the early hour. There weren't many local walkers as driven and disciplined as Carole.

The figure was so hunched against the wind into a green shiny anorak that it could have been of either gender. But even if Carole had been able to see enough face to recognize someone of her acquaintance, she still wouldn't have stopped to talk.

There were social protocols to be observed on an early-morning walk along the beach at Fethering. When one met another human being—almost definitely proceeding in the opposite direction: everyone walked at the same pace; there was very little overtaking—it was bad form to give them no acknowledgement at all. Equally, to have stopped and engaged in lengthy conversation at that time in the morning would have been considered excessive.

The correct response therefore was "the Fethering Nod." This single, abrupt inclination of the head was the approved reaction to encounters with mild acquaintances, bosom friends, former lovers, current lovers and complete strangers. And its appropriateness did not vary with the seasons. The nod was logical in the winter, when the scouring winds and tightened anorak hoods gave everyone the face of a Capuchin monkey, and when any attempts at conversation were whisked away and strewn far across the shingle. But it was still the correct protocol on balmy summer mornings, when the horizon of the even sea was lost in a mist that promised a baking afternoon. Even then, to respond to anyone with more than "the Fethering Nod" would have been bad form.

For other times of day, of course, and other venues, different protocols obtained. Not to stop and chat with a friend met on an after-lunch stroll along the beach would have been the height of bad manners. And Fethering High Street at mid-morning was quite properly littered with gossiping acquaintances.

Such nuances of social behaviour distinguished the longtime residents of Fethering from the newly arrived. And it was the view of Carole Seddon that anyone privileged to join the local community should be humble enough to keep a low profile until they had mastered these intricacies.

From what she'd seen of the woman, she rather doubted whether "Jude" would, though.

Nor did the figure who passed her that morning seem aware of what was required. With an averted face and not even a hint of "the Fethering Nod," he or she deliberately changed course and broke into a lumbering— almost panicky—run up the steep shingle towards the Yacht Club.

Gulliver's barking once again distracted Carole. Quickly bored with the unresponsive figure in the anorak, the dog had rushed off on another of his pivotal missions to rid the world of seaweed or lumps of tar-stained polystyrene, and disappeared round the corner of a breakwater. Invisible behind the weed-draped wooden screen, he was barking furiously. Beyond him, the sea, having reached its twice-daily nadir, was easing back up the sand.

Carole wondered what it would be this time. Gulliver's "sensibleness" went only so far. A crushed plastic bottle or a scrap of punctured beach ball could suddenly, to his eyes, be transformed into a major threat to world peace. And, until forcibly dragged away, he would continue trying to bark the enemy into submission.

But that morning it wasn't a bottle or a scrap of beach ball that had set Gulliver off. As Carole Seddon saw when she rounded the end of the breakwater, it was a dead body.

# 2

HE WAS MAYBE in his fifties, though his pallor made it difficult to tell. The flesh of his face, framed by matted greying hair and the sharp separate stubble of a three-day beard, was bleached the pale beige of driftwood. It seemed to Carole a mercy that his eyes were closed.

His mouth, though, hung open. To the right of the bottom jaw, a tooth was missing. It had been missing a long time.

The inside of one exposed wrist was pockmarked with old and new scar tissue.

The body was hunched uncomfortably against a barnacled wooden stanchion of the breakwater. At first sight the man might have crawled there for protection, but the unnatural conformation of his limbs denied that supposition. He hadn't got there by his own efforts. He had been manipulated and abandoned by the sea.

His clothes—jeans and a grey jumper—were soaked heavy. The sea had borne away one of his trainers, exposing a poignantly vulnerable sports sock, ringed in blue and red. Laced round his upper body was an orange life-jacket, stamped in faded black letters "Property of Fethering Yacht Club."

Instinctively, Carole looked up towards the small white-balconied clubhouse at the top of the beach by the sea wall. In front of it, guarded by a stockade of white railings, were drawn up rows of sailing boats, securely covered for the winter. She knew that if she moved closer, she would be able to hear the incessant clacking of rigging against metal masts. But there'd be nobody at the club so early in the morning. The first-floor bar-room's dark expanse of window looked out blankly to the sea.

Despite his life-jacket, any theory that the man had been the victim of a sailing accident was belied by the two wounds in his neck. Washed blood-free by the sea, they were thin, like the lines of a butcher's cleaver in dead meat, exposing the darker flesh beneath.

Never for a moment did it occur to Carole Seddon that the man was not dead. She felt no urge to kneel by the body and feel for pulses. It wasn't just squeamishness. There was no point.

Anyway, it was better to leave the corpse undisturbed for the police to examine.

Carole was distracted by more barking. Having drawn her attention to it, Gulliver had immediately lost interest in the body. He'd found a supplanting fascination in the sea itself and was now trying to catch the waves, fighting them back with all the optimism of a canine Canute. He'd managed to soak his body through in the process.

One sharp call was enough to bring the dog to heel. He dissociated himself from the sea, looking round in-nocently as if he'd only just noticed its vast expanse.

Carole stood back as he shook the tell-tale brine out of
his coat. Then he rolled over in a mass of seaweed and
something else more noxious. Carole registered dully
that Gulliver would need a bath when they got home.

She gave one last look to the dead man by the breakwater, then started resolutely up the beach, Gulliver trot-
ting maturely at her side.

It was only half-past seven when they got back to High
Tor. Carole had woken early that morning, slow to adjust to the recent change from summertime, and got up
briskly, as she always did. Thinking too much at the
beginning of the day could so easily become brooding.
It had been dark, the night's full moon invisible, when
she and Gulliver left for their walk, and it was still
gloomy when they returned, the kind of November day
that would never get properly light. And never warm up
either.

Carole bathed the dog before calling the police,
splashing him down with a hose outside the back door.
She knew, if she didn't, the house would smell of rotting
seaweed for weeks. Gulliver never made a fuss about
being bathed. He seemed positively to enjoy the process.
Maybe it was the intimacy with his mistress he valued.
Carole Seddon was not given to sentimental displays,
least of all to animals, so Gulliver enjoyed the ration of
contact he received from the necessary scrubbing and
drying. In the cold weather she was particularly careful
to get the last drop of water out of his coat.

When the dog was shining clean and snuffling into
sleep by the Aga, and when Carole had mopped up the
inevitable wet footprints he had left on the kitchen floor,

it seemed natural for her to continue cleaning the kitchen. As a result, it was after nine before she went into the sitting room to confront the telephone.

She had gone through the walk back from the beach, as well as the mechanical processes of bathing Gulliver and cleaning the kitchen, without allowing herself to think about what she had seen. She had kept an equally tight control on her body, not permitting it the slightest tremor of reaction to the shock. As she had done frequently before in her life, Carole Seddon kept everything firmly damped down.

She dialled 999 and asked for the police. In simple, unemotional sentences, she gave them the necessary information. She described her actions precisely, the direction of her walk, the time she had returned, the fact that she had bathed her dog and cleaned the kitchen. She pinpointed the exact position where the body had been found and gave her considered estimate as to how long it would be before the returning tide reached that point. She gave her address and telephone number, and was unsurprised when told that someone would be round to talk to her.

Carole Seddon put the phone down and sat in an armchair. She did not collapse into an armchair. She sat in one.

And then she heard the strange noise from outside. Perhaps it had just started. Or it could have been going on unheard for some time, so intense had been her concentration on the task in hand.

The sound was a rhythmic dull thudding, something being hit repeatedly. Carole rose from her chair and moved tentatively towards the front-facing window. Through it, she saw Jude in the adjacent front garden.

Her new neighbour had spread a slightly threadbare rug over a structure of boxes and was beating it with a flat besom brush. Though still wearing a trademark long skirt, Jude had removed her loose-fitting top to reveal a bright yellow T-shirt. Her large bosom and chubby arms shuddered with the efforts of her carpet-beating. In spite of the cold, her cheeks were red from the exercise.

Carole's instinctive reaction was one of disapproval. There was something old-fashioned in Jude's carpet-beating. The scene could have come from a film of back-to-back terraced houses in the 1930s. *Northern* terraced houses. The possibility, suddenly occurring to Carole, that Jude might come from "the North" prompted a visceral recoil within her. "The North" still conjured up images of unwanted intimacy, of people constantly "dropping in," of back doors left unlocked to facilitate this "dropping in." It wasn't the kind of thing that happened in Fethering.

Back doors were kept firmly locked. Approaches to people's houses were made strictly from the front. And, except for essential gardening and maintenance, the only part of a front garden that was used was the path. Even if the space caught the evening sun, no one would dream of sitting in their front garden. And it certainly wasn't the proper place to do anything domestic, like beating a carpet. Passers-by, seeing someone engaged in such activities, might be forced into conversation.

In Fethering, except for chance meetings on the High Street, social encounters were conducted by arrangement. It was inappropriate to meet someone without having received planning permission. A prefatory phone call—ideally a couple of days before the proposed encounter—was the minimum requirement.

These thoughts were so instinctive that they took no time at all to flash through Carole Seddon's mind, but they still took long enough to allow something appalling to happen. Jude, taking a momentary respite from her efforts with the besom, had turned and caught sight of her neighbour framed in the window. Eye contact was unavoidable.

For Carole then to have repressed a half-smile and little flap of the hand would have been the height of bad manners. Her minimal gesture was reciprocated by a huge wave and a cheery grin.

If she had left the contact there, Carole knew she would have appeared standoffish. And, though standoffish she undoubtedly was, she had no wish to appear so. She found her hand and face doing a little mime of "I'll come out and say hello."

"My name's Carole Seddon. Welcome to Fethering. If there's anything I can do to help out, please don't hesitate to tell me."

"Thanks very much." Carole found her hand grasped and firmly shaken. "My name's Jude."

"Yes . . ." Carole awaited the gloss of a surname, but wasn't given one. "You'll find we're a friendly lot round here," she lied.

"Good." Jude chuckled. It was a warm, earthy sound. "I get along with most people. Most people do, don't they?"

Carole granted this alien concept a thin smile. "Well, if I can tell you where things are . . . shops, drycleaners, you know . . . I'm only next door, so just ask."

"Thanks. I'm sure I'll find my way around pretty quickly."

"Mm . . ." Carole found the openness of Jude's dreamy brown eyes slightly disconcerting.

"Equally," her neighbour said, "if there's anything I can do to help you out, you'll say, won't you?"

Carole nodded at this token offer with gratitude, however incongruous might be the idea of her suddenly turning for assistance to someone she didn't know. The woman had only just moved to Fethering, for goodness' sake. Any support being offered should go from the established resident to the newcomer, not the other way round.

Surely Jude didn't imagine her neighbour was about to confide in her? Carole was hardly likely suddenly to start spilling the beans to a stranger about what she'd seen on the beach. But even as she had the thought, she was surprised how much she did want to talk about the shock she had received that morning. And there was something in those brown eyes that invited confidences.

"Anyway"—Carole shook herself back on track— "better get on. Things to do."

"Yes." Jude grinned easily. "Me too. House is crammed full of boxes. God knows how long it'll take me to sort it all out."

"Moving's always a nightmare."

"Still, I can do it at my own pace. No hurry."

Carole smiled as if she endorsed this view. But she didn't. Of course there was a hurry. One couldn't live in mess. One had an obligation to get one's house tidy as soon as possible. If people weren't aware of the necessity for hurry in life, society would break down completely.

"See you soon then." Jude gave a relaxed wave and hefted her besom for a renewed assault on the carpet.

"Yes. Yes," said Carole, turning in slight confusion back towards her front door.

Inside the house, she berated herself for how little solid fact she had got out of the conversation. She wasn't that interested, of course, but there were things one ought to know about a new neighbour.

She hadn't even elicited a surname, for goodness' sake. Jude. Just Jude. That wasn't very satisfactory. And then again, what was the woman's status? What was her age? Was she married, single, divorced? Was there a regular man on the scene? Carole realized that, uncharacteristically, she hadn't even checked out Jude's ring finger. Something compelling about those big brown eyes made it difficult to divert one's gaze elsewhere.

Did Jude have a job? A private income? A pension? Carole knew none of these things. Not that she was interested, but it was the kind of information that might be important at some stage.

Good heavens, Carole realized, she hadn't even found out whether or not Jude came from "the North."

# 3

"SO WHY WERE you walking on that part of the beach, Mrs. Seddon?"

Carole didn't like Detective Inspector Brayfield's tone. She was the one who'd reported the body, after all. If anything, she deserved congratulation. Certainly not this hint of suspicion in her interrogator's voice.

Also, why were there two of them? Not just the Inspector in his almost dandyish single-breasted black suit. There was also the uniformed WPC, Juster, who hadn't said much but was clearly taking everything in. She sat on a straight-backed chair, tensely alert. Was there some new directive that the police always had to work in twos, even for routine inquiries? Maybe it was a gender thing. Allegations of sexual harassment would not be risked if a male police officer was never left alone with a female witness.

But the explanation didn't seem adequate. Carole still had the feeling that their encounter was adversarial, as if the police were expecting more from her than mere corroboration of what she'd already said over the telephone. She had dealt with a great many police officers in the course of her work at the Home Office but had never before felt this aura of mistrust.

"I always go for an early-morning walk along the beach. I have a dog." Gulliver hadn't provided a visual aid when the police arrived. He was still sleeping off his walk at the foot of the Aga. As a guard dog he was hopeless. His first instinct was not to deter entry, but to give any new arrival at the house a fulsome welcome. "And I always take my dog on the beach first thing."

" 'First thing' was rather early this morning, wasn't it, Mrs. Seddon? Can hardly have been light when you set off."

"I woke early. It always takes me a bit of time to adjust when the clocks change."

"I understand," said the Inspector, who clearly didn't. "So why did you go to that particular part of the beach this morning?"

"It wasn't a *particular* part of the beach. It was just where I happened to be walking." Exasperated by the scepticism in Detective Inspector Brayfield's eye, Carole went on. "There are only two directions in which you can go along the beach. Off Seaview Road there's a path which goes down by the Yacht Club. At the end of that you're on the beach and you have the choice of turning left or turning right. Left you go virtually straight into the sea wall, so this morning, like most mornings, I decided to turn right."

She wasn't meaning to sound sarcastic, but she knew that's how the words were coming out.

"For any particular reason?"

What was it with that word "particular?" "No," Carole snapped. "For no particular reason."

"Are you sure you're all right?" It was WPC Juster this time, her voice showing the professional concern of someone who's done a counselling course.

"Yes, I'm quite all right, thank you!" Why were they treating her like some semi-invalid?

"How old are you, Mrs. Seddon?" Juster went on.

"I don't really see that it's any business of yours, but I'm fifty-three."

"Ah," said the WPC.

"Ah," the Inspector echoed, as if that explained everything.

What was this—some kind of medical assessment? Had they written her off as a menopausal hysteric? Surely not. She had told them everything in a manner that was unemotional to the point of being dull. What were they trying to insinuate?

Though these questions ran through her mind, being Carole Seddon, of course she didn't voice any of them. Instead, she took the initiative. "Presumably," she said, "when a body like that is found, it's photographed *in situ* first, and then taken off for forensic examination?"

Detective Inspector Brayfield, stroking the knot of his brightly coloured silk tie, agreed that that would be the normal procedure. But he wasn't to be deflected from his dissection of her story.

"You say there were cuts on the man's neck and scar tissue on the inside of his wrist?"

"Yes."

"Which might suggest he had been an intravenous drug user?"

"Quite possibly."

"Do you know much about intravenous drug users, Mrs. Seddon?"

"No, I don't. But I do know enough to recognize that that was a possible explanation of the scars."

"From things you've seen on television?"

"I suppose so, yes."

Brayfield nodded, as if this too was of profound relevance. Then he said, "Could we just recap once again exactly what happened this morning?"

"Oh, for heaven's sake!" She couldn't help herself. But, feeling the intense scrutiny of the two police officers after her outburst, she took a deep breath before saying, "Yes, yes, of course."

"Was there anyone else around on the beach this morning when you took your walk?"

"Apart from the dead body?"

"Apart indeed from the dead body. Do you recall seeing anyone else?"

"No, I don't think I did . . ." She screwed up her eyes with the effort of recapturing the scene. "Ooh yes, yes, there was someone."

Carole was aware of WPC Juster tautening in her chair and realized how guilty she must sound, first forgetting, then remembering. But she was damned if she was going to feel guilty. She had nothing to feel guilty about. She was just doing her duty as a public-spirited citizen. Never again, though. Next time she found a dead body, she'd walk away and leave some other unfortunate passer-by the task of breaking the news to the police.

"So who was this?" asked Detective Inspector Brayfield evenly. "Who did you see?"

"It was someone in a shiny green anorak with the hood tied up tight. They were walking into the wind, you see. They hurried straight past me."

"Hurried?"

"Almost ran."

"Uh-huh. And was it a man or a woman?"

"I couldn't tell."

"Really?" Though deliberately ironing out the intonation, he still couldn't remove the last wrinkle of scepticism. "You didn't speak to this person?"

"No. I just gave them a nod."

"And did they speak to you?"

"No."

"Or give you a nod?" Carole shook her head. "That's
a pity, isn't it?"

"Why?"

"Well, obviously if we had any means of tracking
down this other person on the beach, then we might have
another witness of your dead body, mightn't we?"

"Yes."

"Which might be very useful." Before Carole had
time to say anything, the Inspector moved abruptly on.
"So you came straight back here from the beach?"

"As I told you, yes."

"But before calling the police, you bathed your dog?"

"Yes."

"Why?"

"Because he was covered with seaweed and soaked
with saltwater. If I hadn't given him a bath, the whole
house'd smell."

"Hm. And then, after washing the dog, you cleaned
your kitchen." The Inspector ran a hand over his chin,
as if checking the quality of his morning's shave. "You
don't often find dead bodies on the beach, do you, Mrs.
Seddon?"

"No, of course I don't!"

"So, given the fact that it's an unusual—and probably

rather a shocking—thing to happen to you, can you understand why I'm surprised that you bathed your dog and did some of your housework before reporting it?"

"I can see that, with hindsight, it may sound rather odd, but at the time it seemed the perfectly logical thing to do."

"Did it?"

"Maybe I was in shock. Maybe I needed to do something mechanical, something mundane, to calm myself down."

"Or maybe, Mrs. Seddon, you just needed time to work things out."

"Work what out?"

"What you were going to say when you rang the police."

"I didn't need to work that out. I just had to say exactly what I'd seen."

"The body on the beach?"

"Precisely."

"And to direct us to where that body was lying?"

"Yes."

"Well, Mrs. Seddon, everything you've told us this morning makes perfect sense."

"I'm glad to hear it."

"We followed your directions to the letter. They were very clear." Carole nodded in acknowledgement of the compliment. "We went down to the breakwater you described and everything was absolutely fine . . . *except* for one small detail."

"And what was that?"

"When we got to the breakwater, there was nothing there. There was no body on the beach, Mrs. Seddon."

# 4

CAROLE SEDDON FELT upset after the police's departure. They had come to the house with an agenda; their semaphore of little nods and eyelid flickers had been prearranged. Having arrived believing her to be a hysterical attention seeker, nothing she could say was going to make them leave with any change in their attitude.

That's what hurt—that they had thought her anything less than sensible. Throughout her career in the Home Office, Carole Seddon had prided herself on being a safe pair of hands. Male colleagues had paid her the ultimate compliment of appearing unaware of her gender. Even at times of crisis, when she returned to work after the birth of her son, when her marriage to David was turning horribly sour, she had never let her emotions show in her professional life.

And here she was faced with a detective and a WPC being *understanding* about her mental state.

There was nothing wrong with her mental state. Certainly nothing wrong with her hormonally. What stage she was at with her menopause was nobody's business but her own. And yet the attitude of the two police officers had undermined her confidence. She knew she wasn't a hysteric, but the fact that someone could imagine her to be a hysteric upset the carefully maintained equilibrium of her life.

The unease didn't dissipate during the course of the day. She went through the motions of her normal routine. Did a bit of housework for the rest of the morning. Forced down some soup and a hunk of granary bread at lunchtime, then settled to the regular mental aerobics of the *Times* crossword. But her brain was sluggish, slow to dissect words into their component parts, slow to make connections between them. She completed one corner, but could fill in only a few stragglers on the rest of the grid. The crossword, usually finished within half an hour, was set aside for completion later in the day.

Round four, she took Gulliver out for a shorter walk, through the back gate to do his business in the rough ground behind the row of cottages. Jude and her carpet were no longer in their front garden, but, Carole noted with disapproval, the structure of boxes still was. Her new neighbour would have to learn. People in Fethering didn't leave anything in their front gardens, except for staddlestones, tasteful statuary and—in one rather regrettable instance—gnomes.

Gulliver seemed to have caught his mistress's mood, sloping along by her side with none of his usual frenetic attacks on invisible windmills. The light too was depressing. True to its early promise, the day had never felt like day, and its leaden sky was now thickening into a November night. The cold stung her exposed cheeks and she shivered. Her circulation hadn't got properly going all day.

Still Carole Seddon couldn't lose the unpleasant aftertaste of her morning's visitation by the police.

Despite the sour mood they'd engendered, the thought did not for a moment occur to her that she might be in the wrong. There was no doubt that she had seen the body on the beach. The fact that the police hadn't found it was down either to their incompetence or—more likely—to the interference of some outside agency. Maybe they'd taken too long, arriving after the tide had come in far enough to move the body on. Maybe someone had moved it deliberately.

Once the body had been found—as she knew it would be—Carole Seddon was determined to get a very full apology from the West Sussex Serious Crimes Squad. Public-spirited citizens should not be treated like criminals.

Though the prospect of receiving some ultimate moral compensation was a comforting one, when she returned home Carole still felt unsettled. As she put on the lights and drew the curtains, she even asked herself if she was overreacting, if she actually *was* in an emotional state. Maybe a delayed response to the shock of seeing the dead body and to the implications of the wounds on its neck?

Uncharacteristically, she wanted to talk to someone about the whole incident. For a brief, irrational moment, she even contemplated confiding in her new neighbour. She couldn't forget the unusual quality of empathy she'd seen in those wide brown eyes.

But that was ridiculous. Even if Carole Seddon had been the kind of person who talked to her neighbours

about anything more weighty than the weather, she
didn't even know this woman.

These uncharacteristic thoughts were interrupted
when the doorbell rang.

She had received no early warning over the previous
couple of days. No acquaintance was due to come round
for tea. It must be someone selling something, Carole
concluded as she approached the front door. Probably
one of those men with a zip-up bag full of dishcloths,
oven gloves and plastic storage boxes who would flash
some laminated card of authorization. If it was, she'd
send him off with a flea in his ear. There was a consen-
sus view in Fethering that all such visitors were lookouts
for criminal gangs. Carole Seddon wasn't about to have
her joint cased for the benefit of burglars.

By the time she opened the door, she had built up a
healthy head of righteous steam against the expected
salesman and was surprised to be confronted by a thin,
haunted-looking woman she had never seen before.

"Did you find a body on the beach this morning?"

Now Carole knew why she had let the woman in. Her
instinct was always to get rid of unexpected callers—
particularly callers in grubby jeans and purple quilted
anoraks. But something in the woman's eyes had indicated that her visit was serious, maybe even important.
Carole had ushered her stiffly into the sitting room, sat
her down and waited till the reason for her presence was
explained.

Now she knew she'd done the right thing. In the same
armchair where Detective Inspector Brayfield had sat
that morning, disbelieving her story of having found a

body on the beach, here was a woman actually asking about her discovery.

"What makes you think I did?" Carole responded cautiously.

"I know you did." The voice was uneducated South Coast, not from the more discriminating purlieus of Fethering. "It was a woman with a beige raincoat and a Labrador," she went on. "You fit the description."

"Whose description?"

"Never mind that. Look, I know it was you, so we can cut out the bullshit."

Carole Seddon appraised the woman in front of her. The face had about it a deadness the colour and texture of papier mâché. The hair was flat and dull like tobacco. Only the eyes were alive, burning with a desperate energy.

"The police have been to see me this morning," said Carole evenly. "According to them, when they looked, there was no body on the beach."

"I'm not interested in the police. You know and I know there was a body on the beach this morning. Down at the end of the breakwater."

While it was gratifying to have her story corroborated, Carole still wanted to know where the woman had got her information. "Were you watching me? Was it you who I saw walking away from the body?"

"I didn't go on the beach this morning." The woman dismissed these irrelevant details and hurried on to what really concerned her. "Did you take something from the body? Something out of his jacket pocket?"

"No, I certainly didn't. I didn't touch it." Carole spoke with the affront of someone whose upbringing did not countenance theft, least of all from the dead.

"Are you sure?"

"Of course I'm sure!"

"Listen, it's important."

"It may be important, but the fact remains that I did not take anything from the body I found on the beach this morning!"

"There wasn't no knife?"

"Knife? I didn't see any knife."

This answer seemed to provide a moment of reassurance. The woman was silent, her eyes darting from side to side as she considered the next tack to take. "Do you know where it went?" she asked eventually.

"The body?"

"Of course the body."

"I've no idea."

"After you seen it, did you see anyone else go near it?"

"No. I went home and rang the police. And—as I've just told you—when they finally came to see me, they said they hadn't been able to find the body."

This news too seemed to reassure the woman, but only for a moment. Her tone changed. There was overt aggression in her next question. "What were you doing down on the beach, anyway?"

"I was taking my dog for a walk."

"Oh yes?" The woman could do scepticism just as well as Detective Inspector Brayfield. Then, abruptly, she asked, "Did the police say they'd come back?"

"To see me again? No."

"If they do come back, you're not to tell them anything about it."

Carole was getting exasperated. "About what, for God's sake?"

"About what you seen on the beach. About you see-ing anyone moving the body."

"I've told you! I didn't see anyone moving the body!"

"If you're lying and I find out you snitched to anyone about what you seen, there'll be trouble."

"What kind of trouble?" asked Carole, almost con-temptuously.

"This kind of trouble," said the woman with a new, sly menace in her voice.

As she spoke, she reached inside her quilted anorak and pulled out a gun.

# 5

CAROLE WAS TOO affronted to feel any fear. "Put that thing away!" she ordered. "What on earth do you think you're doing? This is Fethering, not Miami Beach."

The woman waved the gun threateningly. "You shut up! I think you'd better cooperate with me."

Carole rose from her seat and moved towards the telephone. "I'm going to call the police."

"Do that and I'll shoot you!"

The words stopped her in her tracks. Carole turned to look at the woman, assessing the risk of the threat being carried out.

Something she saw in the wild, darting eyes told her that the danger was real. The woman's expression wasn't natural. Perhaps she was under the influence of some drug. Indeed, that would make sense of her erratic behaviour since she'd arrived at the house. She wasn't entirely in control of her actions.

Which being the case, she was quite capable of using the gun. Carole returned silently to her seat.

"So tell me what you did see," the woman demanded.

"I didn't see anything other than what I've told you about."

Apparently coolness wasn't the best response. It seemed only to inflame the woman more. Waving the gun with increasing—and rather disturbing—abandon, she said, "Cut the crap. You're nothing in this. You get shot, it doesn't matter. So long as the police never find out who moved the body."

Her speech was slurring now, becoming something of a ramble. But that didn't make its content any less disturbing. Being shot by someone coherent or being shot by someone rambling didn't make a lot of difference, Carole realized. You were still dead.

"They'll never find out from me," Carole said calmly, "because I don't know who moved the body."

The woman looked puzzled. "Whose body? My son's body? My son's not dead." Then, with another worryingly casual wave of the gun, she slurred, "You could be lying."

"Yes, I could be, but I'm not."

"Does this gun frighten you?"

"Of course it does. I'm not stupid."

"Sometimes," the woman maundered on, "people get shot just to keep them quiet. To make sure they don't say anything."

This is ridiculous, thought Carole. I am sitting in my own sitting room—in Fethering of all places—and a woman I've never seen before is threatening to shoot me with a gun. People will never believe me when I tell them. On the other hand, of course, I may not be around to tell them.

Though her brain was working fast, her body was

paralysed. Carole could do nothing. The gun was still pointing straight at her and a new, dangerous focus had come into the woman's eyes when . . . the front doorbell rang.

There was a momentary impasse. Then the woman hissed, "Don't answer it."

"But everyone knows I'm here. The lights are on. If I don't answer, they'll get suspicious and call the police."

The barrel wavered while the woman weighed this up. Then she relented. Flicking the gun towards the door, she said, "See who it is. Don't invite them in, though."

"All right. I won't."

As she went towards the front door, Carole reflected wryly on Gulliver's qualities as a guard dog. Two people—one at least of whom was carrying a gun—had rung her front doorbell in the previous half-hour. And Gulliver hadn't even stirred from his cosy doze by the Aga.

Carole opened the front door. The frost had set in fiercely while she'd been indoors and the cold air scoured her face. In the cone of light spreading from the overhead lamp stood Jude. Her blonde hair was covered by a floppy hat and she appeared to be wearing some kind of poncho.

"Carole, hi. I wondered whether you fancied going down to the Crown and Anchor for a drink?"

Under normal circumstances, the knee-jerk response would have been, "No, thank you. I'm afraid I'm not a 'pub person.' " But the presence of a gun toting, possibly drug-crazed woman in her sitting room disqualified the circumstances from being normal. "Well . . ."

But that was all she had time to say. There was the clatter of a door behind her. Carole rushed back to find her sitting room empty. The sound of the back door slamming shut drew her through into the kitchen. That too was empty. From his position at the foot of the Aga, Gulliver looked up blearily. A real help, he was.

She moved with caution towards the window over the sink and peered into the encroaching darkness. There was no sign of the woman, but the gate at the end of the garden flapped open.

Carole turned back to see Jude framed in the kitchen doorway. That wasn't the Fethering way, her instincts told her. To come into someone's house without being invited, that wouldn't do at all.

"So what about a drink?" asked Jude casually.

To her surprise, Carole Seddon found her lips forming the words, "Yes. Yes, what a good idea."

# 6

CAROLE WASN'T A "pub person" and it was a long time since she had been to the Crown and Anchor. When they first bought the cottage, while she still had a husband, they had gone once or twice for a drink before Sunday lunch. But that period of cohabitation with David in Fethering hadn't lasted, and pub-going didn't seem appropriate to her single status. Except for a couple of visits on those rare occasions when her son came to see her, Carole hadn't stepped inside the Crown and Anchor for at least five years.

To someone who didn't know Fethering, it might seem strange that there was only one pub. Though the Crown and Anchor had been adequate for a fishermen's village, the residential sprawl that had developed seemed to demand more watering holes. But they had never appeared. The Victorians were puritanical about drinking and later residents had been drawn to Fethering by the attractions of its privacy rather than its communal amenities. When the Downside Estate developed, plans were submitted for a new pub up in that area, but traditionalist influences prevailed and the applications were repeatedly rejected. By then the residents of Fethering were determined to ring-fence their village and prevent further expansion of any kind.

Besides, a short country drive to the east, to the west, or north into the Downs gave access to a wide range of characterful hostelries. There was no need for more pubs in Fethering.

Carole certainly hadn't been in the Crown and Anchor since the new management took over. Though established for nearly three years, in Fethering they were still known as the "new" management. And even though there was only one of them, that one was always referred to as "they."

In fact, it was a "he," and he was one of the reasons why Carole hadn't been in the pub recently. Ted Crisp had arrived with a reputation, and since his arrival in the village it had been amplified by local gossip.

Carole knew him by sight. His hair was too long, he had a scruffy beard and shuffled around in jeans and sweat-shirts. She had from time to time vouchsafed the most minimal of "Fethering Nods" when meeting him in the village shop, but had never exchanged words. The reputation Ted Crisp carried did not endear him to her.

There was the drinking, for a start. An occupational hazard for publicans, everyone knew, but in Ted Crisp's case it was rumoured sometimes to get out of hand. Not all the time, to be fair, but every now and then he was said to go on major benders.

Reports of his behaviour towards women were also exchanged in hushed voices among the lady residents of Fethering. Though the village was hardly at the sharp end of the political-correctness debate, Ted Crisp's attitude was not approved of. It was one thing for a quaint elderly gentleman to call a lady "love" or chivalrously to tell her not to worry her pretty little head about things that didn't concern her. It was something else entirely for a man hardly even into middle age to make coarse comments of an overtly sexual nature.

And, according to Ted Crisp's burgeoning reputation, that was what he did. No doubt that kind of thing went down well enough with the younger women, who would snap back at him in kind. But then what did you expect from girls who thought nothing of going into pubs on their own? There was probably no objection from the older brassy divorcees in the village either. But sexual innuendo wasn't the sort of attention that someone of Carole Seddon's background and character would appreciate. Her state of shock might have driven her into the Crown and Anchor that evening, but that did not mean that she was about to engage in vulgar badinage with its landlord.

Jude appeared to be untrammelled by such inhibitions. With an, "I'll get these," she gestured Carole to a table, bustled up to the bar and greeted Ted Crisp as if she'd been a regular for years. Carole looked around the bar with some surprise. She'd expected something more garish, with flashing slot machines. Instead, she could have been in a comfortable family sitting room. And there was no piped music—a surprise, and a blessing.

"How're you then, young Jude?" Ted Crisp asked, with what Carole categorized as a lecherous leer.

"Not so bad, Ted," came the easy reply, reinforcing the impression that they'd known each other for years. Maybe they had, thought Carole. Maybe theirs was a relationship which went back a long way. Maybe there was even a "history" between them.

But the landlord's next words ruled out that supposition. "And how are you liking the upright citizens of Fethering? Or am I the only one you've met yet?"

"I've talked to a few people." Jude gestured across to the table. "You know Carole, of course?"

There's no "of course" about it. He doesn't know me, thought Carole. He knows who I am, but he doesn't *know* me. All he knows is that I've never been in his pub before. Could this be a moment of awkwardness?

It wasn't. Ted Crisp extended a beefy arm in a wave and called, "Evening, darlin' " across the bar. Carole felt a little frisson of embarrassment. She wasn't anyone's "darlin'." Still, the bar was fairly empty. She could recognize nobody there likely to spread to other Fethering residents the news that Carole Seddon had allowed herself to be called "darlin' " by Ted Crisp.

"So what're you going to get pissed on tonight?" the landlord asked.

"Two white wines, please," said Jude.

"Large ones?"

"Oh yes."

Carole had a momentary urge to remonstrate. Whenever given the choice between large and small—whatever the commodity on offer—she instinctively opted for small. But she did feel rather shaken and trembly this evening. Maybe it was one of those moments when she needed a large glass of wine.

For the first time she let her mind address itself to what had recently happened in her sitting room. Locking up the house and maintaining small talk with Jude as they walked to the Crown and Anchor had effectively blocked off the encounter. Now she allowed the shock to assert itself.

The main shock was not the behaviour of the woman with the gun but her own reaction to it. Carole Seddon had just been the victim of a serious threat, almost an assault, in the privacy of her own home. It was not the kind of incident that should go unreported. If nothing else did, her long experience in the Home Office told her that the police should be informed as soon as possible about unhinged people wandering the countryside with guns.

And yet Carole felt no urgency to contact the police. This morning's interview had put her off them in a big way. She didn't relish further scepticism, further aspersions being cast on the state of her hormones.

Besides, when she thought about it, she realized she had as little corroborative evidence for the second incident as she had had for the first. The body on the beach had disappeared. There was only her word for the fact it had ever existed. And exactly the same applied to the woman with the gun. Carole was the only witness of the woman's arrival, of what she'd said in the sitting room and of her departure. Carole didn't even know whether her new neighbour had heard the closing of the doors when she arrived at the house. Jude certainly hadn't said anything about it.

And that was the way things should stay, for the moment at least. There was no point in asking Jude whether she'd heard anything. It would lead only to further questions and explanations. Carole needed time to work out her next move. Whatever had happened was her business, possibly even her problem. It wasn't something in which she needed to involve anyone else.

There was a roar of raucous laughter from the bar.
Ted Crisp had just made a joke which seemed to have
amused both Jude and the man slumped on a bar stool
beside her. His grey hair was thinning and the way he
attacked his large Scotch suggested it wasn't his first of
the evening.

Now she could see his half-turned face, Carole
knew who the man was. He'd been living in Fethering
longer than she had. Rory Turnbull. Dentist with a
practice in Brighton. Lived with a sour-faced wife in
one of those huge houses on the Shorelands Estate.
Carole knew the couple well enough to bestow upon
them more than "the Fethering Nod;" she would actually talk if she met them. But the conversations they
shared never strayed on to any subject more contentious
than the weather.

"It's the only philosophy worth a fart," Ted Crisp was
saying. "Eat, drink and be merry . . ."

"Don't waste time with the eating," said the dentist.
"Drink, drink and be merry—" the landlord chuckled as
Rory Turnbull went on "—for tomorrow we die."

There was a change of tone in his last words, as if
he were suddenly aware of their meaning, and that broke
the conviviality of the moment. Jude moved away from
the bar, cradling the two large glasses of wine and two
packets of crisps.

Right, thought Carole, forget the body, forget the
woman, now's my opportunity to find out something
about my new neighbour. I don't know anything. Here's
my chance to fill in the gaps.

Jude placed the wineglasses and dropped the crisps
on to the table. "I'm starving," she said. "Takes it out
of you, hoicking all that stuff round the house."

"I'm sure it does." Carole wondered whether she should repeat her offer of help, but didn't.

"I'll probably order something to eat soon," Jude went on. "Haven't begun to get my kitchen up and running yet."

"Takes time, doesn't it?" Life in Fethering had refined Carole's skill in the deployment of meaningless platitudes.

"If you fancy joining me in a bite . . ."

"No, no, I'll be eating later," said Carole quickly.

But the thought of food was appealing. Suddenly very hungry, she opened her bag of crisps and put a greedy handful into her mouth. The lunchtime soup and bread seemed an age ago. She took a long swallow of wine.

"You look as if you could do with that," said Jude.

"What?" Surely the woman wasn't suggesting she had a drink problem? But when she looked into the big brown eyes, Carole saw no criticism, only concern.

"You look like you've had a bit of a shock."

"Well, yes, I suppose I have," Carole found herself saying.

Jude was silent. She didn't ask any question, she offered no prompt, and yet Carole found herself ineluctably drawn to further revelation. "The fact is," she said, "I did have rather a shock when I went for my walk on the beach this morning . . ."

And it all came out. The body. The interview with Detective Inspector Brayfield and WPC Juster. Not only the facts either. She told Jude exactly how diminished the police had made her feel.

And Jude simply responded. She didn't push, she didn't probe, she didn't even appear to be waiting for more. Carole could have stopped at any moment.

But she didn't. She went on. She went on to tell of the woman who'd arrived on her doorstep earlier that evening. Of their conversation. Of the gun. Of the woman's disappearance.

"You didn't hear anything? It was just after I opened the door to you."

Jude shook her head. Blonde tendrils hanging from the bird's-nest of hair tickled her shoulders. It must be blonded, Carole thought again. She must be my age. Well, nearly. It can't be natural.

"No, I didn't hear anything," said Jude. "Not a thing." Surely she's not disbelieving me too, thought Carole. But the panic was quickly allayed. "Then, you get to know the sounds of your own house, don't you? You hear things other people wouldn't notice."

"Yes, that's true."

For the first time since the revelations had started, Jude asked a question. "You say the woman appeared as if she was on drugs?"

"Yes. Well, she was certainly odd. She was on *something*. I mean, I don't know much about drugs, except for what I see on the television . . ."

"No."

". . . but she did seem to be out of control. Which was why I was so worried about what she might do with the gun."

"I'm sure you were." And then Jude expressed her first opinion of the evening. "I should think drugs are probably behind the whole thing."

"What do you mean?"

"The body on the beach. The woman with the gun. There's a lot of drug business down here. Long tradition of smuggling on the South Coast. Once it was brandy, silks, and tobacco. Now it's cannabis, cocaine and heroin."

Carole chuckled. "You seem to know a lot about the subject."

"Yes," said Jude.

# 7

THE PUB DOOR clattered open, making both of the women look up. The newcomer was a short man of about seventy. The dark-blue reefer jacket and neat corduroy cap bestowed a deliberately naval air. A wispy white beard on the point of his chin gave his head the shape of some root vegetable newly plucked from the soil.

"Evening, mine host," he said as he strode towards the bar.

Carole recognized Bill Chilcott, another High Street resident. He hadn't noticed her as he came in. She wouldn't have minded if things stayed that way. Since Carole Seddon wasn't a "pub person," she didn't want the impression to get round that she was. Anything observed by Bill Chilcott would immediately be passed on to his wife, Sandra, and soon all Fethering would know.

"Evening, Bill." Ted Crisp reached for the pump handle. "Your customary half?"

"Yes, thank you. And my customary half-hour away from the little woman. Actually, Sandra's deep into

some programme about neighbours redecorating each
other's front rooms, so she's as happy as a pig in . . . in
its element." He chuckled at his careful euphemism, then
noticed the other man at the bar. "Rory. How're you
doing?"

"Been better," the dentist grunted.

"Still, at least you didn't get breathalyzed, eh?"

"No, no." His face twisted ironically before he said,
"Thank you for that."

Ted Crisp handed Bill Chilcott his customary half.
"What's all this about the dreaded breathalyzer then?"

"The Bill was staking out Seaview Road last night.
Stopped Sandra and me on our way back from line-
dancing. I was fine, hadn't had a drop, but on the way
home I saw Rory's car coming towards me, so I flashed
him down to warn him there was a trap ahead. Of
course," Bill Chilcott went on innocently, "I had no idea
whether you'd been drinking or not . . ."

"No."

"So what did you do, actually?"

"Parked the car by the Yacht Club and walked home.
Last thing I need at the moment is trouble with the police."

"Last thing any of us need." Bill Chilcott shook his
head ruefully. "I think it's a bit much, the police breath-
alyzing right down here in Fethering. Up on the main
road, that's fine, but here . . . Nanny state gone mad, eh?
Mind you, if you want my opinion . . . the police
shouldn't be wasting their time harassing respectable
motorists. They should be concentrating on the young
people round here. There's so much vandalism. I hear
there've been more break-ins at the Yacht Club."

"Have there?" Rory Turnbull looked shocked.

"Who'd you hear that from?" asked Ted. "The Vice-Commodore?" He said it teasingly, deliberately prompting a predictable reaction.

It came. Bill Chilcott's tuber face turned purple with anger. "You know I don't give the time of day to that old idiot! No, it was something Sandra heard along the grapevine, from one of our regular swimming group at the Leisure Centre. So no doubt the police'll soon be inspecting down the Yacht Club . . . too late. As ever, shutting the stable door after the horse has gone. If you want my opinion . . ."

But on this occasion the Crown and Anchor was spared another of Bill Chilcott's opinions. Rory Turnbull's stool had clattered against the counter as he rose to leave. "Better be off," he announced brusquely.

"Back to the lovely Barbara, eh?" said Ted Crisp.

"Yes, back to the lovely Barbara," the dentist echoed in a doom-laden voice.

"See you soon, eh?"

"Oh yes. I'll be back." He made it sound like a death sentence as he fumbled to get his arms into the sleeves of his padded coat.

Carole looked down at their wineglasses. Unaccountably, they'd both become empty.

"Think we need another of those," declared Jude, rising to her feet.

Carole was out of practice with pub etiquette. "No, I'll get them," she said, a little late, following Jude to the bar.

The outer door clattered shut behind Rory Turnbull.

"Wouldn't like to be his first appointment in the morning," Ted Crisp observed.

"Why? What's he do?" asked Jude.

"Dentist."

"Oh." She turned towards the closed door. "I should've talked to him. I need to register with a dentist down here."

"If you take my advice, go for one with a steadier hand. I'm afraid friend Rory's been knocking it back a bit the last few months." Ted Crisp chuckled. "I'd say you saved his bacon with that warning about the breath-alyzer, Bill. Rory seems well marinated in the Scotch these days."

" 'Fraid so."

"Sorry, Bill, should have introduced you. You know Carole, don't you?"

"Of course."

Was she being hypersensitive to detect a slight raising of one white eyebrow? Oh dear. Her presence in the Crown and Anchor would be all round Fethering the next morning.

"And this is Jude, who's just moved in to the High Street too."

"Oh, hello. Bill Chilcott." He flashed her a row of too-perfect dentures. "You must be in Woodside Cottage."

"That's right."

"Needs a lot of work, doesn't it?"

"In time. No rush."

Carole empathized with the old-fashioned reaction he gave to this laxity.

"Poor old Rory, though," Ted Crisp went on. "Mind you, don't blame him. Must be a bloody depressing business, looking at rotten molars and breathing in everyone's halitosis all day."

"Presumably the money's some compensation," Carole observed drily. "You don't see many poor dentists, do you?"

The landlord shook his head, bunching his lips in a silent whistle of disagreement. "Don't you believe it. Living from hand to mouth, the lot of them."

"They're certainly not. They're—"

But the sound of Jude and Bill Chilcott's laughter stopped Carole.

" 'Hand to mouth.' Dentist joke," Ted Crisp explained.

Carole said nothing. She'd never been very good at recognizing jokes.

"Anyway, from the amount he's been putting back in here recently, I'd say Rory Turnbull was not a happy man. Sorry, I'm forgetting I'm here to work. Two more large white wines, is it?"

"Yes," replied Jude, and Carole didn't even feel the slightest instinct to ask for a small one. "Rory Turnbull?" Jude mused. "And you said his wife's name's Barbara?"

"That's right."

"Why, do you know her?" asked Bill Chilcott.

"No. Just I had a card through the letter-box yesterday. From a Barbara Turnbull. Asking me to go to some coffee tomorrow morning. As a new resident of Fethering. Something connected with All Saints'."

"That'd be Rory's wife," Carole confirmed.

"And I think, if you go, you'll have the pleasure of meeting my wife, Sandra, there in the morning. She'll be going after our swim."

"Oh, good."

"Barbara Turnbull's very active in the church locally. She and her mother, Winnie. Very devout."

"That's probably what drives old Rory in here," said Ted. "Needs to swill out the odour of sanctity with a few large ones. So you going to this coffee morning then, Jude?"

"Oh yes."

"Joining the God squad, eh?"

"Not sure about that. I just want to find out everything about Fethering. A new place is always exciting, isn't it?"

Though not sure that she agreed, Carole didn't raise any objection as they settled back at their table with the refilled glasses. But realizing she'd been given a good cue to find out a bit more about her neighbour, she asked, "Are you religious?"

Jude let out a warm chuckle. "Depends what you mean by religious."

"Well . . . church-going?"

The chuckle expanded into laughter. "Good heavens, no."

Having elicited one small piece of information, Carole pressed her advantage, "I don't know anything about you, actually . . . Jude." She managed to say the name with only a vestigial hint of quotation marks around it. "Are you married?"

"Not at the moment. What about you?"

"Have been. Divorced." Carole still felt a slight pang when she said the word. It wasn't that she regretted the loss of her married status or that she wished David was still around. Very much the opposite. She knew she was much better off without him. But being divorced still seemed to her to carry an overtone of failure.

"How long ago?" asked Jude.

"Ooh, ten years now. No, twelve. How time flies."

"Any children?"

"One son. Stephen. He's nearly thirty. I don't see a lot of him. What about you?"

Jude looked at her watch, seeming not to hear the return question. "I'm really starving," she said. "I've got to order something to eat. Are you sure you're not going to?"

"Well," said Carole.

They both ended up ordering fish and chips. By then, Bill Chilcott, having made his customary half of bitter last exactly his customary half an hour, had left the pub with a hearty, "Cheerio, mine host."

The two women's conversation for the rest of the evening moved away from their personal details. Jude was intrigued by the two dramatic events of Carole's day and kept returning to the body on the beach and the woman with the gun, offering ever new conjectures to explain them. Only once had Carole managed to get back to her neighbour's domestic circumstances.

She'd said, "So you're not married at the moment?"

"No."

"But is there someone special in your life?"

But this inquiry had prompted only another throaty chuckle. "They're all special," Jude had said.

Carole's recollections of the end of the evening were a little hazy. Of course, it wasn't just the alcohol. She may have drunk a little more wine than she usually did—quite a lot more wine than she usually did, as it happened—but it was her shocked emotional state that had made her exceptionally susceptible to its effects.

She comforted herself with this thought as she slipped into stupefied sleep.

The other thought in her mind was a recollection of

something her new neighbour had said. Carole couldn't remember the exact words, but she felt sure Jude had suggested their working together. If the police weren't going to show any interest in doing it, then the two of them should find out who killed the body on the beach.

# 8

CAROLE WAS WOKEN by Gulliver's barking. This was unusual. Normally, when she went downstairs to make herself a cup of tea, he was still comatose in his basket by the Aga. And the idea that he might have been barking to alert her to some intruder in the house was laughable. Such behaviour was not in Gulliver's nature.

As she looked around her bedroom, Carole realized something else was odd. The curtains were not drawn and thin but bright daylight was trickling through the windows. She raised an arm to check her wristwatch, but couldn't see the hands without her glasses. She fumbled and found them on the far edge of the bedside table, not neatly aligned on the near side where she left them every night.

She squinted to focus on the watch. A quarter to ten! Good heavens!

She sat up sharply, and then realized how much her head was aching.

Carole hurried into some clothes and rushed Gulliver

out onto the open ground behind the house. The grass was still dusted with frost and her ears tingled in the cold air.

The speed and relief with which the dog squatted at the first opportunity made her realize what a narrow escape her kitchen floor had had.

She couldn't blame the dog. He'd been very good, exercising all the control of which he was capable, while his mistress overslept. She couldn't blame anyone but herself.

Except, of course, for her new next-door neighbour. It was Jude who'd led her into self-indulgence at the Crown and Anchor. Maybe Jude wasn't such a suitable companion after all. Carole decided that any future communication between them should be strictly rationed.

She felt a little tremor of embarrassment. She had talked far too much the previous evening, confiding things that she had never confided to anyone else.

No, Jude was definitely a bad influence. Carole couldn't remember when she'd last had a hangover.

At first she'd decided she wouldn't take anything for the pain, just brazen it out. But after an hour or so, ready to succumb, she had gone to the bathroom cabinet, only to find it empty of aspirin. Oh well, that was meant. Serve her right. She couldn't take anything.

Half an hour after reaching that conclusion, though, she had decided she'd have to go to the shop to get some aspirin.

As she set out, neatly belted up in her Burberry, Carole heard a heavy regular thudding which she knew didn't come from inside her own head. There must be some construction work happening somewhere in the

Fethering area. Whatever it was, the noise didn't make
her headache feel any better.


The shop was not a village shop in the old sense of the
expression, though it occupied the site where a proper
village shop had once stood. That old shop, incorporat-
ing a post office, had been run by an elderly couple and
very rarely had in stock anything anyone might need.
But that didn't matter. The people of Fethering drove in
their large cars to do their major shopping at the nearby
out-of-town Sainsbury's or Tesco's. They used the village shop only when they'd run out of life's little essen-
tials—milk, bread, cheese, ketchup, cigarettes or gin—
and to collect their pensions. Many of them went in to
buy things they didn't need, just so they'd have the opportunity for a good gossip.

But that was no way to run a business and in the late
1980s, when the elderly couple retired, the old shop was
demolished, replaced by a rectangular glass-fronted
structure and called a supermarket. It was one of a local
chain called Allinstore—a compression that someone in
a meeting must once have thought was a good idea of
"All-in-store." This verbal infelicity was untrue under
the Trades Description Act (in fact, the store's local
nickname was "Nowtinstore"), but it was also sympto-
matic of the lacklustre style which epitomized Allinstore
management. The only detail the new shop had in common with the old one was that it very rarely had in stock
anything anyone might need, but people still went in to
buy things they didn't need, just so's they'd have the
opportunity for a good gossip.

In the transformation of Fethering's shopping facilities the village had also lost its post office, which led to a lot of complicated travel arrangements on pension days. And Allinstore had become an outlet for the National Lottery, thus enabling the residents of Fethering to shatter their hopes and dreams on a weekly basis.

The architect who'd designed the new supermarket (assuming such a person existed and the plans hadn't been scribbled on the back of an envelope by a builder who'd once seen a shoebox) had placed two wide roof-supporting pillars just in front of the main tills. Whether he'd done this out of vindictiveness or had simply been infected by the endemic Allinstore incompetence was unknowable, but the result was that many shopping hours were wasted and much frustration caused by customers negotiating their way around these obstructions. Mercifully Allinstore did not supply its shoppers with trolleys, only wire baskets, but many of its elderly clientele brought in their own wheeled shopping containers and these added to the traffic mayhem around the pillars.

Carole, aspirin packet in hand, was stuck behind one of them, out of sight of the tills, when she heard a familiar male voice say, "Apparently they found a dead body on the beach this morning."

She craned forward, encroaching on the elderly lady with a wheeled basket in front of her, and saw Bill Chilcott.

"Really?" said the girl behind the till, with the same level of interest she would have accorded to the news that there were no more toilet rolls on the shelf.

"Oh yes," he asserted. "Heard it on the BBC local news this morning."

Carole leaned over the elderly lady in front of her. "Morning, Bill."

"I don't know," he said, unnecessarily loudly and with what he imagined to be a lecherous grin. "Crown and Anchor last night, Allinstore this morning. We can't go on meeting like this. People will start to talk."

"Yes." Carole dismissed the pleasantry with a curt smile. "What's this about dead bodies?"

"I heard it on the radio when Sandra and I came back from our swim at the Leisure Centre. A dead body found washed up on Fethering beach."

"Did they say who it was? Or what had happened to him?"

"They didn't even say whether it was a 'him.' Probably be more on the lunchtime news. Mind you, if you want my opinion . . ." It was a mystery why Bill Chilcott always made this proviso; he was going to give his opinion anyway. "I should think it's one of those *weekend sailors.*"

He loaded the words with contempt. Though the precise details of Bill Chilcott's naval background were ill-defined, he never missed an opportunity of saying that seafaring should be left to the professionals. "Some idiot who took out a pleasure boat without sufficient knowledge of local conditions and *got what was coming to him.* If you want my opinion, they should impose some kind of regulations on the kind of people who're allowed to take boats . . ."

But as Bill Chilcott's hobbyhorse gathered momentum, Carole stopped listening. In spite of her headache, she felt a glow of vindication. She looked forward to grovelling apologies from Detective Inspector Brayfield and WPC Juster. There had been a body on the beach.

# 9

JUDE FOUND THE Shorelands Estate rather spooky as she walked through on the way to Barbara Turnbull's coffee morning. It took a lot to cast down her spirits. The frosty greyness of the morning hadn't done it. Nor had she had any adverse reaction to the wine of the night before. She'd drunk no more than a usual evening's intake. But Jude had a feeling that spending any length of time in Shorelands could bring her spirits down very quickly indeed.

Though laid out on lavishly spacious lines, the predominant feeling the estate gave her was one of claustrophobia. The main entrance gates looked as if they were never closed, but they were nonetheless gates. The "20 mph" speed signs and the "CRIME ALERT IN OPERATION" notices on lampposts gave Jude the feeling of being under surveillance.

This was reinforced by the contents of a display board which she stopped to read. Behind glass, under a neatly painted wooden sign reading "Shorelands Estate," was a list of regulations for residents. Since these included orders as to how visibly washing could be hung out to dry and times at which lawn-mowing was permitted, Jude felt relieved that Shorelands was a part of Fethering way out of her price range.

Though of massive proportions and, in most cases, with much-sought-after sea-backing locations, none of the houses appealed to her either. The estate was far too upmarket to go for uniformity. Each house was very positively different from all the others, and each failed to appeal to Jude in a different way. Every conceivable architectural style was represented, but in a manner that seemed more parody than homage. Whether with Tudor beams, tall Elizabethan clusters of chimneys, geometric Georgian windows, Alpine chalet gables, thatched roofs or the turrets of French châteaux, all the houses seemed firmly rooted in the time of their construction, the unglamorous 1950s.

The architectural style echoed in the Turnbulls' home was Spanish. The wrought-iron gates in the high white-painted walls might have led into the vineyards of some well-heeled Andalusian grandee, were it not for the coy metal name-plate with a squirrel motif which revealed that the house was called Brigadoon. And the authentic Spanishness of the frontage, with its heavily embossed door, terracotta pots in niches and gratuitous curlicues of wrought iron, was also let down by two quaint Victorian lampposts and by the metal expanse of the double garage's up-and-over door.

The house into which Jude was admitted had been recently "improved" by an expensive interior designer. No attempt had been made to continue the Spanish theme inside. The carpets toned with the walls; the walls were suitably complemented by the discreet pastel patterns of the curtains. Each item of furniture knew its place. The strain of all this tastefulness was almost tangible. To Jude the interior of Brigadoon had the homely charm of an intensive care unit.

But her impression of the decor was only fleeting. As ever, she was much more interested in people than in things, and immediately focused on the woman who had opened the door to her with a brisk, "Ah, hello, you must be the new owner of Woodside Cottage. I'm Barbara Turnbull. I'm sorry, I didn't know your name, so I hope you didn't mind my just addressing the card to 'The New Resident.' But you said on the phone you're called 'Jude.' "

"That's right."

"Jude . . . er . . . ?" the hostess fished.

"Just Jude's fine."

Barbara Turnbull was in her fifties and was one of those women who'd spread sideways. She walked with a slight swaying motion, but carefully, as if afraid her bulk might knock things over. Her hair, dyed a copper-beech colour, had been recently cut short. She wore a broad green skirt and little matching waistcoat over a blouse with an ivy design. Her stout legs ended in improbably small, flat blue shoes with decorative buckles. There were a lot of rings on her hands. Uniform beige make-up covered her face, and her lips were highlighted by lipstick of an only slightly darker beige.

"I'm afraid the house is a complete tip," she said, as she hung up Jude's coat and led her through the hall. Barbara Turnbull's remark was completely at odds with the evidence. The house looked as if individual motes of dust were removed with tweezers every hour on the hour. "My cleaning lady, Maggie, couldn't come in this morning. Just called five minutes before she was due to arrive to say she'd got some problem with her son. Honestly, people are so inconsiderate."

"Her son couldn't help being ill, could he?" Jude suggested.

"That's not the point. Maggie should have had some contingency plan ready for that eventuality. Anyway, I'm not sure he was ill. Some other problem, I wouldn't be surprised. He's very neurotic, from all accounts. Maggie seems to have no control over that boy of hers. Psychological problems . . . But then . . . *single parents.*" Barbara spoke the words as though no further explanation were needed. Jude might have taken issue with her, but they had reached the door of the large front sitting room and she was ushered inside.

"Now, hello, everyone," said Barbara loudly. "This is 'Jude,' who's recently moved in to Woodside Cottage in the High Street. I'll just tell you who everyone is."

"Don't bother." Jude knew she'd never remember a whole catalogue of anonymous names. She'd do much better talking to the other guests individually, matching names with personalities. "I'll work it out as we—"

Too late. Barbara Turnbull was determined to go through the full list. There were about a dozen, all women, with an average age of well over sixty. Jude got the impression that few of them had ever had jobs beyond looking after husbands and children. They were dressed as though their lives had become one long stationary cruise. Most of the faces looked deterrent, one or two more approachable. All of them wore too much make-up.

". . . and this is my mother, Winnie." Barbara Turnbull's guided tour finished on the smallest and oldest person present. "Winnie Norton. Now, 'Jude,' why don't you sit and have a chat to Mummy while I get you some coffee. How do you like it?"

"Just black, please."

"Any sweetener?"

"No, thanks."

"Right you are, 'Jude.' Just black it is."

"So how do you like Fethering?" asked Winnie Norton. Her hair, a blue that was picked up by the veins on the back of her hands, had been engineered into a rigid structure like spun sugar. The eyes were black and unashamedly curious. From the Yorkshire terrier on her lap peered another pair of black and unashamedly curious eyes. They took in Jude, not liking what they saw, and a low growl rumbled from the tiny silken body.

Winnie Norton wore a tweed suit whose dominant colour was turquoise. There were even more rings on her hands than on her daughter's, but they hung loosely on the thin talons.

"Seems fine from what I've seen of it so far," Jude replied.

"Did you know the area before you moved here?"

"Not well."

"Well, you'll find Fethering's very welcoming," said Winnie Norton. The dog, unwilling to endorse this view, yapped petulantly. "Quiet, Churchill." She tapped his nose gently before going on, "Yes, very welcoming . . . to the right sort of person."

"Ah."

"Of course, in the old days, before the war, only the right sort of person moved here, but since they developed that Downside Estate . . . well, something of an *element's* crept in." The little black eyes scrutinized

Jude, trying to gauge the risk of her being an "element."

The smaller set of black eyes on her lap had already made up their mind. Jude was definitely an "element." He yapped ferociously, baring his vicious little teeth.

"Now do be quiet, Churchill," said his mistress mildly. "We have to be on our best behaviour for a coffee morning, don't we?"

The yapping subsided into a malignant rumbling.

"Have you lived here long, Mrs. Norton?" asked Jude.

"All my life in the area, yes."

"But not all that time here at Shorelands?"

"Oh, I don't live on the estate. No, when I sold the big house after my husband died, I bought one of those new flats near the Yacht Club. Spray Lodge—do you know where I mean?"

"Sorry. Still getting my bearings."

"It's a very nice block. The residents do have a degree of control over who moves in."

"Ah."

"Well, you have to these days, don't you?" Winnie Norton chuckled. "All kinds of people have got the *money* to move into somewhere like Fethering now."

"Yes." Jude realized that, if she didn't quickly move the subject in another direction, she'd come to blows with the old lady. "Do you have any grandchildren, Mrs. Norton?"

"No. Barbara and Rory didn't want children."

"Ah." Churchill barked approval of this situation, while Jude looked around the vast sitting room. "So it's just the two of them living in this house, is it?"

"Rory does very well," said his mother-in-law, as if that answered the question. And perhaps, Jude reflected, by Winnie Norton's standards, it did. Rory Turnbull was making a lot of money as a dentist; therefore it behooved him to buy a large house on the Shorelands Estate. That was a fact of life, nothing to do with how much space he and Barbara actually needed. "Of course," the old lady went on, "he never really was our sort, but Barbara's done wonders with him."

Jude began to understand why Rory Turnbull needed his intravenous drip of whisky down at the Crown and Anchor. But Winnie Norton was prevented from casting down more of her poisoned pearls of wisdom by the arrival of her daughter with Jude's coffee.

"Now you mustn't monopolize our guest, Mummy. Incidentally, 'Jude'—" like Carole, Barbara Turnbull still couldn't quite say the name without a penumbra of quotation marks (a fact which amused its owner hugely)—"we are hoping that Roddy himself will drop in later."

"Roddy?"

"Canon Roderick Granger, to give him his full title. He's the vicar of All Saints'. A tower of strength locally." Barbara lowered her voice and gave the newcomer a look whose beadiness matched her mother's and Churchill's. "You are a believer, aren't you, Jude?"

"Oh yes."

The easiness of the reply brought visible relief to Barbara Turnbull's face. "Thank goodness for that. In these benighted times there are lots of people who don't even put 'C of E' on forms."

"I didn't say I was a believer in the Church of England," Jude pointed out.

Her hostess looked horror-struck. "You're not Catholic, are you?"

"No, I'm not."

Another sigh of relief. "There are a lot of them down here, you know. Arundel's quite a centre for the Rock Cakes."

"Is it?"

"Mm. It's a Catholic cathedral there, you know." Barbara moved on. "You'll find All Saints' is a friendly church, with quite a lot of social activities. Roddy's very keen on that side of things. He always says it's too easy for church-goers to get po-faced about religion." A little chuckle. "He's such an amusing man."

If what she'd just heard was an example of the vicar's wit, Jude wasn't convinced. What was clear, though, was that, in her hostess's eyes, Canon Roderick Granger could do no wrong. She was almost coquettish when she talked about him. It was quite possible that the Canon was held up to her husband as an exemplar of all the things that Rory Turnbull wasn't.

"Anyway," Barbara went on, "if you don't see him this morning, you'll catch him at the morning service on Sunday. Roddy's sermons are quite something. Lots of jolly good laughs on the way, but a real core of serious truth."

"I'm not a church-goer," said Jude.

"Oh."

"I don't want you to get the wrong impression. I accepted your invitation because I wanted to meet some local people, not because I'm ever likely to step into All Saints'."

Barbara Turnbull gaped like a beached fish.

"But I've nothing against the Church of England," Jude reassured her with a huge smile. "Everyone should

be allowed to believe in what they want to believe in—
don't you agree?"

Barbara's expression showed that she certainly didn't
agree. Allow everyone to believe in what they want to
believe in? That, her look seemed to say, is a short cut
to anarchy.

But her transparent thoughts remained unvoiced. "Do
let me introduce you to some other people, 'Jude.' " This
time she managed to get a double set of quotation marks
round the name.

With the newcomer in her wake, Barbara bore down
on a bird-like woman with spiky white hair who was
saying, "And this is meant to be a civilized country. I
ask you, is it civilized to park a boat trailer so that the
mast goes over the hedge into one's neighbour's garden
by a full three inches? I mean, is that the action of a
civilized human being? I'd say it was the action of a
boorish lout, if you want my opinion."

"Sorry to interrupt," Barbara Turnbull cooed, "but I'd
like to introduce you to someone who's a very near
neighbour of yours, Sandra."

The bird-like eyes darted to take in Jude and form an
instant opinion of her.

"This is Sandra Chilcott." It was said in best hostess
manner. "And here's the new owner of Woodside Cottage, whose name is . . ."

"Jude," said Jude, taking Sandra Chilcott's thin hand
in hers.

"Jude, of course! I've heard all about you from Bill.
Though, of course, being a man, he didn't tell me anything very interesting. I really do think men walk around
with their eyes closed, don't you, Jude? They never notice anything." She smiled slyly. "Didn't take you long

to find your way to the Crown and Anchor, though, did it?"

Jude was then introduced to the two women either side of Sandra, who'd acted as audience for the diatribe about her neighbour. "Well, 'Jude,' " one of them asked, "have you come down to Fethering in search of the quiet life?"

"No, not really. I think quietness is an internal thing, don't you?"

The two women looked at her in some puzzlement, as Sandra took her cue. "If it's quietness you're after, I'm not sure that you've come to the right place. You'll find quite a lot of exciting things happen in Fethering."

"Really?"

"Oh yes." Sandra Chilcott warmed to her task as news-bearer. "For example, this morning a dead body was found on the beach."

# 10

"YIPPEE!"

Carole gave her visitor an old-fashioned look. Her head was still aching and she still blamed Jude for leading her astray. It was a bit premature for her new neighbour to arrive again so soon at her door—and unannounced. And particularly shouting, "Yippee!" That wasn't the way things were done in Fethering.

"What is the cause of your celebration?" Carole asked, rather frostily.

Jude was blithely unaffected by the deterrence in her tone. "You were right. There was a body on the beach. I met Bill Chilcott's wife, Sandra, at Barbara Turnbull's—and she'd heard about it on local radio."

"Yes, I heard too. I met Bill in Allinstore."

"So you're vindicated, aren't you?"

"Well . . ."

They'd been standing on the doorstep almost long enough for the situation to become awkward. Carole would have to either invite her neighbour in or quickly invent some excuse and get rid of her.

But Jude solved the social dilemma before it developed. "Anyway, I was thinking there's bound to be something about it on the local news at lunchtime." She looked at her watch, a huge white dial which appeared to be tied on to her chubby arm with a broad velvet ribbon. "In two minutes. So I think we ought to watch that."

"Yes." Carole had been intending to do so anyway. But before she had time to say, "Thank you very much for the reminder. I'll see you later," and close the door, Jude had grabbed her by the hand.

"So come on, let's go and watch it at my place."

"What?"

"I'll knock up something for lunch. And we can open a bottle of wine."

"In the *daytime*?" Carole responded instinctively.

"Sure, why not?"

"I think I probably had quite enough wine last night."

"Oh, feeling the effects, are you?" There was no judgment, only sympathy in the way the question was posed. "In that case you definitely need a hair of the dog."

"That reminds me. I was going to take Gulliver out for—"

"Come *on*!" And Carole's hand, still being held, was given a quite definite yank.

"But I haven't got my coat!" wailed Carole.

"We're only going about five yards."

As she locked her front door and followed Jude down the symmetrical flags of her garden path, Carole managed to convince herself she was going simply because it would be good to talk about her traumatic discovery of the day before, and not because she wanted to have a snoop inside Jude's home.

Her neighbour's front path was an ill-fitting jigsaw of uneven red bricks, through whose interstices moss and weeds protruded. "Got into a terrible state, hasn't it?" Carole observed. "You'll have to get this sorted, won't you?"

"Oh, I quite like it like that." The breeziness with which Jude committed this blasphemy to the standards of Fethering suggested that it wasn't said for effect, that she really meant it.

She pushed the dark-wood front door open with an elbow and beckoned Carole to follow her inside. Good heavens, she hadn't even locked it. The fact that Jude had gone only next door didn't excuse this lapse. Suppose Carole had invited her in? Fethering High Street was a Neighbourhood Watch Area and, as everyone locally knew, the average burglary took less than three minutes.

And, dear oh dear, as she passed through the hall, Carole noticed that Jude's voluminous handbag was on a table right by the front door. Where had Jude come from to have such a cavalier attitude to the serious business of security? The thought reminded Carole once again that she still didn't know where Jude had come from. In fact, she knew very little more about her neighbour than she had the moment they first met.

The sitting room into which she was ushered was low and, because the old leaded windows hadn't yet been replaced by sealed double-glazing units, rather dark. Though Carole had never been inside Woodside Cottage during its previous occupancy, she'd assumed that the old lady would have had more of the basic modernization done. There was no evidence of central heating radiators, though an open fire crackled cheerfully from the gate (without a fire-guard in front of it, Carole noted, awarding her neighbour another black mark for domestic security).

Jude snapped on a couple of lights with dangly paper shades and illuminated what appeared to be an over-stocked junk shop. She crossed to a portable television perched on a pile of old wooden wine-crates and switched it on. "News is on One," she said. "Fiddle with the aerial if the picture's fuzzy. I'll go and open the wine."

And she disappeared into the kitchen before Carole could say that she didn't really need wine at this time of day. As the television came to life with a picture that was indeed fuzzy and as she moved the aerial on top of the set around to improve it, Carole took in the crammed contents of the room.

No surface was unlittered. There were piles of books and papers and knickknacks everywhere. And there didn't seem any theme or coherence to what was on display. Carved African animals jostled with brass hand-bells and green marble-stoppered bottles. Silver-framed photographs of stiff Victorians consorted with china cats and glass candlesticks. Eggs of exotically veined stone lay beside Russian dolls and spinner's bobbins.

Snuggled in the midst of this chaos were a small sofa and two armchairs. It was impossible to tell whether they were a matching set, though their varied outlines under the brightly patterned throws that covered them sug-gested otherwise. Further pieces of furniture were also hung with gratuitous drapery. The room was like the nest of a kleptomaniac magpie.

One must make allowances, thought Carole magnan-imously. The poor woman moved in only a couple of days ago. She's just had everything dumped in here. When she's got the stuff distributed around the house, this room'll look a lot tidier.

"Do sit down," said Jude, bustling in from the kitchen. One hand held a bottle of red wine, the other two glasses and a corkscrew that she was busily plying. As she slumped into one of the heavily draped armchairs, she looked around with satisfaction. "At least I've got this room done," she said.

Carole's jaw dropped. The decor was *intentional*. The confusion expressed how Jude *wanted* the room to look. But, even if Carole had been so ill-mannered as to say anything, there wasn't time. Jude sprang up again and shoved the wine and glasses into her neighbour's hands. "Here, you pour this."

Then she crossed to the still-fuzzy television and, with a cry of, "Come on, behave yourself, you little bastard!" gave it a resounding thump on the side. The picture immediately resolved itself into crystalline clarity.

Her timing had been perfect. The local news had just started. It was fronted by the kind of gauche female newsreader who makes you realize that, bad though network presenters may be, there remain unimaginable depths of the television barrel yet to be scraped.

But Carole and Jude didn't notice the girl's incompetence; they were too caught up in what she was actually saying.

"A body was found on the beach at Fethering this morning by a woman walking her dog."

"Only a day late," Jude chuckled.

"It wasn't me," Carole objected.

"The body," the newsreader droned on, "has been

identified as that of sixteen-year-old—" Carole's jaw dropped—"Arran Spalding . . ."

As the name was mentioned, a picture of the dead boy filled the screen. One of those school photographs, posed against a vague cloud-like backdrop. The caption showed that, though it had been pronounced "Arran," his name was spelt "Aaron." Aaron Spalding, with his floppy blond fringe and cheekily crooked grin, looked nearer twelve than sixteen. Probably he had been when the picture was taken. Self-conscious adolescents don't like being photographed; what showed on the screen was perhaps the most recent image available. But the innocent wickedness of his face added a poignancy to the fact of the boy's death.

The newsreader's voice continued drably: ". . . who lived in Fethering and who had been missing for the past twenty-four hours. The cause of death has not yet been established, but the police have not ruled out foul play."

Then, with one of those awkward jump-cuts beloved of local newsreaders, she moved on to the allegation that a recent spate of deaths among ducks in the area had been caused by ferrets.

The two women looked at each other in amazement. Carole noticed with even more amazement that half the contents of her wineglass had somehow disappeared.

"But it's . . . I mean . . ." she spluttered. "It was a middle-aged man, the body I saw. No way could it have been mistaken for a teenager."

"It wasn't mistaken for a teenager," said Jude firmly. "There have been *two* bodies on the beach. First the middle-aged man you saw, then this poor kid."

"You don't think there's any connection between them, do you?"

Jude cocked her head thoughtfully to one side. "There's no reason why there should be. It'd be a remarkable coincidence if they were connected. Then again, it's already a coincidence that two dead bodies have appeared on consecutive days. Logic dictates that the two incidents have nothing to do with each other, but my instinct says they have. And," she concluded mischievously, "in a straight fight between logic and instinct, I'd go for instinct every time."

"Hm . . ." Carole might have called the odds rather differently. "Well, this poor boy's death is nothing to do with me. It's not as if I even found the body. Some other woman with a dog. I wonder who it was . . . And, as for the first body, the police don't even believe that existed."

"But it did!"

Jude sounded aggrieved, almost as if it was *her* story that was being doubted. Carole realized, with a sudden warm feeling, that her neighbour had never for a moment questioned her account of what she had found.

"Since that body did exist," Jude went on, "there are two rather important questions which have yet to be answered. One—whose body was it? And, two—where is the body now?"

Carole shrugged. "Two questions to which, I'm afraid, we can never know the answer."

"Don't you believe it." Jude rose determinedly and switched off the television. Then she picked up the bottle and refilled the glasses, which had both unaccountably become empty. "I think we should find out the answers to those two questions."

"Us?" said Carole. "But surely murder—if it is murder—that's a job for the police."

"Have you been impressed by how the police have reacted so far?"

"No, but . . ."

There was a gleam in Jude's big brown eyes. "I think this could be rather fun." Then, briskly, she announced, "I'll get us some lunch. There's a sort of Turkish salad I do in the fridge. Aubergines and yoghurt and what-have-you. That sound all right?"

"Sounds great," Carole replied. "Are you vegetarian?"

"Sometimes," said Jude easily, as she disappeared into the kitchen, leaving Carole to wonder when she'd found the time to buy aubergines. There was no way that Allinstore's stock would have aspired to anything so exotic.

The Turkish salad was excellent and somehow, by the time they'd finished it, the wine bottle was empty too. Carole felt very warm and cosseted in the draped sofa in front of the glowing fire. She yawned.

"Wiped out?" asked Jude.

"A bit. At least my headache's gone, though."

"Never fails." Jude chuckled. "Go and have a little sleep."

Carole was shocked. "During the *day?* But I'm not ill."

Her neighbour shrugged. "Please yourself." Then she looked thoughtful. "I wonder who your body was . . ."

"No idea."

"No, but we're going to find out."

"Were you serious? What you said before lunch? About *us* investigating this?"

"Of course I was. Why, don't you think it's a good idea?"

To her astonishment, Carole found her lips forming the words, "Yes, I think it's a very good idea."

"Excellent. So where do we start?"

Carole looked blank. "Don't know. I'm afraid I haven't got much of a track record as an investigator."

"No, but you have a track record as an intelligent woman who can work things out for herself."

"Maybe."

"So what information do we currently have about your body on the beach?"

Carole stretched out a dubious lower lip. "All we have, I suppose, is the fact that he was wearing a life-jacket that was printed 'Property of Fethering Yacht Club.' "

"Right." Jude clapped her hands gleefully. "Then it seems pretty obvious to me that the first thing we should do is go down to Fethering Yacht Club."

"But we can't do that," Carole objected.

"Why not?"

"Because we're not members."

"Oh, for heaven's sake!" said Jude.

# 11

IN THE SNUGNESS of Woodside Cottage they hadn't noticed the weather worsening, but when they emerged the afternoon had turned charcoal grey and relentless icy rain swirled around them. The wind kept animating new puddles on the pavement into flurries of spray. The cold wetness stung their faces.

"Sure you wouldn't rather have that sleep?" Jude suggested teasingly.

"No," came the crisp reply. Affront at the idea of sleeping during the daytime, though unspoken, remained implicit. "I'll just get my coat and we'll go to the Yacht Club."

Carole hardened her heart against Gulliver's pathetic appeals to join them—he'd go for a walk in any weather—and wrapped her Burberry firmly around her. Soon she and Jude were striding into the horizontal rain towards the Fethering Yacht Club.

Fixed to the gatepost of one of the High Street houses they passed was a plastic-enclosed notice which read, in professionally printed capitals, "THIS FRONT GARDEN IS

PRIVATE PROPERTY. TRESPASSING, AT ANY LEVEL, IS STRICTLY FORBIDDEN."

"What the hell does that mean?" asked Jude.

Carole chuckled. "It's the Chilcotts."

"Bill and Sandra?"

"The very same. They're having a feud with their next-door neighbour."

Jude recollected the fag-end of conversation she'd heard at Barbara Turnbull's. "About where he parks his boat?"

"About that or about anything else they happen to think of. It's a battle that's been running for years."

"And does the neighbour respond in kind?"

By way of answer, Carole pointed to a notice, hand-written in marker-pen capitals, which was pinned to the gatepost of the next house. It read, "ALL TRESPASSERS WILL BE TREATED WITH RESPECT AND COURTESY—SO LONG AS THEY'RE NOT THE PETTY-MINDED COUPLE FROM NEXT DOOR."

Jude giggled. "Sounds as if the people this side have at least got a sense of humour about it."

"I'm not so sure," said Carole. "I think it's all in deadly earnest on both sides."

Jude looked into the garden. The trailer of a sailing dinghy with a fitted cover was parked diagonally across the cemented area in front of the garage. Its flattened mast missed the shared hedge between the feuding households by fractions of an inch. "So who's the sailor?" she asked.

"Denis Woodville. It's quite possible we'll meet him at the Yacht Club. He's rather a big noise there, so I've heard. Incidentally, Jude—" Carole was finding, the more she said the name, the less pronounced were the

virtual quotation marks with which she enclosed it—
"what are we going to say when we get there? I mean,
shall I say that I saw one of the club's life-jackets on
the body I found?"

"No, no, no. Don't mention the body—that'll only
cause a lot of unnecessary follow-up questions." Jude
looked thoughtful for a moment, then clapped her gloved
hands together as she found the solution. "Yes! Everyone round here seems totally obsessed by security, so
that's going to be our way in. We'll say we saw some
kids on the beach playing with a Fethering Yacht Club
life-jacket and we wondered if it'd been stolen . . . You
know, whether the club's had any kind of break-in recently?"

"But that's not true," Carole objected.

Jude's brown eyes took on a new vagueness. "True?
Truth is such a relative concept, though, isn't it, Carole?
And telling the truth, the whole truth and nothing but
the truth is the surest way of completely screwing up
your life, wouldn't you agree?"

Carole certainly would not agree. Telling the truth,
the whole truth and nothing but the truth to everyone
had been one of the guiding principles of her life. It was
an approach which had caused occasional awkwardness,
moments when confrontations could have been avoided
by a little tactful finessing of that truth. Indeed, if she'd
been less strict in her adherence to the principle, she
might still have been married. But Carole Seddon had
never given in to the way of compromise. She had always told the complete truth and faced up to the consequences of her actions.

So she didn't give any answer to Jude's question.

• • • •

Rather than going straight down the High Street and turning left on to Seaview Road, they cut along one of the side lanes and approached the Yacht Club along the banks of the Fether. Though it was hardly a day for sightseeing, Carole wanted to show Jude another aspect of the village.

There was a high path along the side of the river, the top of the defences which, further on by the Yacht Club, joined up with the sea wall. Cars were kept off this pedestrian area by serried rows of concrete bollards. Near the path a rusted Second World War mine had been converted into a collecting box for some maritime charity.

It was low tide. The Fether was a truculent sliver of brown water between swollen mudflats, which looked bleakly malevolent in the driving rain.

"Wouldn't fancy falling down there," said Jude.

"No, I think you could have a problem getting out again. Everything sinks into that lot."

Carole pointed out a row of public moorings, pontoons loosely attached to tall posts which rode up and down the water level with every tide. The rectangles of slatted wood lay on the mud, as did a few motor launches, stranded at asymmetric angles. "One of those belongs to Bill Chilcott, I think."

"What's that noise?" asked Jude.

Once again Carole was aware of the heavy thumping which had done so little to help her headache that morning. As they turned a bend of the path, they saw its source. On top of the sea wall, beyond the gates controlled by the Fethering Yacht Club, a cluster of builders' vehicles was gathered. There were a crane, two small vans and a JCB. Huge sheets of corrugated metal were piled by the blue fishermen's chests, and a lot of men in fluorescent yellow jackets and hard hats milled around.

Rising from the centre of this activity, at the edge of the Fether, stood a tall pile-driving machine. The rhythmic thumping sounded as it forced the metal sheets deep down into the mud. Gulls protested overhead, intrigued by the commotion.

"Repairs to the sea wall," Carole explained. "I'd heard it was due to be done some time." She shivered. "What a day for them to start."


From inside the Fethering Yacht Club, but for the dull thudding of the pile driver, you wouldn't have known about the repair work taking place only fifty yards away. The building equipment was as invisible as everything else beyond the windows of the bar. The way the wind whipped the rain about in every direction, sitting in the Fethering Yacht Club that afternoon was like being in a car wash.

Carole's conjecture had proved right and it was Denis Woodville who let them in. He was a tall, angular man with a high domed head surrounded by a little frill of white hair that gave the impression of a joke-shop tonsure. His nose was beaky and he had the sagging, papery skin of a heavy smoker. A politically incorrect Gauloise drooped from yellow-stained fingers and he kept sucking at it, as if desperate to tar up the last few unpolluted cells of his lungs. He perched on a stool and had gestured his visitors to sit on two others. Beside him, on the shelf that ran the length of the sea-facing window, was a balloon of brandy from which he took sips between drags of his cigarette. The bar-room was punctiliously neat and—the adjective could not be avoided—shipshape.

"Wouldn't surprise me at all if they'd nicked one of our life-jackets," he said after Jude had glibly produced her lie. "Lot of bloody kids always trying to break into this place."

Denis Woodville's accent was unusual, upper class on the surface but very carefully spoken, as if he was afraid he might at any moment betray a less cultured voice beneath.

"And into the boats," he continued, gesturing outside.

Though the windows were blinded with rain, Carole and Jude had seen what he was talking about as they approached the clubhouse. Rows of dinghies on trailers were regimented on a cement rectangle in front of the building, all zipped up to the necks of their masts in sturdy fitted covers.

"Bloody awful times we live in," Denis Woodville went on. "Nobody has any respect for property any more. Kids aren't brought up with any respect for anything, that's the trouble. May not be a fashionable sentiment, but bring back National Service, I say. A couple of years of doing what they're told, thinking about other people rather than themselves for a change—that'd bring the little buggers into line."

His taking a reflective swallow of brandy enabled Carole to ask, "Is this clubroom open right through the winter?"

"Yes. Every day. Normally a few regulars come in at midday, but when the weather's like this . . ." He shrugged. "Won't put off the evening crowd, though,

I'm sure. Actually, just as well there's no one in this lunchtime, because we've recently lost our barmaid—finished work on Friday. And you can't really have the Vice-Commodore pulling pints, can you?" He chuckled at the incongruity of the idea.

"So are you actually the Vice-Commodore?"

The note of awe that Jude had injected into her voice had the right effect. Denis Woodville preened himself as he replied, "Yes. I am. Hotly contested election for the post last year, but I won through. Members of this club still appreciate the old-fashioned values of integrity and common sense, you know."

"I'm sure they do. Are there a lot of members?" Jude asked ingenuously.

"Couple of hundred. Not all very active. Some're London folk who're just weekenders down here. We tend to be a bit careful about the kind of people we let in. Open the doors too wide and you could end up with all kinds of riff-raff, eh?"

"I suppose you could," said Jude, in a manner that might have implied agreement.

"And it's all run by volunteers, is it?" asked Carole. "You don't have any permanent staff?"

"We club officials give our services free," the Vice-Commodore replied grandly. "Obviously, expenses taken when required by the Treasurer and so on. That's Rory Turnbull, he's our Treasurer. Dentist chap. You know him, don't you, Mrs. Seddon?"

"Yes."

"He's got problems at the moment, you know . . ."

"Oh? Problems with what?"

"Club accounts. Don't tally, I'm afraid. It's the

bloody accountant's cock-up. Honestly, these days you can't even trust the professionals. Just scrape through their bloody exams and then reckon they've got a meal-ticket for life. And when they get their sums wrong, it's the client who has to pay, of course. Do you know, the accountant who looks after the club has managed to mis-lay over a thousand quid somewhere during the last year. Rory's on to the case and it's getting sorted, but even so . . . it all takes time, doesn't it? In the old days, if you employed a professional, you could rely on getting a professional job done. Not anymore."

"No," Carole apparently agreed. "It's rather impressive that this whole set-up's run without any paid employees."

"Well, of course, we pay the casual workers . . . cleaners, bar staff . . ."

"Except," said Jude, "you say you haven't got any bar staff at the moment."

"No. Tanya finished Friday, as I said. Did you know her?" Carole shook her head. "Rather large girl. No thing of beauty, and got this great industrial rivet punched through her nose, but polite enough to the members. And didn't drink the profits, just cup after cup of coffee all day.

"Well, anyhow, she suddenly reckons in her wisdom that this place was 'too far from Brighton,' so she's going to look for something closer to home. I don't know, young people nowadays just don't stick at anything. She'd got a perfectly good job here, done six months, members getting to know her, doing very well, and suddenly she decides a twenty-minute train journey is too much for her. Kids've got no tenacity these days."

"So will you be advertising for a replacement barmaid?" asked Jude.

"Yes, have to get round to it. Why, you looking for a job?"

"Might be."

This reply, as well as amazing Carole, seemed to release some warmth in Denis Woodville. He smiled into Jude's brown eyes as he said, "If you want to pursue it, let me have a CV and maybe I can put in a word with the committee."

"I might just do that."

Did she mean it, Carole wondered. Could she possibly mean it? People who had cottages in the High Street of Fethering didn't work behind bars. Once again she realized how little she knew of Jude's background. Maybe her neighbour actually did need a job and maybe she wouldn't be above working as a barmaid. Once again, Carole determined to get a few basic facts about Jude's life sorted out.

The relaxation of Denis Woodville's formality continued. "Would either of you like a drink, by the way?"

"No, thank you," replied Carole firmly, before Jude could once again succumb and lead her further astray.

"Oh." The Vice-Commodore looked wistfully down at his empty brandy balloon. "Well, I'd better not have another one either. Better get back home, I suppose." The prospect didn't appeal to him. "Yes, better close up. Open again at six. The six o'clock regulars never miss a night, come hell, high water or both."

"I gather from Carole," said Jude, "that we're neighbours, Mr. Woodville."

"Please . . ." He raised a veined hand in admonition. "Don't call me Mr. Woodville."

"All right, if you—"

"Vice-Commodore'll do fine."

"Oh. Very well, Vice-Commodore."

"And we're neighbours you say? How's that?"

"I've just moved into Woodside Cottage in the High Street."

"Oh, right. Really? Place needs a hell of a lot of work, doesn't it?"

"I quite like it as it is."

"Do you?" Denis Woodville scratched his bald dome in disbelief. "Good heavens."

"And you're just down nearer the sea? Carole showed me. The house with the dinghy in the front garden."

"That's the one, yes."

"Next door to the Chilcotts." Jude was apparently unaware of the clouding of the Vice-Commodore's expression as she chattered on. "I've only met Sandra and Bill briefly. I look forward to getting to know them better."

"I wouldn't get too excited about the prospect," said Denis Woodville darkly.

"Oh? Is he a member of the club here?"

Carole couldn't decide whether Jude had calculated the effect of her innocent inquiry, but it was certainly explosive.

"Bill Chilcott? A member of the Fethering Yacht Club? Oh, for heaven's sake! We do have quite strict requirements for entry here, you know. The last thing we want is the kind of jumped-up little creep who talks about boats and sailing all the time and in fact doesn't know a blind thing about any of it."

"Ah."

"This is a serious Yacht Club, you know."

"Yes, of course."

"The likes of Bill Chilcott have to moor their boats up on the public moorings. Bloody *weekend sailors!*"

The Vice-Commodore seemed belatedly to realize that this diatribe wasn't the approved method of welcoming a new resident. Swallowing his spleen, he announced formally, "Anyway, I do hope you'll be very happy in Fethering." And then, in apparent contradiction of much he'd already said, he went on, "You'll find people round here are very friendly . . . I'm sorry, I didn't get your name when you came in . . ."

"Jude."

"Ah. Jude what?"

"People just call me Jude." Carole had a little inward seethe at another missed opportunity to get more information, and was surprised to hear Jude go on, "Did you hear about that poor boy who drowned, Vice-Commodore?"

"What? Oh yes, of course I did. Another 'Fethering Floater.' "

"Sorry, what does that mean?"

"Bit of local folklore you could call it. Based on a peculiarity of the tides round here. Fether's not much more than a stream really, but it's got a nasty kick at high water. Moves pretty damn fast. Strange thing is, though, you'd have thought it'd take a body out a long way to sea. But no. Anyone who's so unfortunate as to fall into the Fether—or so damn stupid as to jump into it—some cross-current gets them, and they usually turn up on Fethering beach within twenty-four hours. They're your 'Fethering Floaters.' Name goes back hundreds of years, I've been told. A bit ghoulish . . . Still, nice to have a few local traditions, eh? Something for the tourists to get their teeth into."

The Vice-Commodore seemed unaware of any potential bad taste in his remarks, given Aaron Spalding's recent death. He looked at his watch and said for the second time, "Anyway, ladies, I think I'd better be closing up for the afternoon. So, if you'll excuse me . . ."

"Yes, of course."

Carole and Jude stood up.

Outside the weather had, if anything, worsened. The rain had turned to stinging sleet and the day was dwindling into darkness. It was also bitterly cold. Soon the sleet would stop and a major freeze-up set in. Denis Woodville let the two women through the small gate beside the clubhouse and reached into his pocket for the key to its padlock.

"So, if you see any more Fethering Yacht Club property round the place, you let me know. And I'll get on to the police sharpish. These little buggers have got to be caught and taught some sense of responsibility. They've got to learn to respect other people's property, and if it took horse-whipping to achieve that end . . . well, you wouldn't hear any complaints from me. What about you?"

Gracefully, Carole avoided answering the question by saying, "Thank you so much for your time, Vice-Commodore. If we all work together, I'm sure we can make Fethering a much more secure place to live in."

"Absolutely certain we can. May I accompany you back up to the High Street, ladies?"

"Well, since we're all going the same—"

"That's very kind," said Jude, "but in fact we were

going to have a walk along the beach before it gets completely dark."

"Were we?"

"Yes," Jude informed Carole firmly.

# 12

"ARE YOU REALLY looking for a job as a bar-maid?" Carole couldn't help asking as they pressed on into the icy gloom.

"Good heavens, no," Jude replied. "I just said that to keep the old boy sweet."

"So what, do you have a job or are you retired?"

"Ah, you mean what do I live on?"

Carole wouldn't have put it quite that crudely, but she admitted that yes, that was more or less what she meant.

Jude chuckled. "Like the rest of us, I live on money. And money comes and money goes, doesn't it?"

This did not come within Carole's definition of an adequate answer, but she had no time to probe further as her sleeve was snatched and Jude's voice hissed in her ear, "It's all right. He's gone."

"What?"

A gloved hand waved up towards the top of the beach. "Our Vice-Commodore. He's out of sight."

"So?"

"*So* he can't see what we're doing." And, tugging on Carole's arm, Jude pulled her round, so that they were both walking back the way they came.

"I wish you'd tell me what we *are* doing," Carole complained.

"We're going back to where you found the body on the beach. The water's far enough out for us to see."

"But we're not going to see anything. The tide's washed over the area a good few times by now."

"That's not the point."

However, Jude granted her no more information until they were standing at the foot of the breakwater, where, in what seemed like another lifetime, a dead man with a missing tooth had lain. Out of sight now in the encroaching darkness, the relentless thudding of the pile driver continued, eerily echoing off the sea.

Jude looked at the water-filled indentation at the foot of one of the breakwater's worn stanchions. "It was here?"

"Yes. Exactly here."

Scrunching up her eyes, Jude looked across the rain-slicked sand to where the pebbles started. "And you say the tide was coming in?"

"Yes."

"So how far was it away from the breakwater when you found the body? How far did it have to come in to reach here?"

"About twenty yards."

"Hm." Jude nodded thoughtfully. "Well, there's no way the body was swept out to sea again."

"How can you be so sure?"

"Because if the incoming tide was going to move him at all, it'd move him *further up* the beach. He wouldn't be swept out till after the tide had changed. And the police came to see you too soon after they hadn't found the body for that to have happened."

The deduction was undeniably true. Carole was surprised to encounter this new, logical streak in her neighbour.

"So . . ." Jude spun on her booted heel and looked around the semicircle towards the village. She stopped, facing the Fethering Yacht Club. "I think we go back up there."

"Hm?"

"For anyone who wanted to hide a body, it's the nearest place, isn't it?"

"But who wanted to hide a body?"

"We don't know that yet, do we?"

It was nearly dark when they got back to the side gate to the Yacht Club. Jude looked around but could see no one in the enveloping gloom. "OK, give me a leg-up."

"But we can't break in. I mean, particularly after what Denis Woodville was saying."

"Nobody's going to see us, Carole. And if he does find any evidence of our intrusion, he's going to put it down to the local youngsters. 'Kids these days just have no respect for property,' " she announced in an uncannily close echo of the Vice-Commodore's tones. "Come on, give me a leg-up."

With Carole's help, Jude negotiated her long skirt over the gate and then helped her neighbour to join her inside the compound. "Now, let's have a look at all of these boats."

"What are we looking for?"

"A loose cover. A sign that one of them's been broken into."

"You think the body might have been hidden in one of the boats?"

Jude looked around. "See anywhere else suitable?"

In the last threads of daylight, they felt their way along the rows of dinghies, Carole starting from one end, Jude from the other. On most, the blue covers were firmly battened down, either fixed with cleats or pulled tight by threaded cords. Above the two women, the wind sang in rigging and steel halyards clattered endlessly against metal masts.

"Could be something here!" Carole called out.

Jude was quickly by her side.

"Look!" Carole pointed to the rim of a boat cover, where a piece of rope dangled loose.

"Pity we haven't got a torch. It's really hard to see."

"I have got a torch," said Carole, trying to keep the smugness out of her voice. "I always carry one in my raincoat pocket. There's no streetlighting on the High Street."

"Isn't there? I hadn't noticed."

Carole reached into her Burberry pocket and the beam of light was quickly focused on the trailing rope. It ended in a sharp right angle.

"Been cut through," said Jude.

The severed cord had been rethreaded through the eyelets of the cover in an attempt to hide the break-in. Jude started quickly to unpick it.

"Should we be doing this?" asked Carole plaintively.

"Course we should. We are doing it anyway. And nobody can see us."

It was true. The wet darkness around them suddenly

seemed total. The floodlights focused on the sea-wall repairs were only fifty yards away but looked pale, distant and insubstantial. Someone would have to be very close to detect their tiny torchbeam.

Freeing a corner of the cover, Jude flipped it back like a bedspread from the stern of the boat. "Shine the torch here," she said. "No, here!"

The thin stream of light picked out a name in gold lettering: *Brigadoon II.*

"I wonder," said Jude. "Do you think there's a kind of person who would give their boat the same name as their house?" She didn't wait for an answer. "Come on, let's get the rest of this cover off and have a look inside."

"What are you expecting to find in there? The body?"

"It's a possibility."

Carole shivered. The possibility was macabre. But she couldn't deny that it was also exciting.

When they had peeled the cover right back, however, they found no body. Just the moulded fibreglass interior of a dinghy's hull. In the central channel a rectangle of trapped water gleamed against the torchlight. Its surface was frozen hard.

But the ice didn't stop an acrid smell from rising to their nostrils. "Standing water," Carole observed. "It's been leaking in for some time."

She ran the beam of the torch carefully over the inside of the boat. It revealed nothing they wouldn't have expected to find there.

"Just check if there's anything under the water."

Putting a foot on one of the trailer wheels, Jude hoisted herself with surprising ease over the side and into the dinghy. With a gloved fist, she hammered through the sheet of ice. Then, removing her right-hand glove and supporting herself on the other arm, she felt down into the bottom of the boat. She winced at the cold of the water.

"Something here." She produced a nut and bolt, rusted immovably together, and handed them to Carole. "Don't think that helps us much."

She reached down again through the cracked ice into the fetid water and felt her way systematically along the trough. "I think that's probably it. Be too easy if we— Just a minute . . ."

Carole craned over the side of the boat, trying desperately to see what her neighbour had uncovered. Jude's dripping hand raised her trophy into the torch-beam. "Look at that," she said with triumph.

It was a large, robust Stanley knife, clicked in the open position. The light gleamed on the shiny triangle of its blade.

"Wonder how long that's been there . . . ?"

"Not very long," said Carole. "Blade like that would rust very quickly. And . . ."

"What?"

"The woman who drew a gun on me wanted to know if I'd found a knife."

"Yes. So she did."

Jude slowly turned the knife over in her hand. On the other side of the handle words had been printed in uneven white paint-strokes. They read: "J.T. CARPETS."

# 13

"SO WHAT HAVE we got?" asked Jude.

They were back in Carole's house, sitting in front of her log-effect gas fire. She had chosen the system because she knew it would be a lot more sensible than an open fire. None of that endless business of filling coal scuttles, loading log baskets and sweeping out grates. But for the first time, with her new neighbour installed in a sofa in front of her virtual fire, Carole felt a little wistful for a grate glowing with real flames.

She had felt uncertain about inviting Jude in for a cup of tea, but the unalterable rules of reciprocal hospitality dictated that she should. The trouble was, when you invited someone in, you never knew how long they were going to stay. A drink with Jude in the Crown and Anchor had escalated, without apparent effort, into supper and a lot more drinks in the Crown and Anchor. With someone like Jude, who could say what "a cup of tea" might escalate into?

And once inside the house, with Gulliver greeted and fed, the unalterable rules of reciprocal hospitality dictated that Carole should at least suggest the option of something other than "a cup of tea." In Jude's house she'd been offered wine, so when she returned from the kitchen to the sitting room, she said, "I've put the kettle on, but if you'd rather have a glass of wine . . ."

This had prompted a quick glance at her large watchface from Jude and a, "No thanks, I don't want anything. Bit early for me to start on the wine, anyway. But don't let me stop you."

The response had caught Carole on the back foot, seeming to imply that if anyone had an over-enthusiasm for alcohol it was her. But Jude's brown eyes contained no censure or patronage. Carole was coming to the conclusion that her new neighbour was a very unusual person. Certainly in Fethering.

"We've got the knife," said Carole, picking up from Jude's question. "But whether that has any relevance to the body on the beach, we just don't know, do we?"

"Let's start from the other point of view," said Jude. "If we assumed that the knife *did* have something to do with the body . . . would that help?"

"It depends *what* it had to do with the body."

"All right. Well, your woman with the gun mentioned a knife, so that's a start. But suppose it actually belonged to the dead man . . . that it dropped out of his pocket while he was hidden away in the boat?"

"We don't know he *was* hidden away in the boat," Carole objected.

"No, but let's assume that too. Think about it. Where else could the body have been hidden where the police wouldn't see it?"

"The boats are the obvious place, I agree. Or I suppose there are those chest things on the sea wall, where the fishermen keep their stuff. They're kept padlocked, but if someone was prepared to break into a boat, they'd be equally ready to cut through a padlock."

"Yes."

"Surely, though, if the police were looking properly for the body I told them about, then they'd have gone up to the Yacht Club, wouldn't they?"

"Ah, but were they looking properly? Or had they already marked you down as a hysterical fantasist before they got to the scene?"

Carole was affronted. "I don't see how they could possibly have done that. When I rang them, I was extremely unemotional and controlled."

"But you did say that you'd bathed Gulliver before calling them."

"Yes. Yes, I think I did."

Jude shrugged. "That was probably what did it."

"How? But . . ." Carole didn't pursue the objection. "All right, *assuming* the body was hidden in the boat after I found it, that does raise a few other questions, doesn't it?"

"Like who hid it there?"

"Certainly."

"And, more to the point, Carole, who removed it from the boat before we looked under the cover this afternoon?"

"Yes. And, still maintaining all the assumptions about there being a connection, the only clue we have to help us answer those questions is the Stanley knife . . ."

"Which might have belonged to the dead man . . . or might have belonged to the person who left the body there . . ."

"Or might have belonged to anyone else in the world," Carole couldn't help saying.

"Ssh. Ssh." Jude spoke very soothingly, as if she were some kind of therapist. "We're just letting our ideas flow. Hold back on the logic for a little bit longer."

"All right."

Jude's brows wrinkled as her mind focused. "Anyway, the knife couldn't have belonged to anyone else in the world. There are geographical limitations, logistical limitations . . . No, when you come right down to it, there are very few people to whom that Stanley knife could have belonged. Hm . . ." She twirled a tendril of blonde hair thoughtfully between finger and thumb. "I suppose in fact the most likely person to have dropped the knife—is the boat's owner . . ."

"Who *might* be Rory Turnbull . . . assuming we go along with the theory that he would give the same name to his boat as his house."

"Let's go along with that for a moment." As she concentrated, Jude seemed to go in an almost trancelike state.

"Well," said Carole with no-nonsense practicality, "easy enough to find out who owns the boat. We simply ask our friend the Vice-Commodore."

Jude dragged herself back to reality. "Alternatively, I haven't registered with a dentist down here yet. Now I've met Barbara Turnbull and her mother, I'd like to know more about Rory."

"All right. He's a bit of a sad case, as you saw in the pub. Anyway, you pursue that line of inquiry." Carole moved into the delegating mode which had served her so well during her Home Office career. "Meanwhile, I'll find out about J. T. Carpets. Start with *Yellow Pages*, then see where I go from there."

"Good," said Jude. "That sounds very good." Then, with another look at the moon-face of her watch, she stood up. "I must be off."

And within a minute she was out of the house, leaving Carole to wonder why she had to be off so suddenly. And to realize that, after all her worries about Jude staying too long, she wouldn't have minded her staying a little longer.

The red light on the answering machine was flashing when Jude got back to Woodside Cottage. Just one message. From Brad, saying he hoped she'd settled in all right to her new home and lots of luck for the next stage of her life. And it'd be good to see her.

Yes, she thought, it'd be good to see Brad too. Been a while. She'd call him later. First, though, she dialled a local number.

"Hello?" The voice was politely deterrent.

"Barbara, it's Jude."

"Oh?"

"Jude from the coffee morning. New resident of Woodside Cottage."

"Of course. How nice to hear from you." The words were entirely automatic, invested with no element of sincerity.

"It was such a pleasure to meet you and your mother." Jude's words, though completely untrue, sounded sincere. "Thank you so much for inviting me."

"We always like to make newcomers welcome here in Fethering . . . in the hope we're going to swell the All

Saints' congregation." The reproof in the voice, at Jude's failure to espouse the Church of England, was hardly disguised.

"Well, I just wanted to say that I appreciated it, and thank you for going to all that trouble." Jude knew she was being over the top. Providing coffee and biscuits for a dozen people was hardly the most onerous assignment since records began.

But apparently it had seemed so to Barbara Turnbull. "Yes, well, one likes to make an effort. And I've just about finished clearing it up now. I told you I'm completely without help, didn't I?"

"Sorry?"

"Maggie, my"—Barbara had the usual middle-class difficulty with how one referred to staff—"my 'lady who does,' didn't come in today."

"Oh yes, you did say."

"And what's more, I've just heard from her to say she won't be in tomorrow either. Still some problem with her son. I don't know, it's so thoughtless. I told her, in no uncertain terms, that she couldn't assume that the job at Brigadoon would stay open forever. Have you found someone?"

The abrupt change of direction threw Jude. "Sorry? Found someone?"

"To do your cleaning."

This prompted a peal of laughter. "Oh, really, Barbara! I'm not going to have a cleaner. Can't afford to, apart from anything else. And I think I can probably manage myself. Woodside Cottage is absolutely tiny."

"Yes." There was a wealth of nuance in the monosyllable, as Barbara Turnbull moved her new acquaintance a few more notches down her social ranking system. "Well, it was a pleasure to meet you, and I do appreciate your ringing."

But Jude wasn't yet ready to have the conversation terminated. "One thing I wanted to ask . . ."

"Yes?"

"I'm not registered with a dentist down here and I wondered whether your husband—"

"Rory isn't taking on any new National Health patients," his wife asserted quickly.

"No, I wasn't imagining I could get a National Health dentist down here. I just wondered if you could give me the number of his practice."

Unable to find any fault with the concept of getting her husband more work, Barbara Turnbull gave the number. Jude, in a spirit of devilment, then brought her own end to the conversation. "And I hope that you'll let me repay your hospitality and that you'll come and have coffee here with me at Woodside Cottage one morning."

"Yes. That'd be delightful. I'll look forward to it," said Barbara Turnbull, meaning the exact opposite.

# 14

IT WAS STILL office hours, so Jude rang through to the surgery number Barbara Turnbull had given her. She explained that she had just moved to the area and was looking for a dentist with whom to register. Once it had been established that she was prepared to pay for her treatment, the woman at the surgery became much more accommodating and asked when Jude would like to make an appointment. As soon as possible. Well, they had actually had a cancellation for the following morning.

Jude said that would be absolutely fine, couldn't be better. "And that will be Mr. Turnbull I'll be seeing, will it?"

"Sorry?" For the first time the voice sounded a little fazed.

"Mr. Turnbull. He was the dentist that was recommended to me. My appointment is with him, is it?"

"Possibly." But the voice was cagey. "It may be one of his partners. We tend to allocate new patients according to who's free."

"Surely the appointment is with one dentist or the other?"

But the voice did not wish to pursue this.

"See you in the morning. Thursday the eighth, ten-twenty. Goodbye."

Bit odd. Still, at least she wasn't going to have to wait long for her appointment. Jude smiled softly to herself and then keyed in Brad's familiar number.


The first bit of Carole's research also went smoothly. J. T. Carpets were listed in the *Yellow Pages*, with an address not far away in East Preston. When she rang, the phone was answered by a voice which implied that it was very near the end of the working day and she had been about to get off home.

"My name's Mrs. Seddon and I'm ringing because I found something which I believe is your property."

"What's that then?"

"It's a knife . . . a Stanley knife . . . and it says 'J. T. CARPETS' on it."

"If it says 'J. T. CARPETS' on it, then there's a strong chance that it does belong to J. T. Carpets, I'd have said." The girl's voice was poised just the right side of insolence. But only just. "Did one of our fitters leave it in your house?"

"No. I found it . . . on the beach." No need to be too specific.

"Oh, all right. So why're you telling me?"

"I just thought you might want it back."

"Not that bothered," said the girl. "I mean, it's only a Stanley knife. Not like it's the only one in the building."

"Oh."

Some residual compassion in the girl responded to the disappointment in Carole's tone. "I mean, if you're passing the office, drop it in by all means," she conceded magnanimously.

"But none of your staff has reported the knife missing?"

"Oh, come on, if they've lost company property, they're hardly going to go shouting to the boss about it, are they?"

"No, I suppose not. So you have no idea which member of your staff might've mislaid the—"

"Listen, lady. You drop it into the office, that'd be very public-spirited of you. If you don't, the company's not going to go to the wall—right? And, since it is now after half-past five, I'll say thank you very much for calling and *goodbye!*"

The phone was put down with some vigour. Carole felt uncomfortable. The patronizing tone been all too reminiscent of Detective Inspector Brayfield's. And Carole was also left with the feeling that she had a lot to learn about being a detective.


Jude's appointment turned out not to be with Rory Turnbull. She was told when she arrived at the smart reception area that she'd be seen by a Mr. Frobisher. While she waited, Jude was aware of much toing and froing among the receptionists and dental nurses, as though the impact of some offstage crisis was being minimized for the watching patients.

The man who greeted her when she was ushered into his surgery was about forty and fit-looking, with an unreconstructed Australian accent. He was immaculately clean in white coat and rubber gloves, and his surroundings matched him. All the equipment was shiny and new. Even his dental nurse looked as though she'd been recently delivered and only just removed from her wrappings.

"I was put on to this practice by Barbara Turnbull," said Jude, as she was settled into the chair and floated into a prone position.

"Oh yes?" said Mr. Frobisher, without much interest.

"So I thought I might be seen by Mr. Turnbull."

"There are three of us in the practice. We tend to share out the new patients. I hope that's all right with you . . ."

"Yes, yes. Absolutely fine. So is Mr. Turnbull in today?"

"No, he isn't, as it happens." Was Jude being hypersensitive in detecting a slight resentment in Mr. Frobisher's reaction to his colleague's absence? He sat astride his mobile stool and focused the overhead light on her face. "So, Mrs.—"

"Please call me 'Jude.' Everyone does."

"Very well then, Jude . . . any problems with your teeth?"

"No, I just wanted to get registered."

"Fine. Well, I'll have a quick look and confirm everything's OK."

For the next few minutes, Mr. Frobisher's probing around her mouth made further conversation impossible. He called out a few notes to the dental nurse, who clicked them in on a keyboard.

There was an interruption when one of the receptionists entered with a sheaf of printed papers. Some silent semaphore with Mr. Frobisher caused him to break away from his examination of Jude's teeth. With an "Excuse me a moment," he crossed to look at what the receptionist had brought in.

"No, that has to be wrong."

"It's in black and white, Frobie."

"Must be a misprint. Tell them I'll come and have a word in a couple of minutes, OK?"

He crossed back to his patient as the receptionist left the surgery. "Sorry about that. We're having an inspection by the RDO—that's the Regional Dental Officer. Routine stuff, but they always manage to disrupt the whole place."

"What is it that they—"

"Now, open wide again please."

So Jude was unable to find out more about the workings of Regional Dental Officers. And Mr. Frobisher gave her little opportunity for further conversation when the examination was concluded.

"Good. No serious problems at the moment. Couple of places where the gums're looking a bit red, though. Look after your gums and it makes my job of looking after your teeth a lot simpler."

"Yes," said Jude contritely.

"Make an appointment to see one of our hygienists on your way out, will you?"

"Sure. I—"

"Now, if you'll excuse me, I'd better go and sort out this RDO."

She couldn't make him stay. And even if she had been able to make him stay, Jude wasn't sure what questions she would have wanted to ask Mr. Frobisher.

"Tell reception to apologize to the next appointment,"

he told the nurse as he left the room. "Only be about five minutes."

On the coastline train that rattled through an unbelievable number of small stations and rattled past an even more unbelievable number of bungalows on its way back to Fethering, Jude tried to comfort herself with the fact that there was nothing wrong with her teeth. But the predominant feeling in her mind was one she shared with Carole—that she had a lot to learn about being a detective.

# 15

THE CROWN AND Anchor was on the way back from Fethering Station. Jude knew she shouldn't really, but the thought of grabbing a bite to eat there rather than knocking something together at home was appealing. She could be an excellent cook when she felt like it, but she very rarely did feel like it.

Jude knew she shouldn't really spend the money either. But what the hell? Tomorrow would be soon enough to start her economy regime. She went into the pub.

There were maybe half a dozen people scattered around the sitting room that was the Crown and Anchor's interior. Most were tucked away in alcoves, their presence betrayed by a glimpse of elbow or a murmur of chatter. The room looked comforting, as did the lugubrious grin Ted Crisp gave her from behind the bar.

"Couldn't keep away from me, eh, young Jude? My old animal magnetism doing its stuff?"

"Something like that."

"So what can I do you for? Or are you just after my body?"

"I was thinking of lunch."

He accepted this philosophically. "First things first. And first thing's got to be a drink, hasn't it? Wodger fancy—apart from me, of course?"

"Glass of white wine."

"Large, I take it?"

"Why not? And something to eat. Nothing very big. Do you do sandwiches?"

"We not only do sandwiches, we also do baguettes. Bread rolls with delusions of grandeur, no less. List of fillings on the board."

Jude looked at the selection written out in multicoloured chalk. "I'll have the tuna and sweet corn, please."

"You won't regret it. Good choice, that. One tuna and sweet corn baguette!" he shouted out towards the kitchen. "Normally write the orders down. Not when we're slack like this, though."

"Who've you got cooking today?"

"No idea. She's a woman. Knows her place. Never comes out of the kitchen."

Jude could sense a degree of calculation in his words. Ted Crisp was sizing her up, testing the level at which she'd be offended.

She denied him the satisfaction of a response. "You ever been married, Ted?"

"Used to be. You can tell. I'm still round-shouldered. Didn't take, though." The landlord shook his shaggy head gloomily. "Like an unsuccessful heart transplant. My body rejected it." He was silent for a moment. "Actually, that's not true. My body didn't reject her. She rejected me. Walked out after three months. With a double-glazing salesman. 'But he's so transparent,' I said. 'Can't you see right through him?' She didn't listen. Said she wanted the security. Wanted to be with someone who didn't always come staggering in at four in the morning . . ."

"Having been out drinking?"

"Having been out *working*, I'll thank you very much, young Jude. And maybe a bit of drinking after the working. But the human body is like an old clock, you know. It needs to unwind."

"So what did you do that kept you out till four every morning?"

"Stand-up. I was on the circuit. When I moved here was the first time I'd ever been in a *downstairs* room in a pub."

"That explains a lot, Ted."

"Like what?"

"Your jokes. They sound like they come from someone who *used* to be a comedian."

He screwed up his face in a mock-wince. "Ooh, you know how to hurt, don't you? Anyway, you're right. I wasn't a huge success on the circuit. It's a business where you're only as good as your last joke, and, as you've so diplomatically pointed out, my last joke was bloody terrible. So . . . about four years too late, I saw the wisdom of what my former wife'd said and went for security. Sold up the house, borrowed far too much from the brewery to get this place and . . . here I am."

"Do you miss it?"

"Stand-up?" He screwed his lips into a little purse of disagreement. "Nah. No different here. As a pub landlord, I still get heckled and shouted at and have glasses thrown at me by a bunch of drunkards."

"Not in Fethering, surely?"

"Don't you believe it. Come Saturday night, they've all tanked up at home on the old Sanatogen Tonic Wine, they've got their pensions in their pockets and evil in their hearts. I tell you, you can hardly move in here for the flying zimmer frames. Ooh, here's your baguette." He reached out through the hatch to a disembodied hand from the kitchen. "Get outside of that and you won't hurt, young lady."

There was a clatter from the front door and Jude turned to see Rory Turnbull making a clumsy entrance. He hadn't shaved that morning and looked unkempt.

The dentist weaved his way up to the bar. "Large Scotch please, Ted."

"If you're sure . . ."

The note of warning in the landlord's voice hit a raw nerve. "Of course I'm bloody sure! Otherwise I wouldn't have bloody asked you for it, would I?"

As Ted Crisp turned to get the drink, Jude ventured a, "Hello. We sort of met in here the other night, didn't we?"

"Hm?" Rory Turnbull's eyes had difficulty in focusing on her.

"And actually I went to your surgery this morning. Mr. Frobisher looked after me." Just as well it wasn't you, thought Jude, or my mouth'd be bearing the scars. "Your wife put me in touch."

"My wife?" He seemed puzzled by the alien concept.

"Yes, Barbara."

"Oh, *that* wife." He let out a bark of laughter, as

though this were some huge joke. "Thanks, Ted." He took a long swallow from the glass.

"Why, you got another wife, Rory?" asked the landlord. "Little totty tucked away somewhere?"

The dentist smiled slyly. "I should be so lucky. Don't think you can get away with that kind of thing in Fethering."

"Don't you believe it." Ted Crisp struck his forehead in a mock moment of revelation. "I just realized. Jude! You suddenly appear here in Fethering, nobody has a clue who you are, why you're here . . . You're Rory Turnbull's bit of stuff, aren't you?"

She smiled ruefully. "Sorry. I'm afraid my only connection with Rory is professional—not even that, actually, because I saw his partner rather than him."

"And you say my wife put you in touch?"

"Yes. Everyone needs a dentist, don't they?"

This struck Rory Turnbull as very funny. "I'll say. Oh yes, everyone needs a dentist. Everyone needs someone with a steady hand to probe around their smelly mouth. Everyone needs that frisson of lying in a high-tech chair and just waiting to be *hurt*. And nobody thinks what the dentist needs. Nobody thinks how much it costs him to be there in the surgery every morning, there with the steady hand and the fixed grin and the knowledge that what he's doing is so stressful it's lopping the years off his life, one by one. How many dentists get to enjoy the wonderful pensions they salt away so much for through their working lives? Very few, very few. Because they drop dead, you see. Or if they don't drop dead, they top themselves. Did you know that dentists have one of the highest suicide rates of any profession? And why do you think that is? It's because what they do manages to be both deadly boring and agonizingly stressful at the same time. It's because being a dentist combines—"

But here the maudlin aria was interrupted by a voice from across the pub. "Rory. I only just noticed you were in here. I wonder if you could . . ."

It was Denis Woodville. He was standing next to an alcove where, unnoticed by Jude, he had been lunching with a large young woman dressed in black, who had also risen to her feet. On the seat behind her, where it had been cast off, lay the semicircle of a green anorak.

"No, sorry, Vice-Commodore," said Rory Turnbull. "Can't stay. Have to finish my drink—" he gulped down what remained in one "and do some very important things." Shovelling a pocketful of small change on to the bar counter, he set off unsteadily towards the door, repeating to himself, "Very important things."

"But what I need to talk about's important too!" Denis Woodville turned back to his guest as he made for the door. "Sorry, Tanya. Be with you in a moment!"

The girl had risen from her booth, a lumpen creature in black sweat shirt, leggings and Doc Martens. Hair dyed reddish and cut short, a lot of silver dangling from the perforations in her ears. A silver stud in her nose. She looked anxious.

"It's all right, Tanya, love," Ted Crisp called across. "The Vice-Commodore'll be back. You won't be left to pick up the tab."

"I hope not." Her voice had those slack local vowels which sound uninterested even at moments of excitement. She drifted uneasily towards the bar.

"Though it's not like our Denis to be pushing the boat out like this," Ted went on. "Bit of a tightwad usually."

"Lunch is on Fethering Yacht Club expenses," the girl explained. "He wanted to say thank-you now I've left, and since I didn't have anything else on today, I thought, 'Well, it's a free lunch.' "

"No such thing," said Ted Crisp.

"Sorry?" The girl looked at him curiously.

"A free lunch. No such thing."

"What?"

He spelled it out. "There's no such thing as a free lunch."

"No. You have to pay. In a pub or a restaurant, you always have to pay."

Ted Crisp recognized he wasn't getting anywhere. Tanya was unaware of the reference. "You like some coffee, would you? Seem to remember when you worked behind the bar here, you were virtually on an intravenous drip of coffee."

The girl wrinkled her nose, a manoeuvre which the silver stud made look hazardous. "No, thanks." She looked across to the door. "I hope he's all right."

The landlord chuckled. "I think the Vice-Commodore can look after himself in the face of drunken dentists. Don't you worry. He'll be back in a minute."

No sooner had he said the words than Denis Woodville returned. He was lighting up another Gauloise and looked rather miffed. "Tanya, I'll just sort out the bill for this lot and then we'll be off—all right?"

"Fine," said the girl without interest.

The Vice-Commodore reached into a pocket for an envelope full of petty cash. "Right, Ted, what's the damage?"

While he settled up, Jude attacked her baguette, which was excellent. After the unlikely couple, thin septuagenarian and broad twenty-year-old, had left, she said, "You said Tanya used to work for you too, Ted?"

"That's right. Not of the brightest, as you might've gathered from our exchange about free lunches. No, Tanya's not a bad girl. Been in care, had a tough time when she was growing up, I gathered. But she did the job all right. And a good barmaid is hard to find." His eyes narrowed as he looked across at Jude. "Don't suppose you fancy doing the odd shift in here, do you?"

She chuckled. "Not at the moment. Maybe, if I get desperate . . ."

"Yeah, nobody works for me unless they're desperate." He sighed. "Nobody does anything for me unless they're desperate."

"Talking of desperation, Ted . . ."

"Hm?"

"How long's Rory Turnbull been drinking like that?"

"Only the last few months. Well, only the last few months he's been drinking like that in *here*. Maybe in the privacy of the Shorelands Estate he's been doing it for years."

"Can't see the lovely Barbara being too keen on that."

"No, nor the old witch, her mother." He shuddered. "That Winnie. One of the best arguments for misogyny I've ever encountered."

"Do you know them well?"

"Hardly. Only by reputation, gossip, what-have-you. You hear a lot stuck behind the bar of a pub."

"I bet you do."

"And not much of it's very charitable."

"No. So what have you heard from Rory Turnbull while you've been stuck behind the bar?"

"Well, it's all the same, really. You heard the full

routine today. Goes on and on round the same things—how miserable life is, what hell it is being a dentist, what hell it is being married . . . usual cheery stuff. Tell you, after an evening spent with Rory, my own life seems a bed of blooming roses."

A new thought struck Jude. "Ooh, and he has a boat, doesn't he?"

"That's right. Called *Brigadoon*. Same as his house."

Good, thought Jude. At least one of our conjectures has proved to be right.

But it still doesn't prove any link between the owner of *Brigadoon II* and the body on the beach.

# 16

CAROLE SEDDON HAD woken that Thursday morning with a change of attitude. In Jude's company, caught up in the excitement Jude generated, the idea of playing at detectives had seemed a seductive one. Finding an explanation for the body on the beach had been imperative. On her own, though, Carole found it less compelling. Life, she reflected, is full of loose ends. There are many questions that will never be answered, and a sensible person will recognize that fact and get on with things.

So that morning Carole got on with things. She re-established the routine of her life that her discovery of the body and her meeting with Jude had briefly interrupted.

The weather was better, though still astringently cold and heavily overcast. She took Gulliver for his early-morning walk on the beach, striding resolutely past Woodside Cottage without a sideways glance. On her way back up the High Street, she did slow for a moment by the gate, contemplating a brief call to see if Jude's thinking had progressed at all. But, in spite of the ambient gloom, there were no lights on, so Carole went straight into her own house and started a major cleaning offensive.

The telephone didn't ring all morning. This was not unusual, but that particular morning Carole kept half expecting it might.

She was very sensible and virtuous. She even emptied out the fridge and defrosted it.

After her morning of hard work, she felt she deserved an omelette and a glass of mineral water with the lunchtime news. There was nothing much on the international front. Reports of atrocities in the Balkans or Africa, where she got confused about which side was which—who the aggressors, who the victims—had little power to engage her interest.

The weatherman promised more of the same. The apparent improvement of that morning had been an illusion. More frost was coming. More wind. More gloom as the evenings darkened earlier and the year spiralled down to its close.

At the start of the strident signature tune of the local news, Carole reached for the remote control. But before she pressed the off-button, she heard the voice-over menu of headlines: "Drowned boy's mother blames drug culture."

Carole's button-finger froze.

Another newsreader who'd never make it on to national television appeared in shot. "The mother of teenager Aaron Spalding"—once again the name was pronounced "Arran"—"today blamed the ready accessibility of drugs to young people on the South Coast for her son's death."

A woman's distraught face filled the screen. "Aaron was a good boy. Then he got mixed up with a crowd who was doing a lot of drugs and I'm sure that's what caused his death. He was a good boy . . ." Her mouth wobbled as the tears took over.

But it wasn't what was said that kept Carole frozen in her chair. It was the fact that she'd seen the woman before.

In that very sitting room. Holding a gun.

# 17

ANY THOUGHTS OF giving up trying to be a detective evaporated as if they'd never been there. Now there was something positive to link the two fatalities. The woman who'd come to Carole's house to ask her about the body she'd found on the beach was the mother of the boy whose body had been found on the beach the following day. Also she'd asked about a knife. There had to be a connection.

Carole rushed out of High Tor, not even bothering to lock the front door, and hurried up the garden path of Woodside Cottage. When the bell prompted no response, she hammered on the dark wooden door.

But there was no one in. For a moment she contemplated going down to the Crown and Anchor to see if Jude was having lunch there (which would have been a very good idea, because that was precisely what Jude was doing). But Carole's sensible side prevailed. If she didn't find Jude, she reasoned, then she'd have to stay in the Crown and Anchor and have a mineral water to justify her going in there. And if she did that, there was a real danger it might appear to the other residents of Fethering that she'd become the kind of woman who went into pubs on her own. (The option of just going in and asking Ted Crisp if he'd seen Jude did not occur to her.)

So Carole left a message on Jude's answering machine, asking her to phone back as soon as possible. And then she sat waiting in an agony of frustration, once again made aware of how little she knew about Jude's life. Her neighbour could be anywhere. Maybe she did have a job and was off at work? Maybe she was visiting a family member . . . or a long-term lover? Maybe she owned a second home and had gone there? The possibilities were infinite.

To speed up the passage of time, Carole went to her bookshelves and consulted her reference library. Various works of criminology reflected different Home Office initiatives in which she had been involved. The volume she was looking for had come her way when she had been investigating police training methods. It was a manual about scene-of-crime techniques.

Carole looked dispassionately at the rows of photographs of those who'd come to violent ends. There was nothing gruesome about the task; this scientific layout of wounded bodies detached them from any humanity of which they might once have been part.

At the same time Carole focused on the image of the body she had found on Fethering beach. In particular, on the two cuts that she had seen on the man's neck.

She compared the picture in her mind with the picture on the page, and it confirmed a tiny doubt which had stayed with her since she first saw the corpse.

The two cuts on the man's neck were not deep enough. They were little more than flesh wounds and had not reached any major arteries. He might even have received the injuries post-mortem.

Whatever had killed the man, it hadn't been the wounds to his neck.

Carole had hardly reached this conclusion before there was a furious ringing at her doorbell. Jude was back from the Crown and Anchor.

"We've got to talk to her."

"But, Jude, she'll be in a terrible state. She's only recently lost her son."

"She's also only recently threatened you with a gun. Anyway, I'd have thought the one thing anyone would want to know if they've just lost their son is how it happened. We may be able to help her answer that question."

"She may know already."

"If she does, she can tell us. And also maybe tell us the connection between her son's death and the body you found. Come on, we've got to get to the bottom of what happened, haven't we?"

"Yes, of course we have." Carole had by now completely forgotten her morning's doubts about the wisdom of pursuing the case. "So how're we going to find her?"

"If she's local, she might be in the phone book. The dead boy's called Aaron Spalding, so let's assume she's a Spalding too. Do we have a first name for her?"

Carole screwed up her pale-blue eyes with the effort of recollection. "There was a caption up over the bit of interview they showed. Um . . . began with a 'T,' I think. Yes, it's coming. Theresa. That's right—Theresa."

"Though presumably," said Jude, grabbing the Worthing Area telephone directory and flicking through it, "the entry would be in her husband's name."

"If she's got a husband. You never know these days, do you?"

There were ten Spaldings, none of them with the initial T. Carole and Jude took turns to phone them all and ask to speak to Theresa. None had anyone of that name on the premises. And all of them seemed to regard a wrong number as an infringement of their human rights.

"So where do we go next?" asked Jude. "Ring the television company who did the interview?"

"No, local paper," said Carole firmly. "Comes out today. Always on a Thursday. There's no way they wouldn't cover a story like this."

They negotiated the pillars of Allinstore to buy a copy of the *Fethering Observer*, and didn't have to search far to find what they were looking for. The front page was dominated by the headline: "TRAGEDY OF DROWNED TEENAGER." Beside it, the boyish school photograph of Aaron Spalding appeared again.

"Wonder why it's spelt 'Aaron' and pronounced 'Arran?' " Jude mused.

"Maybe it's a local variation. Influenced by living so near the Arun Valley."

"Maybe. Oh, look, there's the address. It says, 'Mrs. Theresa Spalding, of Drake Crescent, Fethering.' Where's that?"

"Up on the Downside Estate, I'm sure. A lot of the roads there are named after famous Elizabethans. Marlowe . . . Sidney . . . Raleigh . . . Meant to give a bit of class when they were built. Mind you, I think it's the only bit of class they've still got left."

"Not the most desirable part of Fethering then?"

A wrinkle of Carole's nose gave all the answer that was required. "So," she said, "when do we go up to Downside and try to talk to Mrs. Theresa Spalding?"

"No time like the present," replied Jude. "How do we get there?"

"In my car. Unless you want to go in yours . . ."

"Haven't got one." Jude grinned. "Never felt the need."

# 18

FETHERING DOESN'T HAVE an underbelly in the way that, say, Los Angeles has an underbelly, but the Downside Estate is as near as it gets.

The houses there betrayed signs not of real deprivation but of diminishing willpower and ever-tightening budgets. The Downside Estate had been built as council housing, but cut after cut in local authority spending over the years meant that maintenance had been pared to the bone. The buildings had all reached the age when serious structural refurbishment was required, not short-term making-good repairs. Their late-1940s brickwork needed repointing. Windows needed painting, even those where the original frames had been replaced by soulless double glazing. Tiny front gardens were unkempt and littered. Depressed cars crouched against the pavements on failing suspension.

The drab November weather did not add to the estate's charms, as Carole navigated her sensible and immaculately clean Renault towards Drake Crescent. She tried to bite back her instinctive snobbishness, but the compartmentalizing habit of her mind was too strong. Here was a place, she decided, where cultural aspiration stopped at the *Sun* or the football, and hope existed only in the form of the National Lottery.

On the side of every house a satellite dish perched like a giant parasitic insect, leeching away more profits for Sky TV. In Downside no attempt had been made to hide them, whereas on the Shorelands Estate a visible satellite dish would have constituted a social lapse more terrible than walking around with one's fly undone.

"Pretty grim place to live," Carole observed, as she turned off Grenville Avenue.

"Oh, I don't know. I've lived in worse," said Jude, adding yet another to the list of questions that Carole must at some point put to her neighbour.

But this wasn't the moment. "How do we know which house it is?" she asked as the car crawled along Drake Crescent. Unable to disguise her distaste, she added, "Stop and ask someone?"

Jude chuckled. "It wouldn't be such a bad thing to have to do. The people round here are human, you know."

"Oh, I didn't for a moment mean—"

"Yes, you did," said Jude cheerfully. "Anyway, I don't think we're going to have to ask anyone. I'd say it's the house with the television crew outside."

Sure enough, there was a blue and white van bearing the regional station's logo. A couple of dour technicians were rolling up cables and stowing them in the back. An effete young man stood awkwardly by, feeling he should offer to help, but not knowing how.

Jude jumped out as soon as Carole had parked the

car and went straight up to the young man. "Is this Theresa Spalding's house?"

"Yes," he said.

"Have you just been doing a news interview with her?"

"Not news, no. For a documentary. We're doing an in-depth analysis of the teenage drug problem on the South Coast."

"Oh, that'll be interesting," lied Carole, who'd come up to join them. All local documentaries, she knew, were ruined by inadequate budgets, sketchy research and inept presenters. "And you were talking to Mrs. Spalding about her son's death?"

"Yes. She's obviously very cut up about it."

"I'm not surprised," said Jude, starting up the short path that led to Theresa Spalding's front door.

"I'm not sure that she really wants to talk to anyone else at the moment," said the young man. "Unless, of course, you're social workers."

"That's right," Jude called breezily over her shoulder as she pressed the doorbell.

In amazement, Carole followed her neighbour. The young man, seeing his colleagues had finished packing the van, got inside.

It was a moment or two before the front door was opened, and then only halfway. The woman was un-doubtedly the one who'd come to Carole's house, but her face had drained down to a new pallor. The darting eyes were raw with weeping and a hand flickered across in front of her as if warding off some unseen attacker.

"What do you want? I don't want to talk to no one."

"We may be able to help you find out how Aaron

died," said Jude, pronouncing the name "Arran" as everyone else had.

"I don't care *how* he died. My boy's dead—that's all that matters to me. I don't want to talk about it."

She made as if to close the door, but Carole's incisive words stopped her. "Then perhaps you do want to talk about why you drew a gun on me . . ."

The door-closing movement stopped. Through the remaining crack the woman's eyes took in the speaker's face.

"Unless you want the police to talk to you about why you drew a gun on me."

Reluctantly, the crack of the door widened.

"You better come in then."


Theresa Spalding lived in a maisonette. Whether the house had been built like that or subsequently converted into two dwellings was hard to tell. The sitting room, into which Carole and Jude were grudgingly ushered, was dominated by a huge television screen. Throughout their interview, some American sitcom full of overacting teenagers was running with the sound off.

Theresa Spalding gestured to a couple of broken-down chairs, stubbed out the remains of a cigarette and, with trembling hands, shook another out of a packet. She remained standing while she lit the new one. She took a drag, as though gulping in oxygen on the top of Everest.

"Look, I don't know what you want, but I've already got enough grief."

The room was full of traces of her son. A poster of the Southampton football team. A Playstation with a scattering of CD-ROM games by the television. Stephen Kings and similar paperbacks littered on a shelf, along with a neat row of horror videos. A grubby pair of trainers left by the sofa, exactly where he'd kicked them off.

Jude took the lead. There had been no discussion between them, but instinctively they fell into their roles. If Carole, with her threats of police involvement, was the Bad Cop, then Jude was going to be the Good Cop.

"Yes, Mrs. Spalding, I understand—"

"It's not 'Mrs.' I never been married. But if you think that means I didn't bring up Aaron right—"

"We're not saying that . . . Theresa. Can I call you 'Theresa'?"

Carole knew she could never have got away with it, but the woman snorted permission to Jude for her first name to be used. There was something in Jude's manner which made such things possible.

"Thank you. I'm Jude, and my friend's called Carole."

This first use of the word "friend" gave Carole a warm feeling. She wasn't sure whether she was ready yet to reciprocate the compliment, but it was still nice to know that Jude thought of their relationship in that light.

"And we're both desperately sorry about what happened to Aaron."

"Why? What business is it of yours?"

"It wouldn't be our business," Carole responded sharply, "if you hadn't come to my house and threatened me with a gun."

"You needn't have worried. It wasn't a real gun." Theresa Spalding crossed to a dresser and pulled the weapon out of a drawer. She chucked it across into Carole's lap for inspection. No parts of the gun's mechanism moved except for the trigger. A moulded replica. "Just a thing Aaron bought."

"Why did he buy it?" asked Carole.

"Not to do any harm!" Theresa snapped. "He'd never have done an off-licence with it. He wasn't like that. Aaron was just a little boy and little boys like playing with guns. That's just a toy. He bought it as a toy!"

"Yes." Jude's voice smoothed down the flare-up. "But you can see why your use of the gun got us interested. What was so important to make you go to the house of someone you'd never met before and pull a gun on them—even if that gun was just a replica?"

Theresa was sullenly silent.

Carole picked up the baton of interrogation. "What interests me even more is the fact that you mentioned the body that I'd found on the beach that morning. How did you know about that?"

Again there was no response.

"Did Aaron tell you about the body?" suggested Jude gently. "Had he seen it down there?"

"Aaron didn't have anything to do with that bloke dying! Aaron was a good boy . . ." Once again, as in her television interview, these words unleashed a flood of tears from Theresa Spalding.

Jude rose and, with an arm around her, led the woman to sit down. "Cry," she murmured. "It's good. You need to cry."

Then, crouched beside the chair, she rocked the woman in her arms, crooning words whose sound was more important than their meaning. Carole watched the calming process with surprise and a degree of envy, knowing that she did not possess such skills.

Gradually, the shudderings of Theresa Spalding's body became tremors, which twitched away to nothing. She reached into the pocket of her jeans for a crumpled tissue and rubbed it against her nose.

"Ready to talk?" asked Jude.

The woman nodded. To her surprise, Carole found Jude was looking at her, indicating that she was to take over for the next bit.

"Right." Carole had taken her glasses off and was rubbing the lenses on the end of her scarf. It was a mannerism of which she was entirely unaware, but which had been noticed by all her Home Office colleagues, a little ritual she went through before any important interview. "We weren't suggesting that Aaron had anything to do with the death of the man I found on the beach. We just want to know why you were so concerned about that body."

Theresa Spalding said nothing. Jude had calmed her, she didn't mind Jude, but she was still resistant to the Bad Cop.

"It was nothing to do with me. I didn't even see the body. I had no connection with it."

"Apart from the connection through Aaron?" said Jude.

For a moment the woman's face contorted. If the suggestion had come from Carole, she would have shouted some defiant response. Because Jude had spoken, though, she accepted it.

"Yes. OK."

Carole picked up again. "You were particularly concerned about something in the dead man's pocket."

Theresa nodded, still calm. "Yes. Aaron had told me about it. I was just afraid, if the police found it, they'd make the connection with him and come after my boy."

"What was it? What was in the man's pocket?"

She couldn't face answering this question without another cigarette. Carole and Jude watched in silence while she fumbled with the packet and lit up again.

"I don't know what it was, but it was something with Aaron's name on it. They all had to put their names on something. It was part of the test."

The Bad Cop and the Good Cop exchanged glances. The understanding passed that Jude should take over again. "Who's 'they'?" she asked softly.

"The other lads. The ones he was with when they found the body."

"Did they find the body at the Yacht Club?"

Theresa nodded. "Aaron got in about four that morning. I started to bawl him out, but I could see what a bad way he was in. He'd been doing some stuff, I could tell. Weed, I suppose—maybe something stronger. Bit of smack perhaps. He was crying just like a kid. Wasn't much more than a kid, really. Got in with the wrong company, that was all that was wrong with Aaron. What chance did he have, living with me, no man around . . . well, no man around for long? And me always on some medication for the depression and the panic attacks. I did try to look after him. He never got put into care. Times they wanted to, but I wouldn't let them. I brought him up on my own, all on my own."

Jude nodded, soothing, commending the achievement. "So what did Aaron tell you?"

"He said they'd been drinking. He didn't say they'd been doing stuff too, but I knew they had. And then they decided to break into the Yacht Club . . . I don't know what for . . . maybe a bit of thieving or just to smash the boats up. It wasn't Aaron's idea, it was the others. And they broke into one boat and they found this man's body . . . He was dead. He was definitely dead before they found him. And they . . . I don't know what they did to the body, or exactly what they put in his pockets, but it was some test . . . some kind of test . . ."

"A test to prove how hard they were?" Jude suggested. "How tough they were?"

"Perhaps. I don't know. Aaron's been into a lot of this horror stuff, you know, books and films and stuff. A lot of that age are. Black magic stuff, you know. Maybe what they done to the body was something to do with that. You know what kids that age are like—terrified, but it doesn't do to show they're terrified, so they egg each other on to show how brave they are, and they do stupid things. Anyway, whatever they actually did, it ended up with them chucking the body over the sea wall into the Fether. That's all Aaron told me, but he was in a bad way, a really bad way. He'd scared himself something terrible. He kept saying that the body would come back to life, that it was one of the Undead or some such crap, and that it'd come after him. And then he was afraid too the police was going to come and get him as soon as the body was found. I tried to calm him and put him to bed . . . Then I slept for a couple of hours, and Aaron was here when I woke up round eight . . . but later in the morning I went down the shops . . . and when I come back, he was gone . . ." A sob came into her voice. "And that was the last time I saw my boy.

"I still thought he was coming back then, but I wanted to do a kind of damage-limitation thing—stop anyone who knew anything about the body talking to the police. That's why I come round your place with the gun.

"But Aaron didn't come back." She swallowed down the sob welling up in her throat. "It was the drugs. He got into bad company and they started him doing drugs . . . and Aaron couldn't cope . . . not with that and the other things they done. I think he just couldn't take it anymore. He was convinced this Undead body was going to come after him and get him . . . so he must've jumped into the Fether at high tide Tuesday night . . . and that was the end."

She didn't burst into tears this time, but stood, her body shaking with dry sobs.

"Did you tell all this to the police?" asked Carole.

"No, not the half of it. I don't want them thinking my boy'd been messing around with dead bodies."

"So why did you tell us?"

"To stop you telling the police about the gun." There was a naked appeal in the bloodshot eyes she turned on Carole. "That was the only reason I turned it on you. I was trying to frighten you, so's you wouldn't tell the police what Aaron'd done. You won't tell them, will you?"

"No. We won't tell them."

"What about his friends?" asked Jude. "The ones he was with?"

"Friends!" Theresa Spalding spat out the word. "You don't call someone who gets a sixteen-year-old boy into drugs a 'friend,' do you?"

"No, you don't. But who were they?"

"I don't know for definite. There's a bunch that gets together. Could have been any of them. But there's one who I'm sure was involved. Older boy. Aaron worshipped him, thought he was the business all right. Asked him round here once or twice, but I turfed him out. I can always spot a bad 'un. I'm sure it was him who got Aaron into drugs."

"What's his name?"

"Dylan."

"Surname?"

"Don't know. Never heard it."

"Any idea where he lives?"

Theresa Spalding shook her head. "Somewhere local. Went to the same school as Aaron. Few years older, though, like I said. He's left the school. Think he's got a job now."

"Doing what?"

"Carpet-fitter."

# 19

"WHAT COULD BE more logical," asked Carole, "than that someone who has just moved into a new home should be looking to have it carpeted?"

"Fine." Jude nodded cheerfully. "I'll just think of it as an acting job."

"Have you ever acted?"

"Oh yes," said Jude.

"What—professionally?"

"Sort of."

"Oh?" But, frustratingly, no further information was forthcoming. Carole swung the Renault into a parking bay.

J. T. Carpets was a flat, rectangular building on a retail estate just outside East Preston. Nearby was a Sainsbury's, a Do-It-All, a Halfords, a Petsmart, an MFI and a Toys 'R' Us. Here the devoted homemaker could find everything he or she required—provided he or she possessed a car in which to cart it all away. (And in many cases, the devoted homemakers round the Fethering area arrived in huge four-wheel-drive off-road vehicles—essential equipment to negotiate the notorious gradients of the retail estate's car parks.)

Inside the outlet (on retail estates what used to be called "shops" had all become "outlets"), they were greeted by the distinctive smell of rope and rubber which rises on the air wherever new floor coverings foregather. Variegated rolls and piles of carpets were laid out across the floor area. Sample books spread over tables. Small displays of corners of room demonstrated to the unimaginative how some of the carpets would look with furniture on them.

There were few customers. Late afternoons in November were not a favourite time for buying carpets. With the run-up to Christmas, people had other purchases on their minds.

As a result, there were plenty of staff available, and the two women were quickly accosted by a young man in a sharp suit and cartoon-character tie.

"Good afternoon, ladies. What can I do for you?"

Jude was straight into her cover story. "Yes, I'm looking for a hard-wearing carpet for my landing and staircase," she announced.

"Certainly, madam. What sort of quality had you in mind?"

"It's not so much the quality that concerns me as the price. On a tightish budget, I'm afraid."

"Yes. Aren't we all?" He chuckled automatically. "Well, with carpets as with most things, you get what you pay for, but we do have some very competitive offers which you'll find—"

"Excuse me, do you have a toilet?" Carole broke in.

"What?" The young man was totally thrown.

"A toilet. I need to go to the toilet."

"Oh. Well, we don't have public toilets."

"You must have staff facilities."

"Yes, but—"

"I'm desperate. It's my age."

The young man was so embarrassed by this that he immediately called over one of his female colleagues. Jude hid her grin as Carole was escorted out to the office area at the back.

"Now, your cheapest option," the young man continued, blanking out the interruption, "would be a hard-wearing cord . . ."

Jude listened, occasionally throwing in doubts and questions. She moved easily—and with some relish— into the role of a dithery little woman unable to make up her mind. She invented a husband called Kevin whom she'd have to consult about the various options. Had Carole not returned from the lavatory at that point, she would soon have invented a couple of children and an ageing grannie whose opinions also required canvassing.

"Better?"

"Much better, thank you," said Carole, showing Jude a covert thumbs-up sign. "It's awful when you get taken suddenly like that, isn't it? So embarrassing."

"Oh yes."

"How're you doing?"

"This young man has been extremely helpful. He's showed me all kinds of possibilities. I think what I'd better do now is go home and discuss them all with Kevin."

"Good idea," said Carole. It wasn't until they were back in the car that she asked, "Who the hell's Kevin?"

"A necessary fiction. But never mind him. Have you found out what you wanted to?"

"Yes. Dylan is scheduled to be fitting carpets in a house on the Shorelands Estate tomorrow morning. For a Mrs. Grant-Edwards. House is called Bali-Hai. I've memorized all the details."

"How did you find out?"

"There was a duty-schedule board up in the office. Wipe-clean calendar thing with staff names and addresses where they were going to be working. I thought there would be," Carole concluded smugly.

"Well, congratulations. Very convincing. For a moment back there I thought you really did want to go to the loo." Jude was silent for a moment. "Mind you, they might have told you where to find him if you'd just asked."

"Yes," Carole agreed. And then she did something that she did very rarely. She giggled. "But the way I did it was much more fun."


It was six o'clock and the Crown and Anchor had just opened. Carole had initially demurred at the idea of having a drink, but Jude had insisted they needed to talk to Ted Crisp as part of their investigation.

He was going round, wiping down the tables and emptying ashtrays into a bucket.

"Have to do everything yourself, I see," Jude observed.

"That's right. It's tough at the top. Bar staff don't come on till seven during the winter."

"And in the summer?"

"Summers I'm open all day. That's when I make my

money. From all those dads sneaking off and leaving the mums on the beach with the kiddies." He took up his post behind the bar. "What can I do you for? Two large whites, is it?"

"Yes, please," said Jude, and Carole didn't even make a token murmur of dissent. Instead, she moved straight to the purpose of their visit. "Ted," she began and paused for a nanosecond of shock at the knowledge that she, Carole Seddon, was actually standing at the bar of the Crown and Anchor and calling the landlord "Ted," "you heard about that poor boy who was drowned the other day?"

"That Aaron Spalding? Course I did. Couldn't miss it. All over the telly, for a start. And lots of the old farts in here was talking about it and all . . . moaning on about young kids today getting messed up with drugs . . . and saying that kind of thing wouldn't happen if they brought back National Service."

Carole wondered for a moment whether it had been Denis Woodville repeating his opinion, but decided it was probably a universal sentiment among the old codgers of Fethering.

"Did you know him at all? Aaron? Did he ever come in here?"

"Well, he shouldn't have done, because he was underage, but yes, I seen him in here a few times. He'd come in with a bunch of them. They'd sit in that dark corner over there, hoping I wouldn't clock them, and send up the one who looked oldest with a shipping order for drinks. They tried it on a few times, but I was wise to them. I'm not going to risk my licence for a bunch of kids."

"Had you seen them in here recently?"

"Yes, three of them was in one evening this week. Monday, I think."

The night they went on to the Fethering Yacht Club and found the body in Rory Turnbull's boat, thought Carole. "Who were the other two?" she asked.

"One I'd never seen before. Young kid, looked even younger than Aaron. But I know the one they sent up for the drinks." He spoke without enthusiasm. "He comes in here quite often. Eighteen, nineteen I guess, so he can drink legally. But when he comes up and asks for three pints of lager on Monday night, I says to him, 'I'll pull one for you, no problem, but it's going to be soft drinks for your two underage mates over there.' Then he gets dead stroppy and starts swearing at me, so I tell him to get out. He's a nasty bit of work, that one. Deals a bit in drugs and all. I can do without that sort in here.

"Anyway, out they go, no doubt straight down to Nowtinstore, where he buys a dozen cans perfectly legally and they go off and drink them in one of the shelters on the front. At least they wasn't doing it on my premises. I hope they froze their bollocks off out there."

"The police haven't come and asked you whether you saw Aaron, have they?"

"No, but presumably if they was retracing his movements they'd be interested in the next night, wouldn't they? Not the Monday. His body was found on the Wednesday morning, wasn't it?"

"That's right," Carole agreed thoughtfully.

"So who was this older boy?" asked Jude. "Do you know his name?"

"Don't know his second name, but his first name's Dylan."

"Ah." The two women exchanged significant looks.

"What does he look like?"

"Tallish. Thin. Short bleached hair. One big earring."

"Sounds a real charmer," Carole observed frostily.

Jude looked down at her large watch-face and her expression suddenly changed. "Oh, Lord!" she cried. "I'd completely forgotten! I've got a friend coming round this evening! I must dash!"

"So we'll go to the Shorelands Estate first thing?"

"Yes, fine. Communicate in the morning!" And, having gulped down the remains of her wine, Jude rushed out of the pub.

Carole finished her drink more sedately, as Ted Crisp chatted inconsequentially of this and that. She didn't feel relaxed alone with him. Carole Seddon would never really be a "pub person."

She tried not to be interested in who Jude's "friend" might be. They were only neighbours, after all. There was no reason why they should know everything about each other's lives.

"Another one of those?" asked Ted Crisp, as she sipped down the last of her wine.

"No, thanks. I must get back home." But at the door she did manage to stop and say, "Good night, Ted." Just like a regular "pub person" might have done.

# 20

IT WAS AFTER eight the following morning, the Friday. Gulliver had been duly walked and Carole still hadn't heard anything from Jude. They'd agreed to go to the Shorelands Estate early and intercept Dylan when he arrived for work at Bali-Hai. According to the duty roster Carole had snooped at, all fitters were meant to pick up their carpets from the depot at eight in the morning and be at the properties where they were scheduled to lay them by nine.

Her hand reached for the telephone to call Jude, but then she thought, this is stupid, the woman's only next door and I must make an effort to be a little less formal. Something in Jude's casual approach to life was secretly appealing. Carole knew that the ramparts of inhibition she had built around herself would never allow her to progress far down that road, but maybe she could take a few tentative steps.

Going round to Woodside Cottage rather than telephoning would be one such step. So Carole Seddon put on her Burberry and went to knock on her next-door neighbour's door.

To her considerable amazement, it was opened by a man. He had a head of black curly hair, more of which sprouted out of the top of his Guernsey sweater. Between was heavy dark stubble. He had jeans, trainers, blue eyes and a huge grin.

"Morning," he said cheerily. "I'm Brad. You must be Carole."

"Yes, yes, I am."

"Do come in. Jude's just dressing. She won't be a moment."

"Oh, thank you." In a state of bewilderment, Carole followed the man through the cluttered sitting room into the kitchen.

He indicated a plate of toast and marmalade. "I was having some breakfast. Would you like a coffee or something?"

"No, thank you. I've just had some."

"Well, excuse me if I continue munching."

"Of course."

"Do sit down," said Brad, as he lowered himself on to a chair and took a bite of toast.

"Yes, thank you." Carole knew she sounded ridiculously formal. "So, Brad, have you known Jude long?"

"Oh yes. We go way back."

"Ah." Bubbling to the surface of Carole's mind were a whole lot of other questions she wanted to ask. How far back? Where did you meet? Where do you live? Are you a fixture in Jude's life? *What is the precise nature of your relationship?*

"Great place she's got here, hasn't she?" said Brad.

"Yes, yes, it's very nice. Needs a bit of work, of course."

He didn't seem to hear the second part of this response. "No, good old Jude," he said with easy admiration. "Always lands on her feet."

"Does she?"

"Oh yes."

At that moment the subject of their conversation swept into the room in her customary swirl of drapery. She was twisting the blonde hair into a knot on top of her head. "Morning, Carole," she called out blithely. "Brad's introduced himself, I hope."

"Yes."

"Sorry I wasn't ready. You know how it is."

Carole didn't know how it was, and wouldn't have minded a few background details to tell her how it was. But she didn't get any.

"We'd better be off then," said Jude. She leant across the table and planted a smacking kiss on Brad's marmalady lips. "Don't know how long we'll be, but if you're not here when I get back, it's been good to see you."

"You too. Always is."

"The door's on the latch. Just click the thing up and close it behind you."

"Sure. Nice to meet you, Carole."

"And you, Brad." Though she didn't feel that she'd met him at all.

In the immaculate Renault, as they drove off, Carole said, "Brad seemed very pleasant."

"Yes, he's good news."

"He said you and he go way back . . ."

"That's right. He's a good friend."

And Jude snuggled back into her seat, leaving Carole desperately in need of a definition of the word "friend." But Jude didn't volunteer one, and Carole couldn't see any way of getting one, short of actually asking straight out what her neighbour's relationship with Brad was. And she would never in a million years have done that.

The Shorelands Estate house which was receiving the benefit of J. T. fitted carpets was an Elizabethan pastiche with tall windows and bunches of thin, imaginatively topped chimneys. With the inappropriate nomenclature which seemed *de rigueur* in Shorelands, its name, Bali-Hai, was spelled out in rustic pokerwork in an asymmetrical piece of driftwood. In the driveway, behind closed railings, a large green Jaguar squatted, toad-like.

"I think we're in time," said Carole, as she brought the Renault to a halt opposite the house. "No sign of a van yet."

She looked at her watch. Ten to nine. They'd just sit and wait. And chat. Maybe she'd find out a little more about Jude's visitor.

"Brad was the friend you rushed back from the pub to see last night, was he?"

"That's right, yes."

"So he stayed over?"

"Yes. Well, it's a long way back for him."

Back *where*? Though desperate to know the answer, that was another question Carole could never have brought herself to ask.

"He seemed very at home, Jude."

"It's nice when friends feel relaxed staying with you, isn't it?"

"Yes."

Jude looked across and gave Carole a sweet smile. Was there a trace of irony in it? Was Jude actually teasing her, deliberately withholding information, knowing how desperate she was to know about the relationship with Brad? It was impossible to tell.

Jude smiled inwardly. She *was* having a little game with her neighbour. If Carole had come with direct questions, she'd have answered them. Jude had no secrets. But if she wasn't asked, it had never been her habit to volunteer information.

She felt good, though. It was always a pleasure to see Brad, catch up on what he was doing. Old friends, Jude found, became more valuable with the passage of the years.

There was a sudden tapping at the passenger side window. Jude wound it down.

"I don't know what you think you're doing parked here! This is a Neighbourhood Watch area and . . . Oh. Oh, Jude, good morning."

The righteous resident of Shorelands bending down to the car window turned out to be Barbara Turnbull, her large frame swaddled up in an expensive tweed coat.

"Barbara, how nice to see you. You know Carole?"

"Yes. Yes, of course we know each other. Morning, Carole."

"Morning."

"I'm very sorry to have spoken to you like that, Jude, but you can't be too careful. There's been quite a spate of burglaries here in Shorelands and, since there's a bit of an *element* in Fethering these days, we've all been encouraged to accost anyone we see lurking around."

"Sorry. I didn't realize we were *lurking*," said Jude.

"No, obviously you weren't. But it's an unfamiliar car and, since I didn't know who was in it, it did look as though someone was lurking. Apparently, these criminal gangs send people down to check out potential targets. 'Casing the joint,' I believe they call it." Having shared this piece of underworld know-how with her acquaintances, she straightened up. "Anyway, I was just off to my mother's for a cup of coffee and to take her dog for a walk. First chance I've had to get out for days. Been tied up with housework. But thank goodness my cleaning lady's deigned to come back this morning." Barbara Turnbull put a large smile in place over her features. "So nice to see you both."

"And you, Barbara," said Carole. "How's Rory?"

The smile froze in position. "Rory's absolutely fine," asserted Barbara Turnbull, daring anyone to contradict her. "Goodbye."

And with that she navigated her large, top-heavy body off down the road.

"Funny," Jude observed. "When she didn't know who we were, she thought we might be criminals lurking. As soon as she recognizes us, her suspicions cease. How does she know we're not 'casing the joint'?"

"Because we're Fethering residents," replied Carole stoutly.

"Still, I think it's good . . ." Jude mused.

"What's good?"

"All this security-consciousness. All this Neighbourhood Watch stuff."

"I didn't think you'd approve of that."

"Why not?"

"Because you seem to have rather a hippyish attitude to property" was the answer that came instinctively to

Carole's mind. But all she said was, "I thought you'd regard it as snooping."

"Oh, I do. And that's the beauty of it. Everyone in Fethering seems to snoop. I'm sure it's impossible to do anything in this place without *someone* having seen you at it . . ."

"Well . . ."

"Which makes me very optimistic that we're going to find out how our two bodies came to end up on the beach. Someone must've seen what happened. It's just a matter of finding out who that someone is. And I think we—"

"Ssh! Look."

A yellow Transit van had just drawn up outside Bali-Hai. Lettering on the side read "J.T. CARPETS."

"Here we go," said Carole, her hand tightening round the Stanley knife in her raincoat pocket.

Two men got out of the van and went round to open the doors at the back. Both were middle-aged, one almost completely bald, the other with grizzled grey hair.

Jude shook her head ruefully. "Neither of those looks like Dylan."

"No."

"Maybe you read the duty roster wrong?"

Carole was offended. "I did not! There were three of them allocated to this job. Dave, Ken and Dylan."

"Well, there go Dave and Ken." Jude watched the two men, now carrying toolboxes, open the gates to Bali-Hai and go up to the front door. "Looks like Dylan's called in sick."

But, as she spoke, they were aware of the sound of a car approaching fast. It was a Golf GTI, a good ten years old, tarted up with extra chrome and decals. The way it was being driven gave two fingers to the demure "20 mph" signs of Shorelands.

"I think this could be our quarry," said Carole, as she opened the car door.

They were both standing in front of Bali-Hai's railings by the time the boy emerged from his Golf. He fit Ted Crisp's description perfectly. Bleached hair, single earring, "a nasty bit of work."

He looked through them as he came up to the gates.

"Are you Dylan?" asked Carole.

"What if I am?"

"I've got something that belongs to you."

"Oh yes?"

Carole took the Stanley knife out of her pocket and held it in her open palm, with the painted "J.T. CARPETS" uppermost. Both women watched the boy closely. Though he quickly covered it up, his first reaction was undoubtedly one of shock.

"Oh, well, thanks," he said casually, reaching out for the knife. "I can take it in to work with me."

Carole withdrew her hand. "Don't you want to know where we found it?"

"Not particularly." After the initial giveaway response, his manner had become cocky, on the edge of insolence.

"We found it in a boat at the Fethering Yacht Club," said Jude.

A flicker of the eyelid showed he hadn't been expecting that. But again he recovered quickly. "Wonder how it got there . . ."

Carole took over the attack. "We know that you were there on Monday night with Aaron Spalding and another boy."

Dylan's lip curled. "You know a lot. Nosy pair of old tarts, aren't you?"

"Being offensive isn't going to help, Dylan. This is serious. And you know it's serious. Aaron Spalding's dead."

"Yes, I do know that. Stupid kid. Should have known better than to muck around on the banks of the Fether, shouldn't he?"

"And he's not the only one who's dead."

The young man's face became a rigid mask. "Don't know what you're talking about. I've got to get to work." And he made to push past them.

Jude put her hand on his sleeve. "The police might be very interested to talk to you about what happened on Monday night."

"Oh yeah?"

"We have proof that you were with Aaron," Jude went on, lying through her teeth.

Dylan turned back to look her straight in the face. "All right, yes, I was with Aaron. That's not a crime, is it?"

"No."

"We went down the Crown and Anchor, but that tight-arsed bastard of a landlord wouldn't serve the other two, so we pissed off down Nowtinstore and got some cans. We sank a few in one of them shelters on the front and Aaron asked me if I'd lend him my Stanley knife. So I did."

"What did he want it for?"

"I don't know, do I?" Dylan replied, with a shrug of aggrieved innocence. "And then I went home. I didn't go down the Yacht Club. What the other two done after I gone, I've no idea."

"I think the police would want a rather fuller explanation than that, Dylan."

But Carole's bid to frighten him didn't work.

"Maybe they would. But you're not the police, are you?" he sneered. "And I don't quite honestly think the police'd be that interested in what a pair of old biddies like you have to say."

Carole and Jude were rather afraid he was right. Their bluff had been called.

"Now, if you'll excuse me, I do have work to do." Dylan put his hand on the railings of Bali-Hai's gates.

"Don't you want your knife back?" asked Carole.

"Not that bothered. We get through a lot of those. Tools of the trade."

"Then I'll keep it . . ."

"Please yourself."

". . . as evidence."

"Evidence of *what*?" Suddenly he'd seized the lapel of Carole's raincoat and brought his face close up to hers. Her nostrils were filled by a sickly musk-flavoured aftershave. "You two harass me anymore and things could get very unpleasant for you. I've seen you around. Fethering's a small place. Wouldn't be that hard for me to find out where you live. I'd advise you both to get off my bloody back!"

There was no doubting the reality of the threat in his last words. He raised his free hand to Carole's face. She flinched. Dylan chuckled and touched her cheek. Just one touch, very brief, very gentle and very menacing. Then he let go of her coat and turned towards Bali-Hai.

"Who was the third boy?" asked Jude.

"Who indeed?"

"There was you, and Aaron Spalding, and somebody else."

"Spot on."

"Who was it?"

"That's for you to find out. Mind you, I don't think you will."

"Why? Is he dead too?" Jude called after the retreating back as Dylan strode up the drive.

But there was no answer. And the Stanley knife remained in Carole's hand.

"He's lying," Jude hissed, the first time that Carole had seen her angry. "He was with them at the Yacht Club."

"I know."

"But how're we going to prove it?"

"That," said Carole pompously, "has been the problem with crime investigation since records began."

"Yes."

"Having an instinct for what's happened, having a flash of inspiration—that's the easy bit. It's when you try to make the charges stick that most cases collapse."

Jude nodded thoughtfully. Then a slow smile spread across her broad features.

"What is it?" asked Carole.

"You talked about flashes of inspiration. I think I've just had one."

"About what?"

"About finding the third boy. I may be wrong, but at least I've an idea where we can start looking."

# 21

THEY DIDN'T HAVE far to go through the Shorelands Estate to reach Brigadoon. The front garden's Victorian lampposts continued to look incongruous in their
mock-Spanish surroundings.

"I still don't understand," Carole complained as they
approached the studded door. "We know Barbara won't
be there. We know her mother won't be there. And
Rory'll be at work in Brighton."

"It's not them we've come to see," said Jude firmly,
as she pressed the doorbell.

The woman who came to the door was probably late
forties and could have been attractive in different circumstances. She wore jeans and a faded sweat-shirt; her
greying hair was scraped back into a rubber band at the
nape of her neck and her face had the taut, drained look
of total exhaustion.

"Good morning," she said, in a surprisingly cultured
voice, and waited for them to state their business.

Jude took the initiative. "Good morning. This is Car-

ole and I'm Jude. We're both friends of Barbara Turnbull and—"

"I'm afraid Mrs. Turnbull isn't in."

"No, we know that. You're Maggie, aren't you?"

"Yes," the woman conceded cautiously.

"It was you we wanted to have a word with."

Her face closed over. "You're nothing to do with the
Social Services, are you?"

"No, no, we're not. I promise."

But that didn't resolve her suspicions. "I'm sorry. I'm
working." She reached to close the door, but Jude's next
words stopped her.

"We wanted to have a word about your son."

A new wave of exhaustion flooded the woman's
body. Her shoulders dropped. There was a note of fa-
talism in her voice as she asked, "What's he done?"

"That's what we want to find out." Jude pressed home
her slight advantage. "In particular what he was doing
last Monday night."

This did frighten the woman. Her spoken response,
that she had no idea what they were talking about, was
belied by a wildness in her eyes.

Some instinct told Carole this was the moment once
again to produce the Stanley knife from her raincoat
pocket. The woman's eyes grew wilder.

"What's that? Where did you find it?"

The telephone on the hall table rang. Indecision flickered in Maggie's frightened eyes. She didn't want to
invite them in, but equally she didn't want to let them
go until she knew as much as they knew. The phone
rang on. It was clearly not going to be picked up by

anybody else or by an answering machine. "Wait there," she said. "I'll just be a moment."

She picked up the phone and gave the number. "What? Oh yes. Yes, he is here. I'll get him to the phone." She crossed to the foot of the stairs and called up, "Mr. Turnbull! Telephone!"

She put the receiver down and crossed back to the women at the front door.

"I thought Mr. Turnbull would be at work," said Carole.

"He's not well." Dismissing the detail quickly, Maggie came closer and addressed them with a quiet urgency. "Look, I can't really talk now. But I do want to talk." Then, with a mixture of dread and pleading in her voice, she said, "You haven't spoken to anyone else about Nick, have you?"

"No," replied Jude reassuringly.

"Not yet," added Carole, who thought their level of menace should be maintained. Maggie had something to tell them; having hooked her, they didn't want to lose her.

"Carole. Good morning. What're you doing here?"

Rory Turnbull was coming down the stairs. He wore a shapeless towelling dressing gown. He looked raddled, hungover and haunted.

Carole improvised wildly. "We were just calling about a Labrador charity I'm involved in. The Canine Trust."

"If you're looking for a handout, I'm afraid dogs come fairly low down my pecking order of good causes."

"No, we were just . . ." Not wishing to get tangled up in details of her fictitious charity call, Carole moved on.

"You met my new neighbour, Jude, in the pub, didn't you?"

"Did I?" Rory Turnbull's bloodshot eyes showed no recognition but took Jude in, as though he were memorizing her features for future reference. "You will excuse me." He turned to Maggie and asked gracelessly, "Who did you say was on the phone?"

"The BMW garage. Something about a bill or—"

"I'll take it in the study." Without a word to the two women still standing on his doorstep, Rory Turnbull left the hall.

The urgency remained in Maggie's voice as she said, "Listen, I can't talk now. I'm through here at twelve. Could we meet after that?"

"Sure," said Jude. "Where?"

"You'd better come round to my place. It's not far. Spindrift Lane—do you know it?"

Carole nodded. "I do."

"Number 26. Say half-past twelve. I'll be back by then."

"Fine."

"And please don't say anything to anyone." There was a naked appeal in Maggie's eyes as she echoed Theresa Spalding's words. "Nick's a good boy. He is, really."


"I'm wondering why Rory came down," Carole mused as she drove them back to the High Street. "They must have a phone upstairs in a house that size. In their bedroom certainly."

"Come to that, why didn't he answer it in the first place?"

"Asleep? He looked pretty crumpled when he did come downstairs."

"Yes. Alternatively, he may just have been curious as to who was at the door. He heard our voices and came to have a snoop."

"He certainly subjected you to a rather searching look, didn't he?"

Jude nodded and gave a little shudder. "Uncomfortably searching. There's something very strange happening with that man, isn't there? He doesn't seem to be behaving like the pillar of society a Fethering dentist should be."

"Certainly not. He's behaving like an alcoholic."

"Or someone who's in the throes of a nervous breakdown?"

"Maybe. Still, poor old Rory's not really our concern. Except for the fact that his boat was possibly used as a temporary morgue, I can't see that he has anything to do with our body on the beach."

"No, I guess not."

"Though Maggie clearly does have something relevant to tell us. How on earth did you know that she would, Jude?"

"It was just a guess. Intuition, if you like. Barbara Turnbull had said something about Maggie's son having psychological problems and . . . I put two and two together. You know, sometimes you just have a sense of things being connected, don't you?"

"No," replied Carole, who never did.

"Bad luck. Oh, here we are."

Carole brought the Renault to a halt outside Woodside Cottage. She looked at her watch. "Spindrift Lane's only five minutes' walk away. Hardly worth taking the car. Shall I knock on your door about twenty past twelve?"

"That'd be fine."

Carole couldn't help herself from fishing a little. "So you'll have time for a nice cup of coffee with Brad . . ."

"No," said Jude breezily. "I'll have to empty a few more boxes upstairs, I'm afraid. Brad's car's not here. He's gone."

"Oh." Carole couldn't for the life of her have left it there. "But I dare say you'll be seeing him again . . ."

"I dare say," Jude agreed, with an infuriating, but probably not deliberate, lack of specificity.

Carole parked the car in her garage. As she was doing so, she noticed on the mat a little scrape of mud left by Jude's boot. She got out the dustpan and brush which was used only for the car and swept it up.

# 22

SPINDRIFT LANE WAS part of the residential network which spread out from Fethering High Street. While not aspiring to the wealth-proclaiming grandeur of the Shorelands Estate, the houses there bore witness to lives well spent and money well invested. Paintwork gleamed and anything that could be polished had been polished. Even in November, no front grass was allowed to grow ragged and weeds had been banished from the interstices between flagstones in garden paths. The area was a testament to bourgeois values, which are, for the most part, financial values.

Number 26 Spindrift Lane, however, fell short of these values. The front lawn was unkempt, the paint on the window-frames blistered and split. The garden gate sagged, maintaining only a tenuous contact with its hinges. Carole and Jude exchanged looks as they pushed through and approached the front door.

Maggie had changed out of her working clothes into a navy woollen suit. With hair neatly brushed, her appearance matched the educated accent which had seemed so discordant earlier in the morning. As she ushered her two visitors into the sitting room, her mouth was tight with anxiety. Their welcome was polite—she had been well brought up—but not warm.

Carole and Jude were sat down on a sofa in a room that was sparsely furnished and, like the exterior of the house, could have done with being decorated. The grate in the fireplace was bleakly empty. The bunched curtains in the bay window had faded unevenly. There was a portable television, but no video recorder. The room boasted few ornaments, but those there were looked to be of good quality. The two watercolour seascapes on the wall made Carole want to know the artist's name. On the mantelpiece stood a pair of rather fine brass candlesticks and a photograph of a boy aged about fourteen. It was a school one, posed against a cloudy background, like the picture of Aaron Spalding featured in the *Fethering Observer*.

Maggie stood in front of the fireplace and confronted them. "All right. What is all this? What's Nick being accused of?"

"We're not accusing your son of anything," Jude replied calmly. "May I call you Maggie?"

"Maggie . . . Mrs. Kent . . . I don't care. Just tell me what you know."

"You've heard about the death of that boy Aaron Spalding?" A curt nod of acknowledgement. "Well, we have reason to believe that Aaron Spalding, with two other youths, was messing around on the seafront here at Fethering on Monday night."

"How do you mean, 'messing around?' "

"They had a few drinks and then they broke into the Fethering Yacht Club."

Maggie Kent didn't say anything. She still watched and waited, gauging how much they knew.

"We know that one of the other youths was called Dylan. He's training as a fitter with J. T. Carpets . . ."

Carole decided that Jude's gentle approach was too much Good Cop, so she came in heavily in her Bad Cop persona. "And we have reason to believe that the third youth was your son, Nick."

For the first time in their acquaintance, Jude turned a look of reproof on her neighbour. They were going too fast. Maggie Kent didn't look like a woman who'd crumple in the face of bullying. They needed to play her very carefully if they were going to get anything out of her.

Maggie was silent for a moment. The women on the sofa watched her, each afraid that Carole had blown it.

Eventually she spoke. Her voice was quiet and measured. It was costing her a lot to achieve, but she was in control. "Are you suggesting that my son had anything to do with Aaron Spalding's death?"

"No," Jude hastened to assure her. "Certainly not. Whatever happened to Aaron happened on the Tuesday night. We're concerned about events on the Monday."

"Why? Why are you concerned about them?"

Carole took this on. "Because I have reason to believe that a crime was committed that night."

Anger blazed in Maggie Kent's eyes. "And you think Nick did it?"

"No. I'm not quite sure what the crime was and I certainly have no idea at this point who did it. We're just trying to piece together the events of Monday night." There was a silence, before Carole went on, "I've spoken to the police about this, but they seem unwilling to take me seriously."

"Oh? So your aim is not to turn all your information over to the police?"

"No. Not until we know precisely what happened and have a completely watertight case. I'm not going to be treated like a hysterical woman a second time."

"Hm . . ." Maggie Kent nodded, taking in what she'd been told. Something Carole had said had relaxed her. The tension across her shoulders had lessened. She moved restlessly over towards the window and looked out into the November coldness. Then, seeming to reach a decision, she turned back and lowered herself into an armchair.

"All right." There was a new complicity in her voice. "I want to know what happened on Monday night at least as much as you do. But tell me first how you know Nick was involved. Were there witnesses?"

Jude shook her head. "Not so far as we know. It was guesswork and a bit of luck, really. I'd had coffee with Barbara Turnbull and she'd been complaining about how her cleaning lady couldn't come in because of some problem with her son. I just made the connection."

Maggie Kent's lip curled. "And I bet the lovely Barbara was really sympathetic about the situation?"

"From your tone, I don't get the feeling I need to answer that."

"No. I hope she's not a great friend of yours . . . In fact, I don't much care if she *is* a great friend of yours. So far as I'm concerned, Barbara Turnbull is 100 per cent British cow."

Carole had expected Jude to agree with this and was

surprised to hear only a demure, "I don't really know her that well."

"Right. Fine. Well, I've been working for her for seven or eight months and I do know her—quite well enough. I wouldn't put up with her patronizing poison if I had any alternative."

"Aren't there many jobs round here?" asked Jude innocently.

"Not many that don't involve travelling. I don't have transport these days. And I don't want to take on anything full-time yet. I still feel I should be around for Nick . . . you know, when he comes home from school." She bit her lip. "Not that it seems my being around for him is doing that much good."

"Adolescence has always been pretty much purgatory."

Not for the first time, Carole was struck by Jude's instinctive ability to get on someone's wavelength and say exactly the right thing. Maggie Kent nodded, coaxed into confidences. "Yes, and he lost his father at a very difficult time."

"I'm sorry. I didn't realize that—"

"Oh, I didn't mean 'lost' in that sense. Nick's father's still alive—at least, I assume he is, I haven't heard anything to the contrary—but for all the use he is to his son—or to me, come to that—he might as well be dead." She sighed, before launching into a potted history she'd delivered many times before. "Sam—that's my husband—lost his job about three years ago. He worked in the printing industry—managerial job, good salary, all the accessories that go with a nice middle-class lifestyle. House in a desirable part of Fethering, two cars, son at private school, little wife needn't go out to work—all sorted. Then suddenly there's a takeover. Big German conglomerate buys up Sam's company and there's major reorganization, restructuring, redeployment, and all those other words beginning with 're-' which mean basically that people lose jobs. And Sam's out with a year's money.

"He wasn't good at being out of work. Sam was always one of those men who felt defined by his job. That was his status, his sense of identity. Take it away and—as I discovered—there wasn't a lot else there. At first Sam just pretended it hadn't happened, made no changes to the way we lived our lives, kept Nick on at the private school, all that. He seemed to think something was going to happen, some *deus ex machina* was going to swoop down from the skies with a large chequebook and make everything all right again.

"Well—surprise, surprise—that didn't happen. Sam realized rather belatedly that, unless he did something about it, nothing *would* happen. So he applied for a few jobs, but he wasn't good at selling himself. His confidence was so shot to pieces by then, he was going into interviews virtually telling them that he wasn't what they were looking for. Which—all too readily—they believed.

"From then on, it just got worse. The money ran out, Sam started drinking and, to make things even worse, he got into drugs. Cannabis at first—'to dull the pain,' he kept saying—but pretty soon he was on to the hard stuff. Heroin. Under those circumstances, the marriage didn't stand a chance. Rows over money, rows about . . . about anything. Soon we stopped bothering with subjects to have rows about, we just cut straight to the row.

"And then my dear husband walked out. In about

eighteen months Sam'd gone from executive to dosser. I don't know where he is now. Living rough somewhere, I imagine. I wouldn't dare look too closely in shop doorways along the Strand or on street corners in Brighton, in case I recognized my husband . . . assuming of course that I ever went to London or Brighton, and didn't spend all my time incarcerated in bloody Fethering!"

Gently, Jude eased the conversation on. "And you say all this had a bad effect on Nick?"

"Of course it did. Devastating. For a start, he'd always worshipped his father, and suddenly there's this pathetic wreck around the house all the time. And Mum and Dad, who'd always seemed to get on so well, stop getting on well at all. And all Nick's friends are going off on expensive holidays and we can't afford to. And then one day there's not even a pathetic wreck round the house. His father's upped and gone."

"And he hasn't been back since?"

"Not while Nick's been around, no. Sam did come back here a few times the first few weeks, but it was only to try and get money off me. Steal money from me if I wasn't here. He took virtually everything in the house that had any value and sold it off to feed his heroin habit. Even took his passport one time—no doubt he managed to get a few quid for that from illegal-immigrant racketeers. He's just gone." Maggie Kent let out a defeated sigh. "When he started going downhill, I felt dreadful, kept thinking I could save him from himself, that I *should* save him from himself. Now, I haven't got the energy even to think about him. So far as I'm concerned, Sam no longer exists."

"But Nick must've been in an awful state when his father left," Jude persisted gently.

"Oh yes, it was terrible for him. And Sam's departure coincided with running out of money for the school fees, so suddenly Nick's changing schools. I'm not saying anything against state education . . . well, yes, I am, actually. You grow up middle class and your mind rides along certain tracks for so long that it's almost impossible to derail it. Nick was much better taught at his private school than he is now, and he mixed with a much less damaging bunch of kids than he does now. There, I've said it! Deeply politically incorrect and I don't give a damn!"

The outburst had exhausted her further. Maggie Kent sagged in her chair, the anger drained out of her.

"I don't know. I suppose I should move out of here—I'll have to move out of here soon, anyway, the building society will see to that—and buy a little flat somewhere cheaper, and get Nick back into a decent school for his A-levels and . . ." She sighed. "But I seem to lack the will. I keep thinking something'll happen, to sort out this whole bloody mess. Maybe I'm not so different from Sam, after all." She slumped back, defeated.

"So, going back to Monday night," Jude prompted tentatively, "what time did Nick get home?"

"I don't know exactly. Not that late—one, two, I suppose. I was aware of him coming in, but I didn't see him. Quite honestly, I get so sick of all the rows about the time he comes in that if I can duck one I do.

"But he went out again early the next morning and it was what happened then that really affected him. The phone rang when I was hardly awake. Someone wanted to speak to Nick. Young voice, one of his mates I assumed, so I gave the lad an earful about ringing at that hour and got Nick to the phone. I don't know what was said, but it sure scared the hell out of my son. He threw some clothes on and rushed straight out of the house. I don't know where he was going, he wouldn't tell me, but he was shaking like a leaf."

"What time would that have been?" asked Carole.

"Ooh . . . Five past seven, say."

"Uh-huh."

"Anyway, I was worried sick. Though Nick's given me quite a few nasty frights over the last few months, I'd never seen him in that kind of state. But of course I was due up at Brigadoon to be a dutiful Mrs. Mop to the lovely Barbara . . . so I wait around as long as I can. And then, just when I'm about to leave, Nick comes back. He was in a worse state than ever, sobbing like a baby. No, worse than a baby. He was hysterical."

"Did he tell you the reason?"

"No. Oh, I got bits out of him . . . that he'd been out with Dylan and Aaron the night before . . . that they'd had a few drinks . . . I think they did some drugs too. He didn't admit it in so many words, but I'm pretty sure they did. And apparently they were talking about black magic, some gobbledegook I didn't understand, but which seemed to have got Nick pretty scared. Anyway, he told me that they broke into the Yacht Club . . . said it was just a lark, that they didn't do any harm."

"But you reacted this morning when I showed you the Stanley knife," Carole pointed out. "He must've said something about that."

"Yes, Nick mentioned it. He said that Dylan, who works as a carpet-fitter, had his knife with him. But then he seemed to regret saying that and clammed up. I asked if any of the boats had been vandalized and he assured me they hadn't."

"But Dylan was definitely with Nick and Aaron when they broke into the Yacht Club?"

"Oh yes."

Carole and Jude exchanged a look. Neither of them had believed Dylan's disclaimer at the time he said it.

"That was all the night before," said Jude thoughtfully. "But it's Nick's trip the following morning that seems really to have upset him. Did you find out anything about that?"

"Nothing. Not a thing. He kept saying he couldn't tell anyone about it. That he couldn't tell me, of all people."

" 'You, of all people' because you were his mother or because what happened had something to do with you?"

Maggie Kent shrugged helplessly at Jude's question. "I haven't a clue. All I know is that my son was in a terrible state of shock . . . Oh, and I did notice he had sand on his trainers."

"So he'd been on the beach." Carole stated the obvious. "The boy who phoned him that morning, are you sure you didn't recognize the voice?"

"I'd never heard it before. I mean, I could tell it was someone round Nick's age. They all talk ridiculously gruffly. Partly street cred and partly because they haven't got used to their voices having broken. But this wasn't one I recognized."

"Could it have been Aaron Spalding?"

"Possibly. But I never heard Aaron Spalding speak, so I wouldn't know."

There was a silence. Carole and Jude's minds were racing.

"You're sure there wasn't anything else, Maggie?" asked Jude.

"No, sorry. Nick clammed up again. That was all I could get out of him."

"But he didn't go to school on the Tuesday?"

"He was in no state to go anywhere. I stayed here with him, tried to calm him down a bit. Wednesday he stayed here again, but he was more his old self. Then we heard about Aaron's death and I'm afraid Nick just cracked up again."

"Is he at home now?" asked Carole.

Maggie shook her head. "He said he felt up to school this morning. So he went there, and I went to the Shorelands Estate to be patronized by Barbara bloody Turnbull."

"So you really have no idea what the three of them got up to at the Fethering Yacht Club?"

"No, but it was something pretty horrifying, if the effect it had on my son is anything to go by . . ."

"Not to mention the effect it had on Aaron Spalding," Jude murmured.

"What do you mean?"

"There seems a very strong chance that Aaron Spalding killed himself."

Maggie Kent nodded slowly, taking this in. It wasn't an entirely new thought to her. "Yes." Panic flared in her eyes. "I hope to God Nick's all right!"

"He will be . . . He will be."

"If only he'd tell me what happened."

"You still haven't got anything beyond the fact that the three of them broke into the Yacht Club?"

"No, not a thing. And, God knows, it's not for want of trying."

"Do you think," Jude suggested diffidently, "he might tell more to someone who wasn't his mother?"

"He might well, but I think it'd rather depend on who it was who asked him."

"What about me?" asked Jude. "Do you think he might tell something more to me?"

Maggie Kent looked at the blonde-haired stranger on her sofa with amazement, which gave way to deliberation and then assent. "Do you know," she said, "I think he might."

# 23

CAROLE KNEW JUDE was right about seeing Nick on her own, but that didn't take away her sense of frustration. It wasn't jealousy—in the short period of their acquaintance, Carole had come to accept her new neighbour had people skills that she lacked—it was more annoyance at being excluded from any part of the investigation. The feeling brought home to Carole how totally absorbed she had become by the body on the beach. In less than a week the imperatives of her normal, sensible routine had been swept away by the over-whelming need to explain its mystery.

Still, she wasn't going to let her frustration have completely negative effects. Gulliver at least should benefit from her enforced idleness. She would take him for a long walk on the beach.

The dog responded enthusiastically to her attention, making Carole feel guilty that he'd suffered from her recent preoccupations. He scampered about on the sand, scurrying back and forth, covering four times as much ground as his mistress. She walked along parallel to the sea, just below the pebble line, while Gulliver made his sudden, quixotic forays to challenge the unknown foes of flotsam and jetsam.

It was a beautiful afternoon. The weather, as if in apology for its recent bad behaviour, put on a perfect display—white winter sun, evenly pale-blue sky, the full works. It still felt cold—the lack of cloud cover ensured that—but the wind had dropped and the air no longer stung the cheeks. The heavy frosts of the previous days seemed a distant memory. Carole didn't think the night ahead would drop below freezing.

As she walked along, her restlessness eased. Life wasn't so bad after all, she reflected. Looking up to the crystal-clear contours of the South Downs in one direction and, the other way, across the beige sea to the distinct line where it became blue sky, Carole Seddon thought how lucky she was to live in such a beautiful place as Fethering. Amidst the crude cacophony of gulls, she heard the cry of a single curlew, like a piece of tape being wound backwards.

She seemed to see everything with new eyes. The seaweed clusters, stranded along the pebble line, weren't a uniform dull brown; they were a tangle of russets and copper, with the occasional unexpected burst of pimento red and fresh spinach green. Even the reminders of man's presence did not spoil the picture. An abandoned winching mechanism, encrusted with flaking rust and leaning drunkenly sideways, had its own beauty too.

Carole couldn't explain why she was thinking like this. She had many fallibilities, but lyricism was not among them. Yet somehow the combination of the sparkling afternoon, the susurration of the sea and Gulliver's ecstatic barking brought her to a feeling as near peace as her tightly constrained mind ever admitted. She had a feeling the mystery was nearing some kind of resolution.

Carole Seddon looked at her watch. It was nearly four. In a couple of hours, Jude had suggested, they should meet in the Crown and Anchor and she'd bring Carole up to date. Meanwhile, any moment now, less than half a mile away, Jude would be confronting Nick Kent.

"He's coming," Maggie Kent hissed.

She was looking out of the window in Spindrift Lane. Jude rose from the sofa to join her. Three boys in dark trousers and navy anoraks, school bags hanging single-strapped from their shoulders, were running down the middle of the road, tossing a plastic American football between them. They were red-faced from the cold and the exertion.

"I always tell him he mustn't play in the street." But Maggie spoke indulgently; she didn't sound too angry about it. "Not that there's that much traffic down here."

One of the boys stopped by the sagging gate of number 26. He was holding the ball, which he tossed with some unheard but raucous comment to one of his mates. He received a cheerful gibe back and grimaced some response. Jude recognized the face from the photograph on the mantelpiece, though it was at least two years out of date. Nick Kent's features had thickened since and his hair darkened a few shades, but he still looked a child.

As he parted from his friends and turned in at the gate, his persona changed. Quick as the flick of a switch, the jokey face-pulling gave way to an expression of deep anxiety.

There was the sound of the front door opening and slamming shut, the thump of his school bag dropped on the hall floor and the thud of footsteps starting up the stairs.

"Hi, Nick. Could you come in here a minute?"

"Just going to the loo," he called back to Maggie's summons. His voice was roughened by the local accent and the gruffness which his mother had mentioned.

The footsteps thundered on upstairs. A door opened and closed. After what seemed a long time, a lavatory flushed. The door opened and, with seeming reluctance, the footsteps dawdled back down again.

The boy stood in the doorway, registering shock at the unexpected visitor in the sitting room. "What is this?" he asked on a note of panic.

"Nick, this is Jude."

"Oh?"

"She wants to talk to you."

"Well, I don't want to talk to her!"

He turned to bolt, but was stopped by Jude's even voice saying, "I want to talk to you about this knife, Nick."

He wheeled slowly round on his heel, unwillingly drawn to the Stanley knife that Jude held out towards him. When he saw it, his worst fears seemed to be confirmed. The colour left his face and tears welled in his eyes. He collapsed on to the sofa. "Is she from the police?" he asked dully.

"No." Maggie Kent looked as though she wanted to rush across and cradle her son in her arms, protect him from all the evil in the world. But she restrained herself.

"No," Jude confirmed. "I'm not from the police. I'm not trying to cause any trouble for you. In fact, I want to save you from trouble. I want to find out what happened on Monday night. I want to find out what it was that got you so upset on Monday night and Tuesday morning. I think you'll feel better if you talk about it."

Maggie Kent listened with increasing surprise. There was a strange, almost hypnotic quality in her visitor's voice. It relaxed her own tensions a little, and seemed to be having the same effect on her son.

The boy on the sofa was silent, but his crumpled face betrayed complex emotions. He did want to talk, he wanted to end the pain he was going through, blot out the memories which were causing him such anguish. But at the same time he was afraid of the consequences that confession might unleash.

"Where did you get that knife?" he asked finally, his voice clotted with confusion.

"I found it in the bottom of a boat at Fethering Yacht Club. A boat called *Brigadoon II*."

There was a long silence. Nick looked drained, his will sapped.

"I think you'd better tell me about it," said Jude.

"I can't . . ."

"Or perhaps I should take this knife to the police . . ."

Threatening wasn't her usual style but at that moment seemed justified. Its instantaneous effect proved her right. Nick Kent broke down, shedding about five years along with the tears that coursed down his cheeks. Jude could feel the urge within Maggie to go and hug her son, but restrained her by a little shake of the head. With difficulty, the mother stayed where she was.

"So, will you tell me?" Jude gently maintained the pressure.

"I can't . . ." The emotion had eroded the roughness of his voice. His accent now matched his mother's. "I can't . . . not with Mummy here."

Jude looked into Maggie's eyes and could see the hurt there. It was only a small rejection, but Nick was definitely rejecting her.

Maggie Kent, however, was a brave woman, and she accepted the priorities of the situation. "Right. I'll go and put the kettle on." She crossed to the door. "Give me a call when I can come in again." She managed to exclude sarcasm, but she couldn't keep the pain out of her voice.

The door shut behind her. "So, Nick . . ."

"How much do you know?" The tears had stopped. He seemed to have accepted the inevitability of talking.

"I know what you told your mother . . . and a bit more that we worked out for ourselves."

"Who's 'we'?"

"I've been investigating this with a friend of mine called Carole Seddon."

The name meant nothing to him, but it brought a new anxiety. "She's not with the police either?"

"No. If anything, she's extremely anti the police." Another silence. "Come on, Nick. I know you were with Dylan and Aaron. I know you had some beers. I think you probably had some drugs too . . ."

"It was only cannabis," he retorted, his use of the botanical name rather than any slang term making him sound younger than ever. "Dylan had it with him."

"I thought he might have done."

"And he, Dylan, was getting at Aaron and me. Saying

we were just kids, that we were mother's boys, that we were chicken . . ."

"Chicken of doing what?"

"Smoking the . . . the cannabis . . . the weed."

"But you did that. So what else did he say you were scared of doing?"

"Breaking the law. He said we were goody-goodies."

"He said that, for instance, you wouldn't dare break into the Yacht Club?"

There was a hesitation before Nick Kent admitted that this was indeed what Dylan had said.

"And you proved him wrong, and you broke in—or just climbed over the railings, that wasn't too difficult—and you chose a boat at random, which happened to be *Brigadoon II*, and Dylan got out his knife and cut through the rope holding down the cover—"

"How do you know all this?" Panic flared again in the boy's eyes. "You didn't see us, did you?"

"No, I didn't see you. But you told most of that stuff to your mother."

Nick nodded, partially reassured.

"Of course, what you didn't tell your mother was what you found in the boat."

"No." For a moment he looked defiant. "And there's no reason why I should tell you either!"

"No reason, I agree. Though of course I could still take the Stanley knife to the police."

This time the threat wasn't so potent. "So, you take it to the police! That doesn't prove anything."

"No," Jude agreed softly. "Not until they find the body."

This really did shock him. "How did you know about the body?" he murmured in horrified fascination.

Jude heaved a mental sigh of relief. He'd fallen for it. He'd conceded that there had been a body in the boat. She went on, "A man's body I think it was you found in *Brigadoon II*. The body of a man in his fifties. But it's what you did with the body that interests me."

"We were horrified when we found it. There was just moonlight—the moon was full that night—and—" he shuddered—"we could only see this outline. But we knew he was dead. And then Dylan . . ."

"Was Dylan as surprised to see the body as you and Aaron were? Or did he know it was going to be there?"

Nick Kent gave a decided shake of his head. "He was shocked, just like us. Pretended not to be, pretended he was Mr. Cool, but it got to him all right. And then . . ."

The boy was having second thoughts about continuing, so Jude repeated coaxingly, "And then?"

He made up his mind to go on. "And then Dylan had this mad idea. He's into all this occult stuff, you know, black magic, the Undead, all that kind of thing . . . and he said that if Aaron and I wanted to show we were really hard . . ."

"Yes?"

Nick flinched, as though he were trying to flick something off his face. "No, no, I can't tell you."

"Was it something to do with the knife?" asked Jude.

The boy slumped back, resistance gone. The woman seemed to know everything anyway. He might as well tell her. "Yes," he agreed flatly. "He said if Aaron and me were really hard . . . he said cutting a dead man's flesh under a full moon, it'd make us strong . . . and then if we wrote our names in our own blood and left them on the body . . . we'd have special powers . . . if we did it . . ."

"And you believed him?"

"We'd had a lot to drink. And the weed . . . the cannabis, you know. We weren't thinking straight. And Dylan kept saying we were cowards and mother's boys and . . . and then he took the knife and made a cut in the man's neck. And then Aaron took the knife and he made a cut . . ."

"And did you, Nick?"

The boy looked away in embarrassment. "No. I couldn't. I . . . Dylan said I was chicken, and I wouldn't get the power that he and Aaron were going to get, but I . . . I just couldn't . . ."

The boy shuddered, too overcome by the recollection to speak.

"And what about writing the names in blood?"

"Aaron did that. He wrote his name. He wanted to have special powers. There's a girl at school he fancies—he fancied. He wanted to have power over her."

"So he wrote his name and put it in the dead man's pocket?"

"Yes."

"What about Dylan? Did he write his name?"

"No, he said he didn't need to. Because he was the leader and the power would come to him automatically."

Anger seethed within Jude, anger against Dylan. The older boy had egged on the others, probably making up his black magic mumbo-jumbo as he went along. But he wasn't going to incriminate himself by leaving his name around the scene of the crime. He'd allow the gullible Aaron Spalding to do so, though—and no doubt build up the boy's natural paranoia with garish tales of the Undead. Dylan, Jude felt sure, was directly responsible for Aaron's suicide. But she felt

equally sure the older boy would never be called to account for it.

Her only comfort was the fact that it was Dylan
who'd been careless enough to drop his Stanley knife in
the boat. Without that she and Carole would never have
made the connection to him.

"And what about you, Nick? Did you write your
name?"

"No. Dylan said if I was too chicken to cut the man's
flesh, then I didn't deserve to have any special powers.
And they both laughed at me. Said I was just a kid
and . . ." The memory of his humiliation still festered.

"And then what happened, Nick?"

"We . . . I don't know. We suddenly panicked when
we realized what we'd done."

"But you personally hadn't done anything."

"I'd broken into the club. I'd handled the dead body.
We were all in a terrible state. I think the booze and the
weed made it worse. Even Dylan lost his bottle. We
didn't want to leave any signs, any evidence, so we took
the body out of the boat and we . . . and we . . ."

"And you threw it over the sea wall into the Fether."

"How do you know all this?" He was sobbing again.
"You said you didn't see us."

"I didn't. And then you all went your separate ways
home that night—yes?"

"Yes."

"But Aaron rang you the next morning. What did he
say?"

"He said he'd woken up early and he'd panicked
about us having left some clue to what we'd done down
at the Yacht Club . . . and he'd gone down to the
beach . . ."

"And found the body washed up by the tide."

"Yes."

Finally, there was corroboration for what Carole had seen on the Tuesday morning.

"He was in a terrible state. He said the evil was coming back to haunt him, that the body was one of the Undead, and it was coming after him. So I went down to the beach and met Aaron," Nick went on, "and it was still nearly dark and we thought if we put the body back in the boat, then nobody'd ever know that we'd been there . . ."

"And that's what you did?"

"Yes."

Huge sobs were shuddering through the boy's frame. Jude reckoned she had got everything she was going to get out of him. "One final question . . . Your mother said it was after you'd come back in the morning that you were in the really bad state, not the night before . . ."

"She didn't see me the night before, did she? Anyway, I was still full of the booze and the cannabis . . . I just passed out. But the next morning . . . the shock hit me. I knew it wasn't a dream. I knew we'd actually done it. I knew what I'd done."

Something prompted a renewed outburst of emotion, more powerful than any that had come before. The boy's jaw trembled and his whole body shook uncontrollably.

"What is it?" pleaded Jude. "What is it? What was so terrible?"

For a few moments he was incapable of framing any words, just mouthing hopelessly. Finally he managed to control himself. Nick Kent sounded like a very young child as he admitted, "I'd never seen a dead body before."

# 24

"WELL, BEHAVIOUR OF that kind," concluded Carole, sitting back on her barstool in disgust, "is all too typical of the youth of today."

"That's a very Fethering thing to say," said Jude.

"What do you mean?"

"It's the kind of remark I'd have expected from some old codger whose skin's already turned to tweed. Not from someone your age."

"I'm not young," Carole protested. But she was flattered by the implication.

"You're too young to start sounding off about 'the youth of today.' "

"But what Nick Kent and the others did was appalling." She lowered her voice as she catalogued: "Illegal drinking, taking drugs, breaking and entering—probably with intent to burgle—and then mutilating a corpse."

"He wasn't involved in that."

"No, but he was in everything else. Really, Jude, am I supposed to condone that kind of behaviour?"

"No, of course you're not. But you didn't see the boy. You didn't see how much he was suffering."

"From what you've told me, he deserves to suffer. You're not making excuses for him, are you?"

"No, no. I'm just saying that Nick Kent has had a rough deal. And, OK, he drank and smoked dope, and OK, he gave in to peer pressure and behaved disgustingly, but at least you can understand why. Seeing his father fall apart before his eyes can't have been easy."

"Huh," Carole snorted. "I'm sorry. If you're trying to win me round to some woolly liberal idea that there's a psychological explanation for everything, and criminals should take their shrinks to court with them to ensure that they get off with light sentences . . . well, you're not going to convince me. If there's one thing I learned from all my years in the Home Office, it's that there is such a thing as evil within man. And that every criminal who is not technically insane has to take responsibility for his or her own actions."

Jude took a long swallow from her wineglass before replying. This was the nearest during their brief acquaintance that she and Carole had come to a row. It demonstrated how little they knew of each other's attitudes and politics. "I'm not excusing the boy's behaviour," she said calmly. "I'm just saying, from the pain in his eyes, he'd hurt himself by what he'd done much more than he'd hurt anyone else. Now let me get you another drink."

She waved at the unfamiliar girl behind the counter, who came to sort out their needs. There were only the three of them in the bar. "Two large white wines, please. Ted not in tonight?"

"He's in the office out the back, talking to some people who came round."

"Ah."

"Well, I say 'people,' " the girl insinuated. "In fact it's the police."

"Really? What've they come for?"

"I've no idea. I'm not one to pry," the girl replied righteously, as though it were Jude who'd initiated the speculation.

"Some problem with the licence?" suggested Carole, though that wasn't what she was thinking.

The pub door clattered behind them and they turned to see an agitated Denis Woodville approaching the bar.

"Evening, Vice-Commodore."

"Oh, hello, ladies. Is Ted in?" he asked the barmaid.

"He's out the back, talking to some people."

"The police, actually," said Jude, upstaging any second attempt from the barmaid to cast aspersions on her boss.

"Is that so?" The news seemed to be of significance to Denis Woodville.

"Can I get you a drink, sir?"

"Oh yes, all right. A large brandy, please."

"Soda or anything with that?"

"Just on its own, thanks."

"No more break-ins at the club?" asked Carole.

"What?" He seemed distracted. "No, no, I don't think so. Though in fact it does seem that we have been the victim of criminal activity."

He might have elaborated on this portentously delivered hint had not Ted Crisp at that moment appeared through the door behind the bar. He looked as scruffy as ever, but unflustered. If the police presence had had anything to do with his own illegal activities, he wasn't going to let it get to him.

"Evening, Jude . . . Carole . . . Denis . . ." His eyes moved along from face to face. "What're you all looking at me like that for?"

Denis Woodville voiced what the two women would have been too polite to raise. "I gather you've had the police with you . . ."

"Yes. But don't get the wrong impression. I haven't done anything they could touch me for. My record is as driven snow-like as any of Cliff Richard's."

"I wonder if they came to see you for the same reason they came to see me."

The landlord cocked an interrogative eye at the Vice-Commodore. "Missing person, was it?"

"Yes."

The barmaid hovered, all ears. "Oh, love," said Ted, "could you go and get us some tomato and orange juices from round the back? I noticed we was getting low."

With very bad grace, the girl slunk out of the bar. She needn't have worried, though. It was only a temporary delay. She'd hear all the dirt soon enough. The Fethering grapevine was extremely efficient.

"Look, if you both know, you might as well tell us," said Jude impatiently. "Come on, what's it all about?"

Ted Crisp saw no point in secrecy. "The police came in asking if I'd seen Rory Turnbull recently. Same with you, Denis?"

"Yes."

"But we only saw him this morning," Carole protested. "Up at his house."

"Well, maybe you'd better tell the police that," said Ted. "Though in fact they do know he was still at home at twelve, because he paid the cleaning lady when she left."

So the police must already have been out to Spindrift Lane to talk to Maggie. Jude wondered what effect their arrival must have had on the terrified Nick Kent.

"Sometime after twelve, however," the landlord went on, "our Rory buggered off in the BMW. His wife got home round two and immediately raised the alarm."

"What? Was she afraid he'd run off with another woman?" suggested Jude.

Denis Woodville's bald head was firmly shaken. "Can't think so. There's never been any talk of that kind of thing with Rory."

"It's always the quiet ones. These things happen."

"Not in Fethering they don't," said Carole tartly, before continuing, "But why did Barbara raise the alarm? Surely there's no harm in a grown man going off for a drive in his own car when he feels like it?"

"Not usually, I agree, there isn't," said Ted. "But there is when he leaves a suicide note."

# 25

A SILENCE FOLLOWED Ted Crisp's words. Then Jude said thoughtfully, "He certainly had the air of a man who was tired of life."

"Well, comes of being a dentist—living from hand to mouth all the time."

"You've already used that line, Ted." Carole may not have been much good at spotting the humour of jokes, but she could certainly recognize one she'd heard before.

"Sorry. One of the hazards of a publican's life. You've only got so many jokes, and you keep forgetting who was in the bar when you last told them."

"Mind you," Jude went on, as though this exchange hadn't happened, "there's a difference between being tired of life and actually ending it. What kind of major event is needed to push someone over the brink like that?"

"It needn't be a major event," said Carole. "When I worked for the Home Office, I was involved in a survey on suicides in prison. If a victim gets really depressed, often the tiniest reverse or setback will make them do it. They're not rational at that point."

"No, but I'm sure something must've changed in Rory Turnbull's life. I mean, he hated being a dentist. Apparently, he hated his wife too. And I'm certain he hated his mother-in-law. But he'd put up with all of that for years. Why is it suddenly now that he can't take anymore?"

"I could tell you one reason . . ." Denis Woodville spoke with the sly confidence of someone who had secret information to impart. He allowed himself a pause, sure of his audience's attention, then went on, "Did I mention, ladies, when you came to see me at the club, that we'd had a bit of a problem with last year's accounts?"

Carole nodded. "Yes, you said the accountant had made a mistake."

"So I thought. The discrepancy involved was a little over a thousand pounds. Well, I had a meeting with the accountant yesterday and he took me through everything. It wasn't their error. I'm afraid I had to eat rather a lot of humble pie for having even suspected them. No, it turned out that someone had actually been siphoning funds out of the club's bank account."

"Really?"

"The only registered signatories for Fethering Yacht Club cheques are the Commodore, the Vice-Commodore and the Treasurer. Well, the Commodore has been abroad for the last four months, during which time most of the cheques were drawn. I can assure you I haven't been putting my hand in the till—might have helped me out a bit if I had, but I haven't. So that leaves the Treasurer."

He paused for dramatic effect, and was visibly miffed when Carole came in impatiently and upstaged him. "Who is, of course, Rory Turnbull."

"Yes," a tight-lipped Denis Woodville conceded. "So that might give him one reason for doing away with himself. He knew I was meeting the accountants yesterday. I imagine he just didn't want to face the music."

"So he got into his BMW," Ted Crisp speculated, "drove up into the Downs, fixed a tube from the exhaust into the car's interior—"

"We don't know that's what happened, do we?" asked Jude. "The police didn't say they'd found him, did they?"

"No," the landlord agreed. "But from what they were saying, it's pretty clear that's what they were expecting to find."

"But *why* would he have done it?" demanded Carole. "Put his hand in the Yacht Club till? For a thousand pounds? I mean, a thousand pounds would be very nice—none of us would say no to it . . ."

"Certainly not." Denis Woodville's agreement was heartfelt.

". . . but for someone in Rory Turnbull's position— dentist's salary, big house on the Shorelands Estate—a thousand pounds isn't much. Certainly not enough for him to risk public humiliation and possible criminal proceedings. *Why* would he have done it?"

"You'd be amazed." Ted Crisp shook his shaggy head at the recurrent follies of humankind. "Happens all the time—particularly in a place like Fethering. Somebody gets a position of power locally—only in the

Cricket Club or the Yacht Club or something tinpot like that—" he went on, apparently unaware of the Vice-Commodore's bristling—"and they have access to another chequebook, and they suddenly think, 'Ooh, I can get something out of this.' And they milk the funds. Just for the odd hundred they'll do it. I don't know why, but it certainly keeps happening."

"I suppose everyone needs money," Carole concluded. "People may look like they've got plenty, but we can't see inside their bank accounts, can we? We can't know what demands there are on their resources, what foolish investments they may have made, what reckless loans they've taken on. It's one of the last taboos in this country, people actually talking about their financial affairs."

"You're right." Ted Crisp looked at their glasses. "Come on, let's have another drink. This round's on me."

"That's no way to make a profit," Carole observed.

The landlord turned on her in mock anger. "Are you saying no? Are you saying you don't want to take a drink from me?"

She smiled graciously. "No, I'm not. Thank you very much indeed, Ted."

As she pushed her wineglass forward, she felt another little frisson from the knowledge that she, Carole Seddon, was in the Crown and Anchor, exchanging banter with the landlord and calling him by his first name. She'd come a long way in a week.

"Of course, people develop expensive habits too," Ted ruminated, as he poured the drinks. "Rory Turnbull was getting through the Scotch in here like there was no tomorrow."

"But on his income presumably he could afford an alcohol habit."

"He could afford an *alcohol* habit, yes, Carole."

She was quickly on to the slight pressure he'd put on the word. "What do you mean? Are you saying he had another expensive habit? Are you saying Rory Turnbull was into drugs?"

But either Carole had mistaken his intonation or the landlord had decided he didn't wish to amplify the hint. He just said, "Hardly. Don't somehow see him in the role of crazed junkie, do you?" He punctuated the end of such speculation by plonking the two replenished wineglasses on the counter. "There you are—compliments of the management. Treasure this moment. Record it on the mental video cameras of your minds. Because I can assure you, it doesn't happen very often!"

When the round of thank-yous had subsided, Jude looked thoughtful. "It's odd, though, isn't it? Two suicides in a week . . ."

"Two?" asked the Vice-Commodore.

"That boy Aaron Spalding."

"Was that suicide?"

Jude caught Carole's eye and read caution in it. What they had been investigating was private, between the two of them, at least for the time being.

"Well, that's certainly been suggested," said Jude, making her tone more generalized. "I don't know whether there's been an inquest yet. OK, not two suicides—two unnatural deaths. All I'm saying is that for someone like me, who's lived here less than a week, that seems rather a high number. Or is it the usual pattern in Fethering?"

"By no means," Denis Woodville replied. "There's

probably a higher death rate here than in most other parts of the country, but that's simply because of the average age of the residents. Two unnatural deaths like this is most unusual."

Jude's brown eyes signalled to Carole not to worry, she was only floating an idea to see if it got any response, before she asked ingenuously, "Makes one wonder whether there could be any connection between the two."

The suggestion produced a snort of laughter from the Vice-Commodore. "A connection between a highly respected middle-aged man living on the Shorelands Estate and some teenager from Downside? I would think not."

"No," said Jude.

"Hardly," said Carole.

But they were both increasingly convinced that there was a connection.

There was the clatter of the bar door opening and a voice said, "Evening, mine host."

Bill Chilcott had arrived for his nightly half.

Denis Woodville stiffened and downed the remainder of the brandy Ted Crisp had bought him. "Sorry, I must be off," he said. "Suddenly a rather nasty smell around this place."

And, as if his next-door neighbour didn't exist, the Vice-Commodore stalked out of the Crown and Anchor.

# 26

"IT WAS IN Rory Turnbull's boat," said Carole, as they reached the gate of Woodside Cottage. The evening was mild. The frost would probably hold off that night. "The body was put in *Brigadoon II*. That's the only thing we've got linking Aaron Spalding's death and Rory Turnbull's suicide."

"It's not much," said Jude.

Carole sighed despondently. "Maybe there is no connection. Maybe it's just an unfortunate coincidence."

Jude shook her head. "No, there's a link between them. They are connected."

So strong was the conviction in her voice that Carole didn't argue. Instead, characteristically, she moved on to practicalities. "Well, I think we need to know more about Rory Turnbull. What he was like, what was happening in his life, what pushed him over the edge."

"And whether he did have anything to do with drugs."

"You noticed that too? When Ted hinted at something and then clammed up?"

"Oh yes. I'll follow up on the drugs thing tomorrow."

"How?"

"Let's say I have an idea of where to start."

"And I," Carole announced confidently, "will make it my business tomorrow to find out more about Rory Turnbull."

"How'll you do that?"

"Let's say I have an idea of where to start," came the lofty reply.

Carole Seddon could also play mysterious when she needed to.


Carole wasn't a dog person. When she left the Home Office, she'd taken on Gulliver for purely practical reasons. He would give a purpose to the many walks with which she had planned to fill the longeurs of her retirement. Being accompanied by a dog, she would avoid unwelcome questions and speculation. And anyway, people with dogs never look lonely.

It was the same kind of sensible thinking that had made her join the Canine Trust. She didn't feel particularly strongly about the civil liberties of dogs, but she recognized that volunteering for the charity might provide occasional useful work to fill a little more of her time.

The demands were not onerous. She helped out with the Canine Trust local branch's summer fête; twice a year she contributed to their bring-and-buy coffee mornings and she distributed raffle tickets.

Carole discharged these duties punctiliously, as she did everything, but she found her involvement in the charity increasingly dull. In fact, when the latest batch of raffle tickets arrived in the post a few weeks before, she had contemplated ceasing to be a volunteer.

But on the Saturday morning, clutching them in her hand as she walked down the High Street towards the Fethering Yacht Club, Carole positively blessed the raffle tickets. Nothing could have given her a better excuse to call on Winnie Norton.

And the reason why in the past she had tried to avoid calling on Winnie Norton with raffle tickets—because the old lady insisted on inviting her in and subjecting her to a minimum half-hour dose of the Winnie Norton view of the world—was on this occasion a positive advantage.

Spray Lodge was the nearest residential building to the river. Some eight storeys high, its most valued flats looked out, over the Yacht Club and the sea wall which separated the Fether from the beach, all the way to the distant horizon where the water melted into the sky. Normally, Spray Lodge was one of the most desirable of Fethering locations. But when the sea wall was being repaired, the block was uncomfortably close to the monotonous thud of the pile driver. Carole heard the noise increasing as she neared her destination.

Carole no longer took Gulliver on her raffle-ticket-selling excursions. The first time she'd thought he might be useful to establish her credentials as an authentic dog lover, but she had not repeated the experiment. The Fethering residents whom Canine Trust directives instructed her to target were, by definition, other dog owners, and Gulliver's noisy enthusiasm—not to mention combativeness—on greeting their pets had made for slow and uncomfortable progress. Since the first time, therefore, he had remained at home when his mistress went out with her raffle tickets.

Winnie Norton was a dog owner, and presumably therefore a dog lover—assuming she was capable of loving anything other than her daughter. She was the owner of Churchill, whom Jude had encountered at Brigadoon. Carole didn't really count Yorkshire terriers as dogs. They were too small, too silky, too yappy, a kind of bonsai mutant of what, to her mind, a dog should be.

When she buzzed through on the entryphone, she heard Churchill before she heard his owner. He was yapping, as ever. Then Winnie Norton's carefully enunciated tones inquired, "Yes, who is it?"

"It's Carole Seddon. I've got the Canine Trust raffle tickets."

"Oh, splendid. Do come up." And the entryphone box buzzed admission.

Winnie Norton's second-floor flat was relatively small, but every item in it was exquisite. Carole knew that if she referred to any piece of furniture or ornament, her hostess would say, "Oh yes, well, when I sold the big house after my husband died, I had to get rid of a lot of beautiful stuff. Phillips auctioned it, and I've kept only the best, the very best." Then she would chuckle and continue, "There are museums all over the world who'd give their eye-teeth for what's in this room."

And Carole knew if she referred to the sea view, Winnie Norton would say, "Oh yes, well, you see it best from here on the second floor. The people in the flats below just look out over the Yacht Club, and those above get a much less good angle on the horizon. When I sold the big house after my husband died, I insisted that I had to have the best flat in the block with the best view." And then she'd chuckle and continue, "I may be slumming, but at least I'll slum in style."

That Saturday morning Carole was determined to avoid commenting on either the furniture or the sea view.

When she opened the front door of the flat to let Carole in, Winnie Norton was revealed in a cherry-coloured woollen suit with gold braiding and buttons. Her hair, still bearing a bluish tinge, was fixed like stiff meringue on top of her head. With her spare hand, she held Churchill up to her chest. He was once again yapping furiously.

"There, you lovely boy," Winnie cooed. "Look who's come to see you—it's Carole. Look how pleased to see you he is, Carole."

The dog's little eyes glinted a look of pure malevolence at the visitor. Don't worry, you revolting little mutt, thought Carole, it's mutual.

"Now, you do have time to stop for a coffee, don't you, dear?"

It was said defensively, almost challengingly. The last few times Carole had called, she'd managed to wriggle out of staying. This time, however, she gave the right answer.

"Oh, excellent. Now do sit down on the sofa, dear. The kettle's just boiled. Barbara's bought me one of those new fangled cafetières, so I'm getting quite 'with it.' But I must confess, it does make delicious coffee. Oh, and I'll just say the one apology now for that dreadful thumping from the sea wall."

"Don't apologize. You can hear it all over Fethering."

"Yes, but it's much worse from here. I tell you, I've

had a splitting headache for days. It keeps going through the night, you know."

"That's because of the tides."

"Huh. I suppose it has to be done. And, in theory, it's all going to be finished by Monday. Mind you," said Winnie Norton darkly, "I'll believe that when it happens. Now, I won't be a moment getting the coffee. You stay and talk to Carole, there's a good boy."

Winnie Norton poured Churchill down on to the carpet and went through to the kitchen. The dog leapt forward towards Carole, then stopped about a yard away from the sofa, his body tensed backwards. He growled.

"Get lost, you little rat!" Carole hissed.

The dog understood the sentiment, if not the words. He started up his high-pitched yapping again.

"Oh, shut up!"

Again she kept her voice down, but this time the injunction had an effect. With a final look of undiluted hatred, Churchill slunk off behind the sofa.

Carole looked out at the sea. Even though she was determined not to say so in Winnie's presence, the view was undeniably magnificent. She rose and went closer to the picture window. No, from here Winnie couldn't see the end of the breakwater where the dead man had lain. Because of the Yacht Club building, her view of the low-tide beach started farther down.

"Wonderful view, isn't it?" Carole heard from behind her.

"Mm," she agreed, as she turned to help Winnie with the coffee tray.

"Oh yes, well, you see it best from here on the second floor. The people in the flats below just look out over the Yacht Club, and those above . . ."

Damn, out came the whole routine. Winnie Norton didn't need prompting from anyone else. She was self-priming.

While the familiar words were rehearsed yet again, Carole reflected that her hostess wasn't acting like someone whose son-in-law had just committed suicide. Maybe she didn't yet know the news. Maybe Barbara Turnbull had kept it from her mother out of kindness until the facts had been confirmed.

Carole was determined to find out. She waited dutifully for the chuckle and the, "I may be slumming, but at least I'll slum in style," before saying, "I heard a dreadful rumour about Rory in Allinstore this morning." (She certainly wasn't going to tell Winnie Norton that she'd heard it in the Crown and Anchor. Everyone in Fethering knew that Carole Seddon wasn't a "pub person.") "I do hope it's not true."

The light that blazed in Winnie Norton's eye revealed that she knew all the details. And also revealed that she was at least as proficient as her dog at looks of pure malevolence. "It's true, all right. And absolutely typical of the man! Selfish to the end!"

If Rory Turnbull's suicide had been an attempt to make people feel guilty and realize how much they'd undervalued him during his lifetime, the gesture had clearly failed with his mother-in-law.

"But it's definite, is it? I mean, they've found the body?"

"No, not yet. The police're still looking. Typical of Rory again—wasting police time like that. That man's never thought of anyone but himself from the moment he was born. I always told Barbara he was a dubious factor. Not our class of person at all. I could see that from the day I first met him.

"Barbara is, needless to say, distraught," Winnie went on. "What a terrible thing to happen to her. And, if it's confirmed as a suicide, that could well invalidate all the life insurance policies. Selfish, selfish, selfish. What's more, everyone in Fethering will assume that there was something wrong with their marriage."

"And wasn't there?" asked Carole.

"There were faults on his side certainly. The only thing Barbara did wrong in that marriage was choosing an unsuitable man in the first place. But she knows it's a wife's duty to stay by her man. She's discussed her situation with Canon Granger—you know, Roddy—and he has nothing but admiration for the way Barbara has coped. She's behaved like a saint throughout . . . in spite of all the dreadful things Rory did."

"What kind of things?" Carole decided it was going to be quite easy to get the information she was after. Such was the level of spleen Winnie Norton harboured for her son-in-law, the old woman didn't stop to consider why she was being asked all these questions.

"Well, he was always boorish. Had no manners. Someone brought up in the gutter never quite loses the tang of it, you know. Rory was a product of state edu-cation, as you could probably tell. Jumped-up little oik from a secondary modern who managed to scrape into a university and somehow get his dental qualifications. As I said, always a dubious factor. Barbara did all she could to make something of him, but . . . well, you know the proverb about silk purses and sow's ears . . ."

"But what kind of things specifically did Rory do?" Carole persisted. "Was he unfaithful to Barbara?"

"Good heavens, no. Even he wouldn't have dared do that. No, it was more mental cruelty, I suppose you'd call it. He collected pornography, you know."

"Did he?"

"Oh yes. Poor darling Barbara found boxes of the stuff when she was looking through their loft. And that was only the part of it." Winnie Norton shook her head in shocked disapproval. "Rory was up to all kinds of other things as well . . ."

"Like?"

"Like staying out late. Like getting into fights."

"Getting into fights?"

"He came back in the small hours only a couple of months ago and he'd had a tooth knocked out, would you believe? Well, imagine how difficult it was for Barbara to maintain appearances when her husband was walking around looking like a prize-fighter. And then there was the drinking . . ."

"Had he always drunk? Right through their marriage?"

"He'd always had it in him," Winnie Norton replied portentously. "But it was only the last few months it'd got out of hand. And it wasn't just drink . . ."

"What do you mean?"

"Drugs."

"Really?"

"Oh yes." The old lady nodded vigorously. While she did so, her sculpted hair made no independent movement. "Barbara had suspected something of the kind was going on, and I found some stuff in Rory's study."

In other circumstances Carole might have asked what Winnie Norton was doing snooping round her son-in-law's study, but she didn't want to stop the flow.

Winnie seemed to anticipate the thought anyway. "Maybe I shouldn't have been looking into his affairs, but I couldn't go on seeing my daughter suffer like that. So I took things into my own hands, and I found . . . this stuff."

"What kind of stuff? Are you an expert on drugs?"

"Of course I'm not!" Winnie Norton snapped. "But I watch television. There's hardly a drama on these days that doesn't show people taking drugs. So I recognized it when I saw it. In Rory's desk drawer I found a syringe, and some metal foil, and a little packet of white powder. I think he was spending all their money on drugs."

There were a lot of follow-up questions she could have asked, but Carole decided to bide her time until she'd talked to Jude. She'd already been given more than she had dared hope for.

"Well, I'm distressed to hear all that, Winnie," she said blandly. "Do give my condolences to Barbara, won't you?"

If she'd thought this traditional formality would be met by an equally formal response, she was disappointed.

"Condolences!" Winnie Norton spat out the word. "Barbara doesn't need condolences. She needs congratulations. Twenty-eight years of misery and now finally she's shot of him."

"Yes," said Carole. "Of course. Now, about these raffle tickets . . ."

"The Canine Trust, yes, yes, yes." Winnie rose with surprising agility from her chair. "Just get my chequebook." She crossed to a writing desk decorated with intricate marquetry designs. "This is a charming piece, isn't it? You see, when I sold the big house after my husband died, I had to get rid of a lot of beautiful stuff. Phillips auctioned it, and I've kept only the best, the very best." She chuckled, then continued, "There are museums all over the world who'd give their eye-teeth for what's in this room."

Carole smiled graciously. Churchill emerged from behind the sofa and started yapping at her.

# 27

AS SHE'D MENTIONED, Jude had done some acting in her time. She'd done a lot of things in her time. Hers had been a rich and varied life.

On the Saturday morning, while Carole went off to do her bit with Winnie Norton, Jude decided she'd have to call on her acting skills to further her own research. She rang through to J. T. Carpets. Even if no carpet-fitting went on at the weekend, the show-room was bound to be open. And there must be someone working in the office.

There was. Jude put on a voice of excruciating gentility (school of Barbara Turnbull) and went into her prepared spiel. "Good morning. I'm trying to contact one of your carpet-fitters. Named Dylan."

"I'm sorry. The fitters don't work at the weekend."

"Well, could you give me his home address and phone number?" she demanded imperiously.

"I'm afraid it's not company policy to give out our employees' private details over the telephone."

"Then in this case you must make an exception to

company policy. My name is Mrs. Grant-Edwards." Jude was taking a risk that the girl in the office had never spoken directly to the real Mrs. Grant-Edwards. And perhaps less of a risk in assuming that the real Mrs. Grant-Edwards would talk the way she was talking. "I live in a house called Bali-Hai on the Shorelands Estate, where your people have just been fitting a carpet."

"Oh yes?"

"And one of the fitters was this young man called Dylan."

"You haven't found anything missing, have you?"

The anxiety in her voice was a real giveaway. Clearly Dylan didn't have a reputation as the most trustworthy of employees. Jude wondered how many little pilferings had occurred in the houses where he had fitted carpets. And wondered how much longer he would keep his job.

"No, no, it's not that. It's rather the reverse. I've found something of his in the house."

"What?"

Jude had thought long and hard what her cover story should be. She wasn't going to get anywhere with a complaint about Dylan. Inventing some domestic crisis was too risky; his employers were bound to know more about his family circumstances than she did. What was needed was something urgent, but unthreatening, something that would sound as though Mrs. Grant-Edwards was actually doing him a good turn. Jude felt pleased with the solution she'd finally come up with.

"It's a wallet containing his credit cards. And since he hasn't come back to our house looking, I assume he doesn't know where he left it. Well, I know how tiresome it can be to lose one's credit cards. It happened to me last year and caused an awful kerfuffle. So I just wanted to ring him to put his mind at rest."

The approach worked with the girl at J. T. Carpets. "That's very kind of you, Mrs. Grant-Edwards."

"If we don't all help each other out in this life, what will become of us?"

"What indeed? Right, just a moment. I'll find Dylan's home number for you."

The girl gave it. Jude had asked for his address too, but she couldn't justify pressing for that. Her cover story didn't require her knowing where he lived. So she just thanked the girl for her help and put the phone down.

The number had a Worthing code, which meant it was local, and the first two digits were the same as Jude's own, which meant it was very local. Dylan probably lived in Fethering. But whether with his family, a girlfriend or on his own she had no means of knowing.

The next call was going to need a change of persona and she had to get it right. Jude made herself a cup of peppermint tea while she focused on the role she was about to play. In spite of her floaty dress style, Jude was far from being a superannuated hippy, but she had met plenty of the breed. Indeed, during the time she'd lived on Majorca, people who didn't know her well might have reckoned her as one of their number. Most of her acquaintances from that period of her life had long since settled into the worlds of domesticity and employment, often as schoolteachers or in the social services. They remained harmless idealists, benignly ineffectual, posing no threat to society at any level. True, they did break the law on a regular basis, but the one they broke Jude didn't think should be a law anyway.

She concentrated on getting the voice right. Laidback, lazy, full of trailing vowels, that was it. And she'd use her mobile phone, so that the precise location she was calling from wouldn't be revealed if Dylan checked 1471.

She waited till half-past eleven, which she reckoned gave a lad-about-Fethering—assuming that's what Dylan was—time to wake up after the excesses of Friday night, and keyed in his number. She was in luck. He was at home.

"Hi." He managed to invest the single syllable with insolence and menace.

"Is that Dylan?" Jude got exactly the right relaxed diffidence into her voice.

"Yeah. Who wants him?"

"I was given your name by someone. I want to get hold of some gear."

"What kind of gear?"

"Pot." She knew that's what most users of her generation would still call it. "Cannabis."

Dylan laughed harshly. "So you're after some weed, eh? And what makes you think I might be able to help you?"

"I told you. A friend gave me your name."

"I think you'd better tell me who the friend is. Otherwise I might suspect this is some kind of set-up."

Jude took the risk. If Dylan didn't bite, then she knew she'd have lost him. She backed her hunch. "Rory Turnbull."

The silence lasted so long she thought she must've miscalculated. Then Dylan repeated, "Rory Turnbull, eh? Our fine upstanding dentist?"

He didn't mention the fine upstanding dentist's recent disappearance. Which was good news, because it almost definitely meant he didn't know about it. When he did, he'd be on his guard, knowing the inevitability of police investigations into all aspects of Rory Turnbull's life.

"Yes. He said he was a customer of yours."

"Not much of a customer. He bought very little from me. Just a bit of weed on a couple of occasions."

"Oh?"

"I don't carry the stuff he was after."

"He wanted hard drugs?"

"Yes. Smack. I gave him the name of a contact in Brighton and didn't hear from him again. So I guess that's where he took his business."

"Who was that contact?"

Jude realized she had been over-eager even before Dylan responded. "Hey, just a minute, just a minute. I thought you said it was weed—or was it 'pot?'—you were after."

"Yes," she agreed contritely. "Can you help me?"

"Maybe. It depends how much you're prepared to pay."

He quoted her prices for the various grades of goods he had available. She agreed his terms without haggling, and he fixed to meet her in the seafront shelter nearest to the Fethering Yacht Club at seven o'clock that evening.

"How will I recognize you?" he asked.

"I'm very tall, nearly six foot. Thinnish, black hair. I'll be wearing a long brown leather coat and a brown fur hat." Jude felt fairly safe with this anti-description of herself. And, for ethical reasons, her wardrobe contained nothing made of either leather or fur.

"OK. And a name? Or at least something you can identify yourself by, in case there's more than one tall bird in a leather coat down on the seafront tonight."

"Caroline," said Jude.

"OK, Caroline. See you later."

And he put the phone down. As she switched off her mobile, a little tremor of distaste ran through Jude's body.

One thing she knew for certain, though. She would not be anywhere near a Fethering seafront shelter at seven o'clock that evening.

For a moment she contemplated ringing the police and suggesting they make a rendezvous with Dylan at a Fethering seafront shelter at seven o'clock that evening.

But no. Deep though her hatred for the boy was, shopping him to the authorities would have been a very unJude thing to do.

# 28

THAT AFTERNOON, OVER a cup of tea at Carole's, the two women pooled the information they had gleaned. Both had a lot to tell. They had unearthed pretty convincing evidence that Rory Turnbull had been a heroin user. That expensive habit might well have led to his embezzling the funds of the Fethering Yacht Club.

And yet, when they had told each other all their findings, both Carole and Jude were left feeling flat. They had found reasons why Rory Turnbull might have wanted to take his own life, but they'd found nothing that linked him with the body Carole had found on Fethering beach. True, the dentist had had contact with Dylan the drug dealer, and Dylan had been the initiator of the black magic mutilation of the corpse in *Brigadoon II*, but that still did not provide a direct connection. They had no proof that Rory Turnbull knew the body was in his boat, and there seemed no obvious way of getting any.

As they shuffled through the possibilities, even Jude's customary good-natured calm gave way to despondency.

All they were left with was that it had been a bad week for the Fethering body-count. Three deaths, and though Aaron Spalding's might well have been prompted by guilt for what he'd done to the unnamed corpse, Rory Turnbull's seemed to stand on its own.

"Of course, we don't actually know it's a death yet, do we?" reasoned Carole.

"No, not till they've found his body."

"Yes, and who knows how long that'll take? He might have driven out to some disused barn, or into the woods, or driven the car into a pond or into the sea . . ." Carole sighed hopelessly.

"Right." Jude screwed up her eyes and tapped with irritation at her furrowed brow. "Is there something obvious we're missing? Some information we have that we haven't followed through?"

They both concentrated. There was a long silence, then Carole said, "Theresa Spalding!"

"What about her?"

"I've suddenly realized there's something I should have asked her and didn't."

"Hm?"

"I was concentrating too much on Aaron, and I forgot to ask her why she came here in the first place. How did she know I'd found the body? She said I 'matched the description.' She must've talked to someone who saw me. Who though?"

"Hey!" A smile slowly irradiated Jude's features. It was a great improvement. Gloom didn't suit her. "Of course! Why on earth didn't we think of that at the time? Come on, let's go and ask her now!"

They went straight up to Downside in the Renault. The estate didn't look any more welcoming in the dark than it had in daylight and Carole was glad there were two of them in the car. In spite of the cold, a bunch of early teens loitered in Drake Crescent, sorting out plans for where they'd go for their Saturday night—or where they could go for their Saturday night without any money.

A car stopping in the road seemed to qualify as excitement. The kids moved closer, watching the women get out and approach Theresa Spalding's front door. Two of them leaned against the Renault's doors, their exaggerated outlines menacing in puffa jackets. They watched in silence as Carole repeatedly pressed the bell. Only when she banged on the door did one of the kids shout out, "She's not there. They've taken her away."

"Who's taken her away? Where to?"

They all seemed keen to pitch in with information.

"An ambulance come."

"They took her to where the crazy people go."

"She'd totally lost it."

"She's in the nuthouse."

"In the loony-bin."

Carole and Jude exchanged rueful looks. They'd got the impression that Theresa Spalding's level of neurosis was pretty high at the best of times. She'd spoken of always being "on some medication." It was no surprise that her son's death should have destabilized the woman's precarious sanity.

They went back to the car. The two kids in puffa jackets stayed, insolently leaning against the doors till the last possible moment, then eased themselves upright and slouched away. As she started the engine, Carole heard some raucous remark at their expense, followed by a burst of derisive laughter. She shivered.

·    ·    ·    ·

The Saturday evening and the Sunday compounded their frustration. Both of them kept contemplating calling round next door to discuss their investigation further. But both of them knew there was nothing else to say.

So Carole watched Saturday evening television, which only went to confirm her opinion that there never was anything on the television on Saturday evening. On the Sunday she took Gulliver out for longer walks than usual and virtuously tidied the cupboard under the stairs, packing into bin liners a lot of what she now designated rubbish. These activities, preparing a couple of plain meals and reading the Sunday papers served to fill the void of the day.

It was like any other Sunday. As if none of the excitements of the previous week had happened.

Next door, Jude unpacked a couple of boxes of books and stacked them upright in old wine-crates in her bedroom. She did her yoga. She cooked a rather adventurous prawn curry for her one meal of the day, taken round four o'clock. With it she drank half a bottle of wine. She drank the other half during the evening, much of which she spent reading in an aromatic bath, her toe reaching out every now and again to top up the hot water.

Though it was not in her nature to be as uptight as Carole, Jude too felt the tension of unfulfilment.

Nothing could happen until Rory Turnbull's suicide was confirmed to have taken place.

# 29

IT WAS A different receptionist at the Brighton dental surgery the following morning, and Jude was directed to a different waiting room for her appointment with the hygienist. The plate on the closed door read "Holly Draper," and from inside came sounds of girlish chatter.

Jude sat and read a woman's magazine of the kind she didn't know still existed. There was even a special offer for knitting patterns. She wondered how long it had been there.

Then the door opened and the previous appointment was ushered out by a woman who must be Holly Draper. A short unnatural blonde with large honey-coloured eyes, she wore a white overall and latex gloves. A disposable face-mask had been pulled down beneath her chin, perhaps to enable her to talk, though from the way she *was* talking it looked like it'd take a lot more than a face-mask to stop her.

"But that kind of thing seems to happen all the time these days, doesn't it? I mean, who can you trust? You read about all these MPs putting their hands in the till, and they're meant to be our elected representatives, aren't they? And then there are solicitors and . . ."

Jude instantly identified Holly Draper's conversational method. It involved firing out a fusillade of questions and giving her collocutor no time to answer any of them. Perhaps this derived from the fact that most of the people she spoke to in her professional life had their mouths so full of metalwork and saliva-siphons that they couldn't have replied even if they'd wanted to.

Whatever its cause, Holly Draper's monologue style was excellent news for Jude. Just get her on to the right subject.

And even that might not prove to be too difficult. As her previous appointment sidled along the wall in desperate hope of escape, the hygienist was saying, "Well, you'd never have thought it to look at him, would you? Still, it's often the quiet ones, isn't it? Mind you, I can't imagine doing that to myself, can you? Well, I've never wanted to, as it happens. Just as well, isn't it? Have you ever—Oh, right, if you have to be off. Give those notes in at reception and make another appointment for three months' time—all right?"

She turned and flashed a hygienic smile at her next appointment. "Well, hello. You must be—"

"Everyone calls me Jude."

"Oh, right you are. I'm Holly. Jude as in 'Judith,' is that right? It's nice. Nicer than 'Judy,' isn't it? So many Judys around, aren't there? If you'd just like to come through into my little room . . . Lovely. And make yourself comfortable in the chair, will you? And I'll just have a glance at your notes, if I may? Hm, ooh, Mr. Frobisher says we've got a bit of inflammation round our gums, haven't we? Dear oh dear, aren't we a naughty girl? Right, well, I'd better have a look, hadn't I?"

Turning to pick up her examination mirror and toothpick brought a fractional pause, into which Jude managed to insert a line. "Dreadful news about Rory Turnbull, wasn't it?"

"You heard about that, did you? Did you know him?"

Jude once again leapt into the minimal breech. "I've just moved to Fethering, and I did meet him briefly."

"Ooh yes, well, as you can imagine, everyone here was gobsmacked when we heard the news—absolutely gobsmacked. Weren't you?"

"I didn't know him that well."

"Didn't you? Still, after what's happened, we're all asking ourselves if any of us knew him that well, aren't we? It's a terrible thing for someone to do, isn't it?" Before Jude could offer an opinion on the ethics of suicide, silverware approached her mouth. "Now if you could just open for me, could you? And can we pop this in? Could you just hold it, yes? We don't want our mouth filling up with saliva, do we?"

Further conversational prompts would be difficult. But Jude reckoned, having got Holly on to the right rails, the hygienist, in a state of permanently wound-up readiness, could be allowed to run.

"Ooh yes, a few places here where the gums are a bit red. Do you floss at all?" Jude let out a strangled response. Whether it was in the affirmative or negative didn't seem to affect Holly Draper's flow. "Well, you should, because if your gums are healthy then there's a much better chance of your teeth being healthy, isn't there? Now I'm just going to go round and pick out a bit of the muck you've got between your teeth. OK? I'll try not to hurt, but round some of the inflamed bits, I may not be able to avoid it. All right with you?"

Praying that the hygienist's diversion into the professional hadn't derailed her train of thought, Jude gave a gurgled assent to being hurt.

She needn't have worried. While the point of her pick probed away, Holly Draper continued seamlessly, "I mean, I'd never thought Rory was a particularly happy man, had you? And it was no secret that his marriage wasn't made in heaven, was it? But I'd never in a million years have thought he was the kind to do away with himself, would you? Mind you, you never know with people, do you?

"And, after what came out last week, well, it was perhaps a little less surprising, wasn't it? I mean, he must've known the Dental Estimates Board at Eastbourne would catch up with him in time. And when the Regional Dental Officer came to inspect on Thursday, it was clear something was seriously wrong and—" An uncharacteristic moment of caution stopped her. "Maybe I shouldn't be talking about this . . . Could you just shift your chin down a bit please?"

Jude took the opportunity of this movement to manufacture a choking fit. As she spluttered, Holly swiftly removed the plastic tube from her mouth, pulled her upright and patted her back. "Ooh, sorry about that. All right, are we? Take a rinse, why don't you? There, good. Spit it out, mm?"

Jude did as she was told and took advantage of another narrow window in Holly's monologue. She decided the best way to get further information would be to pretend more knowledge than she had. "Yes, somebody in Fethering was talking about the Regional Dental

Officer's inspection. I was really surprised to hear about that."

It had been the right approach. The hygienist picked up her cue perfectly. "Well, it was the scale of it that was so amazing, wasn't it? I mean, getting on for ten thousand pounds of dental work he'd claimed for, but never carried out. He was never going to get away with that in the long term, was he?"

"It doesn't seem as though he was thinking in the long term."

The fact that Jude had managed to slip another line in made Holly Draper realize she shouldn't have left her patient's mouth empty for so long. "Right, could you hold this in place again? There, good. And I'll just keep working round the ones at the back, shall I? Then, when I've finished this, we'll give them a nice clean, shall we?"

Jude was momentarily anxious that the hygienist wouldn't get back to the subject, but once again she needn't have worried. "I mean, it makes you wonder what Rory could possibly have needed all that money for, doesn't it? There's been talk round here of drugs, but he didn't seem the type, did he? You don't associate that with middle-class dentists, do you? And you'd have thought he and his wife'd be very well set up, wouldn't you? Apparently, they've got this great big house over at Fethering—but you probably know that, don't you? And they don't have any kids, so where did all that money go? Maybe it was drugs. What do you think? Or perhaps he had another 'secret vice,' eh? Another woman? Ooh, I don't think so, do you?

"Mind you, we shouldn't really be surprised that he did away with himself. I've been told that dentists are one of the highest-risk professions for suicide. Did you know that?" She giggled. "Not hygienists, though. We aren't daft, are we? Right, now we'll just give them all a nice clean-up, shall we?"

She turned to an articulated drill-like machine and fitted a small circular brush into its socket. This she dipped into a tub of paste. These actions did not for a moment interrupt her monologue.

"No, I don't think he was a bad man, though it was difficult to get close to him. Could you put your teeth together please? OK, take that out. Now this'll taste orangy and it may tickle a little bit. All right? No, as I say, Rory wasn't a bad man. He did some charity work, I believe. One of the girls on reception said he sometimes did free dentistry for down-and-outs out of hours, but he never talked about it. And he could be generous. There was this girl he quite often used to give a lift back to Fethering after work."

"Who was that?" Fortunately Holly had just moved the electric brush away to get a different angle on Jude's mouth.

"Oh, I don't know. Girl about twenty, I suppose. Short hair, sort of hennaed. I think she worked evenings in Fethering, which was why he sometimes gave her a lift. Well, she'll have to find someone else to do it for her now, won't she?

"There, all done, nice and clean, lovely. Look in the mirror. Doesn't that look better, eh? But now I'm going to be a real bully and give you a big lecture about flossing. All right? Can you cope? Are you feeling strong enough?"

      •    •    •    •

Carole's frustration mounted through the Monday morning. What really annoyed her was knowing that the discovery of Rory's body might already have been made but she'd have to wait till the news filtered through to her. Though the Fethering grapevine, based on interconnecting substations like Allinstore, All Saints' Church and the Crown and Anchor, was extremely efficient, it wasn't the same as having a direct line to the police computers.

Still, within the guidelines of Fethering protocol, there was one approach she could make which might lead to further information. She looked up the number in the local directory and rang it.

"Hello?" The voice contrived to sound suspicious and malicious at the same time. In the background something yapped.

"Winnie, it's Carole Seddon."

"Hello, dear."

"I was just ringing to say thank you so much for the coffee on Saturday morning."

"Oh, it was nothing. A pleasure to see you. Be quiet, Churchill, it's only your friend Carole."

"And I just wondered . . . is there any sign of an end to poor Barbara's ordeal?"

"Poor Barbara's ordeal gets worse by the minute. Do you know what she's discovered now? That so-called husband of hers has virtually ruined her financially. Do you know, he'd remortgaged the house without telling her. And goodness only knows where all the money he raised has gone. There's nothing in any of the savings accounts. It's almost as if he was deliberately trying to make life difficult for Barbara. And then to commit suicide, so that she doesn't even get any of the insurance . . . Huh, I always said he was a dubious factor."

"Oh, how awful, Winnie. But when you talk about suicide, I mean, that is definite now, is it? They've found his body?"

"Not yet, but it's only a matter of time. Typical of him to do away with himself somewhere inconvenient, though, isn't it? That man never gave a thought to another human being from the moment he was born. I mean, to have left Barbara destitute . . . Thank goodness my poor little baby's got my money to fall back on. There's my investment income and then, needless to say, I made quite a lot when I sold the big house after my husband died. That's when I started slumming down here, you know—though, mind you, I do like to think I slum in some style." She chuckled, but then her tone darkened as she said, "Thank goodness I never made any of my money over to that man, or no doubt he'd have squandered that too to feed his disgusting habits."

"Did Rory ever ask you to make money over to him?"

"Not in so many words," Winnie replied, with a wealth of implied subtext.

"Oh. Well, look, I hope you do get some good news soon."

"The only good news I can get is the confirmation that that man is dead."

"Wouldn't it be better news to hear that he's still alive—that he hasn't killed himself?"

Winnie Norton was rather stumped by that question. It caught her between the opposite pulls of the polite usages of Fethering society and her own seething hatred. The conventionally humanitarian response she managed to patch together left no doubt as to the true state of her feelings.

# 30

"IT'S ALL TOO easy," Jude announced.

They were walking along the beach on the Monday afternoon. The tide was low, the soft sand, sucking at their feet, made progress hard and slow. Gulliver scampered around them, off on more of his terribly important fool's errands. The two women had brought each other up to date on their individual researches.

"What do you mean, Jude?"

"Look, forget the body you found for the moment. Forget Aaron Spalding and the other boys. Let's just concentrate on Rory Turnbull. Now, the assumption is that he's committed suicide . . ."

"And it seems a very reasonable assumption. He left a note, for a start, saying that that was what he intended to do. And the more we discover about his circumstances, the more impossible his situation seems to have been. His marriage must always have been unhappy—certainly if Barbara had the same kind of attitude to him as his mother-in-law has. And his finances were getting totally out of control. I mean, now we've discovered he'd remortgaged the house and he had no savings left. He must've been really desperate to start fiddling the Yacht Club accounts. And making false claims for dental work on the NHS, that had to be a short-term thing. He knew he'd get found out in time."

"And why was he doing all this? Why did he need all that money?"

"To feed his heroin habit."

"And on what basis do we say he had a heroin habit?"

"Come on, Jude. You got that from Dylan, didn't you?"

"Not really. All I got from Dylan was the fact that he gave Rory a contact name for hard drugs. Rory came to him because he was the Fethering local drug dealer—well known to be, Ted Crisp told us as much. Didn't take us long, did it? Two not-very-streetwise women, and we get on to Dylan straight away, don't we? And all we actually know is that Rory bought a bit of weed from Dylan, and then asked for a contact name to get hold of the smack. We have no proof he ever followed up on that contact."

"But we do. Rory's mother-in-law found evidence—she found the drug equipment in his study. Oh, come on, Jude, we can't argue with this. It all stacks up."

"Yes, it all stacks up." Jude stopped and narrowed her brown eyes to look out over the sea. Now the weather had changed, there was even a trace of blue in the waves. "And I think it all stacks up too conveniently."

"What do you mean?"

"I've known a few drug addicts in my time," said Jude, "and the one thing that distinguishes them is secrecy about their habit. Not when they're with other

junkies perhaps, but they don't want the outside world
to know. And yet we're being asked to believe that a
middle-class dentist leaves evidence of his drug habit
round the house where his mother-in-law can find it.
And where his wife could easily have found it if his
mother-in-law hadn't. Winnie told you that Barbara
snooped around in the loft and found the pornography
he'd stashed away—and he'd made a much bigger effort
to hide that. So Rory knew full well that anything left
round his house was a serious security risk."

"But surely—"

Jude seemed unaware of the interruption as she went
on, "Besides, what Winnie found was so obvious.
What—a syringe, some tinfoil and a packet of white
powder?"

"That's what she said."

"And she also said that she recognized what it was
because she'd seen stuff like that on television. What
she saw was like an identikit shorthand for drug addic-
tion—something that even a genteel, middle-class lady
in her seventies was bound to recognize. No, I'm sorry,
I don't buy it. There's something going on here."

"But what?"

Jude let out a wry little laugh. "If we knew that,
wouldn't life be simple? The only thing I do know,
though, is that Rory Turnbull isn't dead."

"How do you know that? All the evidence points to
the fact that he definitely is dead."

"And that's how I know it. There's too much evidence. I detect a bit of overkill in the planning here."

"Whose planning?"

"Rory Turnbull's, I would imagine. Though what he
was planning and why, I have no idea."

"Well, even if he's not dead," said Carole, "it's no surprise that he's off the scene right now, is it?"

"How do you mean?"

"Retribution was getting dangerously close. He must've known when the Regional Dental Officer would be coming to make his inspection. And when Denis Woodville would be talking to the accountants, come to that."

"Yes." Jude rubbed her chin thoughtfully. "It might in fact have been better from Rory's point of view if those things had come out *after* his apparent suicide. I wonder . . ."

"What?"

"Dunno. Just wonder if he had to change his plans for some reason. But since we don't know what his plans were, such speculation becomes rather difficult. Oh, what the hell? I'm going to paddle."

And suddenly Jude was running down to the sea's edge.

"You're not going to take off your shoes, are you?" Carole called after her. "The water'll freeze your toes off."

"No, no, these boots are supposed to be waterproof!"

Jude jumped into the shallows and kicked about in frustration, raising flurries of spray around her. Gulliver, identifying the kind of game he never got to play with his owner, leapt into the water to join her, barking joyously. Carole stood a few yards above the tide mark, looking old-fashioned.

She gave covert looks along the beach in both directions and up towards the pebbles. There was no one in sight. Thank goodness. Flamboyance of the kind Jude was manifesting wasn't quite the thing in Fethering. Carole reminded herself how glad she was that she wasn't prone to such childish displays. But still she felt a little wistful.

"It's not true!" Jude called out through the spray.

"What's not true?"

"The manufacturer's claim for these boots. They're not waterproof."

"Oh. Well . . ." Carole couldn't think of a response that wouldn't sound smug, so she said nothing.

Jude came out of the sea with a broad grin across her face. "There," she said. "Feel better for that."

Gulliver followed her out. Stopping alongside, he shook himself, covering her with fine spray.

"Gulliver, you naughty boy!"

"It's all right, Carole. I'm so wet already, it doesn't matter. Stay cool."

Carole wasn't sure that she'd ever been cool, so staying cool might have been a problem. But again she didn't say anything.

Jude stood at the sea's edge, unaware of the wavelets lapping away at her heels. She looked up towards Fethering and her brow wrinkled. "I'm sure the solution's very simple . . . if only we could work it out."

"Huh." Carole turned to face in the same direction, but stayed in front of Jude. Although her gumboots were infallibly waterproof, she didn't want to get them wet.

Jude looked across towards the Yacht Club. Behind it, the men who'd been repairing the sea-wall were dismantling their site. The cranes had already gone and other equipment was being loaded on to large flatbed trucks. The builders' work had been done. The wall was shored up and the quick-flowing Fether once again properly contained.

"Let's just think about your body," she said. "What we know of the movements of your body."

"All right. Well, how it got there we have no idea, but we do know that it was lying in *Brigadoon II* on the Monday night when it was found by Dylan, Aaron Spalding and Nick Kent..."

"Then they did their black magic ritual with it and chucked it into the Fether..."

"But, true to form, it became a 'Fethering Floater' and was washed up on the beach the next morning, where I found it..."

"Though the 'someone else' you saw walking away from the breakwater may have found it before you did."

"Possibly."

"And then Aaron Spalding found it, presumably after you did."

"I imagine so."

"He rang Nick Kent and together the two boys manhandled the body back to where they'd found it. By the time the police started looking, the body was back in *Brigadoon II*."

"Yes, though it wasn't there on the Wednesday afternoon when we looked inside the boat."

"No." Jude tugged pensively at an errant strand of her blonde hair. "So, given the fact that moving dead bodies around during the daytime tends to attract attention, it seems reasonable to assume that the body was moved out of the boat on the Tuesday night."

"The same night that Aaron Spalding jumped—or fell—into the Fether."

"Yes. Are those two events connected? Hm..." Jude tapped her chin in frustration. "So where did the body go? Where, come to that, is the body now?"

Her eyes moved restlessly across the horizon of Fethering, and stopped focused on a high thirties house with glass-fronted top floor. As she looked a flash of reflected sunlight caught on something behind the glass. "Who lives there?"

"What?"

"That tall house, Carole. Who lives there?"

"Old bloke. I don't know his name. He's completely housebound, I think."

"But from the top of that house, he can see everything that happens on the beach."

"Well, yes, he probably can, but—"

"Come on!" And Jude had started running up the sand, her wet shoes squelching protests at every step. Gulliver, having recognized another game, also ran, barking enthusiastically.

"But, Jude," Carole wailed, "we can't just burst into his house!"

"Why not?"

"Because we don't know him."

"Oh, Carole! For heaven's sake!"

# 31

THE HOUSE THAT overlooked the beach must once have been in single ownership but had been divided into flats, one on each of its four storeys. Assuming a correlation between the flats and the entryphone buttons, Jude boldly pressed the top one.

There was no response. She was about to press again when an electronic voice from the little speaker said, "Hello?"

"Good afternoon. Are you the gentleman in the top flat?"

"Yes."

"We wondered if we could come and talk to you."

"Might I ask who you are?"

"My name's Jude, and I'm with my friend Carole Seddon. We both live in Fethering. In the High Street. Please. We would like to talk to you."

"About what?" the voice crackled back.

"About things you may have seen on the beach over the last week."

"Uh-huh." There was a silence while the voice

seemed to assess the proposition. Then it went on, "So you are asking me, an elderly, housebound cripple, to open my door to two people I've never seen before . . ."

"Yes."

". . . in spite of the fact that the majority of crimes against the elderly are committed by malefactors who have infiltrated themselves into pensioners' houses on some spurious pretext?"

"Yes," said Jude, with less confidence.

"Come on up," the voice from the box intoned. Then the door buzzed its release. Jude pushed and held it, while Carole sorted out Gulliver. He wasn't going to enjoy being tied by his lead to a garden seat—particularly when he reckoned he was being taken out for a walk—but there was no alternative. As they went inside the building, he gave a couple of reproachful barks at the eternal perfidy of women.

The entrance was at the back, at the foot of a tower which housed a lift and had presumably been added at the time of the conversion into flats. Without the lift, surely no one in a wheelchair would live on the top floor.

"But we don't even know his name," Carole complained as they rose up through the building.

"Then we'll ask him what it is." Jude's tone came as near as it ever did to exasperation.

They emerged on to a small landing. Framed in the doorway opposite, which he had opened ready for them, was a small man in a wheelchair.

Perhaps he wouldn't have looked small if he could have stood up, but, crumpled down as he was, there seemed to be very little of him. He was partially paralysed, his head propped back at a strange angle. His left hand was strapped against the arm of his chair, while his right hovered over a control panel of buttons and levers. He wore a crested blazer and a cravat high around his neck. On his head was an incongruous navy corduroy cap.

"Good afternoon . . . Carole and Jude, was it?"

When he spoke, they realized that not only the entryphone had made his voice sound electronic. He talked through some kind of voicebox. The cravat must have been there to hide a tracheotomy scar.

"Come on in," he said, flicking a control and going into sharp reverse. "Close the door behind you."

"Isn't that a risk?" asked Jude, as they came into his sitting room. "If we were going to rob you or beat you up, nobody would hear your cries."

Carole gave her neighbour a reproving look. What appalling bad taste. Had Jude no sense of the right remark for the right occasion?

But apparently it was exactly the right remark for their host. He let out a bark of electronic laughter and said, "I'm prepared to take my chance with you two. I know appearances can be deceptive, but you don't project the traditional image of teenage tearaways.

"My name's Gordon Lithgoe, by the way. I'd offer to make you tea, but I'm so cack-handed, you'd be better off doing it for yourself. The makings are over there."

"No, thank you. We don't require tea." Carole didn't want the atmosphere to become too relaxed. When they started asking him questions, Gordon Lithgoe might decide to throw them out.

"This is a pretty stunning little eyrie you've got here," said Jude.

It was. The window that took up the entire front wall

dominated the space, as if the sea were part of the decor. The original thirties metal-framed panes were still intact, but outside a more modern set of sliding windows protected them from the worst of the weather. The glow of the bright November afternoon permeated the whole room. There was little furniture; someone in a wheelchair had more use for space than armchairs and sofas. On the walls were pinned large-scale maps of shorelines, creeks and channels; there were a few plaques commemorating various ships; and in rows of bookcases stood the serried blue spines of books that looked as if they must have something to do with navigation.

Most interesting, though, from the point of view of the two women, was the area directly in front of the window. A platform had been built up there, and from it a ramp led down for the wheelchair. On the platform stood a telescope on a tripod. Two pairs of powerful binoculars lay on a nearby table, as well as an open ledger with a fountain pen lying down its middle crease. Some notes were written on the left-hand page.

"Very nautical flavour," Jude went on. "Were you in the Navy?"

"No, no," said Gordon Lithgoe. "No chance of someone like me passing the medical. So I've always had to remain as just an interested amateur."

"Still—" Jude looked around the room again—"this is a wonderful place."

"Just as well," his voice crackled back, "since the only times I leave it these days is to have operations." There was another rasp of laughter. "Apropos of which, ladies, sorry about the cap, but it's prettier than the scars underneath."

"Yes, I'm sure it is," said Carole, ever ready with the required Fethering platitude.

Her recourse to what passed locally for good manners reminded him of his own. "Do sit down." He pointed to two upright kitchen chairs. "Sorry, not very comfortable, but then I have few visitors. The woman who brings my meals never stays. Otherwise, it's the nurse, the occasional social worker, very rarely the doctor and, even more rarely, the odd friend. Have to be odd to come and see someone like me—half man, half electronic gadget—wouldn't they?"

There was not a nuance of self-pity in his words. There hadn't been in anything he had said. He seemed, if anything, amused by his plight.

"Anyway," he said, signalling the end of social niceties, "you are here for a purpose. I saw you deciding to come up here."

"You saw us?" said Carole.

"Oh yes." He suddenly spun the chair on its wheels and shot like a rocket towards the platform by the window. He seemed to be going up the ramp far too fast, but, rather than smashing into the telescope, he came to a neat halt inches away from it. He'd practised the trick many times before.

He didn't need to move the telescope. It was already focused. He edged the wheelchair a fraction closer and his eye was at the lens. "I could see you just like you were in the room with me. Pity I can't lip-read. But anyway your body language told me you'd decided to come up here."

"Do you spend most of the day watching the beach?" asked Jude.

Again, Carole wouldn't have put the question so

bluntly, but Gordon Lithgoe still didn't seem offended. "No, I'm basically looking for shipping. That's what interests me." His working hand fell on to the ledger by his side. "Make a log of all their comings and goings."

"And what about the people on the beach?" Jude maintained her direct approach. "Do you make a log of their comings and goings too?"

He spun the wheelchair round and faced them. Against the brightness of the window, it was impossible to see his expression, and from the even signal of his voice, impossible to gauge his emotion.

"Some," he said. "Not all."

"We're interested in the events of Monday night last week," said Carole. "And then through Tuesday and Wednesday."

There was a moment's stillness, and they were both afraid he was going to clam up. Then, suddenly releasing a brake, he glided the wheelchair down the ramp and swung gracefully round to come to rest beside them. They could now see his face. It was smiling.

"Why do you want to know this?"

Carole replied, "We think there's been something criminal going on."

"And you're not police. Otherwise, as soon as you'd arrived, you'd have flashed that fact at me—along with your ID, wouldn't you?"

"Yes."

"So what are you?"

"Just two people who want to get to the truth of what happened." Even as she said the words, Carole knew how pompous they sounded.

"Oh, hurrah, hurrah." Gordon Lithgoe's sarcasm made itself felt through the electronic crackle. "How very noble. Truth-searchers, eh? Where would this great country of ours be without people who have a sense of public duty?"

"Do I gather you don't have a sense of public duty?"

Again Jude's lighter tone struck the right note. "Not in the obvious way," he replied. "I've seen a lot of things in my life that were probably criminal, and I've never reported any of them. I've seen my role throughout as essentially that of an observer."

"But if someone were to come and ask you? If the police were to come and ask you?"

"That would be entirely different. I would certainly cooperate and tell anything I knew—if asked. But I wouldn't just volunteer information. However"—he drummed his right hand lightly on his sunken chest— "in this case the police haven't come and asked me. They didn't make the deduction that I might have seen something, while you two ladies did make that deduction and have arrived on my doorstep . . ."

"So you'll tell us what you saw?" asked Jude very softly.

"Yes. Of course I will. I assume what you're interested in is the dead body which you—Carole, is it?— found on the beach on Tuesday morning?"

"How did you know it was me?"

"I told you. That telescope enlarges the face of someone on the beach as if they're here in the room with me. I recognized you, anyway. I didn't know your name, but I'd seen you taking your dog for a walk every morning for the last three or four years."

It was uncomfortable to know that she'd been being observed for such a long time. Not, of course, that Carole had ever done anything on the beach of which to be ashamed, but all the same . . .

"What we want to know is what happened to the body after I found it."

"Yes. It was rather active, wasn't it—for one so dead? I'll find the relevant log." He spun the wheelchair across the room to a shelf and selected one from a pile of ledgers. Carole and Jude both marvelled at the extent of his record-keeping. The ledger by the window was half full, but he had to go to another one for events of less than a week before.

He flicked through the book with his good hand till he found the place, then, pressing it to his knee, wheeled himself back towards them. He looked down at his notes. "I was first aware of the body at 6:52. That was first light. But, given where he was on the breakwater, and the fact that the tide had gone all the way out and was on its way back in, he could have been there for a couple of hours before that."

"And I found him about seven, I should think."

"7:02. Then you went back home with your dog." Again, Carole felt a little shiver from the knowledge that she'd been watched. "At 7:06 a boy climbed over the railings of the Yacht Club and raised the cover of one of the boats. He didn't like what he saw inside, I suppose, because he came running out and along the sea-wall, looking down into the Fether. Then he ran down on to the beach, and he found the body at 7:21. He ran back up the beach—don't know where he went to, I couldn't see—but about a quarter of an hour later he came back . . ."

"With another boy?" Jude breathed.

"Yes. The two of them manhandled the body up the

beach, over the railings into the Yacht Club and put it into the boat, the same boat the first boy had looked in."

"And then?"

"And then the boys ran off. Out of vision of my telescope at 7:47. At 10:12 the police arrived, looked along the beach—not very hard—and then they left."

"But what about the body?" asked Carole.

"That's it. That's all I can offer you. Great telescope I've got there, but it doesn't have night sights. If I could afford one with those, I'd get it tomorrow."

"Oh, I don't know." Jude chuckled. "You've got to sleep sometime."

"I don't sleep that much," said Gordon Lithgoe.

"So . . ." Carole sighed despondently. "It looks as though the body was removed on the Tuesday night, under cover of darkness. But by whom and where to, we have no means of knowing."

"Where would you put a body, Mr. Lithgoe?"

There was a scrape of electronic laughter. "I'm glad to say, Jude, that's not a problem I've ever had to address. However, where you'd put a body depends on where you think people are going to look for it."

"Ye-es. With you so far."

"And, among the multiplicity of pastimes available to the human species, carrying dead bodies around is one of the most hazardous. If you get caught doing it, you're facing a hell of a lot of uncomfortable explanations. What I'm saying is that, unless you've got transport, you don't want to move a body far. So if, say, you're hiding a body in a boat, and you think there's a strong chance someone might look in that boat, then you move it to somewhere close by where they're not going to look."

"Into another boat?"

"Possibly. Except if one boat's a security risk, maybe they all are."

"Where else then?"

"Come and have a look." Gordon Lithgoe powered his wheelchair back up the ramp. His right hand slightly reangled the telescope and adjusted the focus. "I don't know. It's a possibility. Have a butcher's."

Carole looked first. She had to arch her back to get down low enough. The telescope was trained on the top of the sea wall, where the repairs had been taking place for the previous few days. The heavy machinery had all gone, as had the workers.

Revealed were the two blue-painted low chests used by local fishermen to store their bait and equipment.

"Bit big," said Gordon Lithgoe, "but otherwise it's the right shape for a coffin, isn't it?"

"Jude, have a look. And of course," Carole went on thoughtfully, "if whoever it was put the body in there just as a temporary measure . . . and they didn't know what was about to happen . . . their plans would have been really screwed up by the builders coming in."

"Yes." Jude rose from the telescope. "They would, wouldn't they?"

"Are you off to have a snoop?" asked Gordon Lithgoe eagerly. "I'd love to watch your exhumation through the telescope. But hurry—while the light lasts."

"Yes, we must go. Mr. Lithgoe, I can't thank you enough—"

"Please call me Gordon."

"No, but you've been so generous with your time."

"Time is not a commodity I need to ration. I have far too much of it. Any visitor is a welcome diversion. As

I said there are people who come and see me occasionally, but—"

"Theresa Spalding," said Jude with one of her sudden
insights.

"What?" asked Carole.

"Theresa Spalding used to come and see you, didn't
she, Gordon?"

"Yes, yes, she did."

"And you mentioned the body on the beach to her?"

"That's right."

"And described Carole?"

"Yes."

"Which explains why she came to your house, Carole."

"It must do, yes."

"But, Jude, you said she *used* to come and see me.
Is she not coming again?"

"I hope she is, Gordon. But she's not well at the
moment. Did you hear, her son died? She's taken it very
badly and she's in hospital."

"Ah." The news seemed to bring him deep sadness.
"I hope she'll be all right. She's had a lot to cope with,
that girl."

"Yes."

"Anyway," Carole broke in briskly, "we must be on
our way. Can't thank you enough for—"

"Carole, there's something we're forgetting!"

"What, Jude?" She spoke testily. She wanted to be
on her way. Gulliver had been left tied up in the garden
for far too long.

"The person you saw on the beach before you found
the body."

"Oh, my goodness, yes."

"Ah," said Gordon Lithgoe, "I wondered if you'd ask about that." He referred again to his ledger. "That'd be the one who saw the body at 6:57."

"Around then it must have been, yes."

"In a shiny green anorak."

"Yes. Who was he?"

"Wasn't a 'he.' It was a 'she.' "

"Really?"

"Young girl. It was hardly light, so I couldn't see when she actually came on to the beach, but she was running down from the direction of the Yacht Club. Seemed to be in a panic, until she found the body."

"What did she look like?" asked Jude.

"Couldn't see the colour of her hair, because she had her anorak hood done up tight. Large young woman, though. And I could see one thing . . . She had a silver stud in her nose."

# 32

WHEN THEY GOT out of the building, Gulliver provided an excellent illustration for the meaning of the
word "hangdog." He was very reproachful.

"I'll have to take him home before we do anything
else," said Carole. "Anyway, I don't want him present
if there is going to be an exhumation."

"No."

They set out back towards the High Street, keeping
on Seaview Road, which was firmer underfoot than the
beach.

"We've got to talk to Tanya," said Jude.

"She's not the only young woman in the world with
a silver nose-stud."

"No, but she's the only one who has a connection to
Fethering Yacht Club. If only we could also find a connection between her and Rory Turnbull . . ."

"Well, he was Treasurer of the club, so she must've
met him there."

"Ye-es. Have we got anything else, though?"

"Hm . . . Ooh, just a minute, we might have. What
about the girl your dental hygienist mentioned?"

"Well done, Carole. How stupid of me! I should've remembered that. Of course! Denis Woodville said she lived in Brighton, so if she was coming to do an evening shift at the club bar, then the timing would be absolutely right for Rory to give her the occasional lift to work when he'd finished at the surgery."

The two women exchanged looks as they strode along. Carole's pale eyes sparkled behind their glasses. "Then we definitely need to talk to Tanya."

"Before we go into the exhumation business?"

"Yes." Carole shuddered. "And I certainly don't think we should do the exhumation bit alone."

"You're not suggesting calling in the police, are you?"

"Certainly not! Not till we've confirmed that the body's there. I can just imagine the expression on Detective Inspector Brayfield's face if we got him to help us burglarize one of those fishermen's chests and found nothing in it except for boathooks and rotting bait. No, I think we should ask Ted Crisp to help us."

"Oh?"

"You sound surprised, Jude. Don't you think it's a good idea?"

"I think it's a very good idea. My only surprise is that you were the one who suggested it."

And it was surprising, when she came to think about it. The Carole of a week before would never have dreamed of making the suggestion.

As they took the left turn into the High Street, Jude went on, "I'll give Ted a call. I'm sure he can slip away from the pub for half an hour."

"It's got to be this evening."

"Hm?"

"When we look for the body." Carole went through the logic. "If Gordon Lithgoe's idea is correct and the body was moved as a temporary measure, then tonight's the first opportunity whoever moved it will have to retrieve it. The building workers have been there all the time since Wednesday."

Jude nodded, then stopped. They were outside Denis Woodville's cottage. Its paintwork and paths were immaculately clean. The dinghy on its trailer was still in front of the garage. On his gatepost a new, meticulously hand-printed felt-tip notice read, "BEWARE! WEEKEND SAILORS IN VICINITY! NEXT DOOR!" And a large arrow pointed towards the Chilcotts' house.

On their gatepost was a new printed notice. In a choice selection of fonts, it read, "DANGER! LITTLE HITLER NEXT DOOR! YOU HAVE BEEN WARNED!" And an arrow pointed back at Denis Woodville's.

"I'd have thought these two were getting a bit close to the libel laws," Jude observed.

"Only if one of them chooses to sue. And I think, deep down, both of them enjoy the game so much that they're not going to risk putting an end to it by court procedures."

Jude chuckled. "You're probably right. Anyway, I'm just going to see if Denis is in . . ."

"To get a contact number for Tanya?"

"That's right. You take Gulliver back. I'll be round in a minute."

The Vice-Commodore was in, though on his home territory he seemed diminished, less assured than he had been in the surroundings of the Fethering Yacht Club. Jude sensed in him a reluctance to invite her in, which was overcome only by ingrained good manners.

When he ushered her through to his sitting room, she could see why. In marked contrast to the neatness of its exterior, the house's interior was distinctly shabby. Some months had elapsed since the sitting room had experienced even the most cursory of cleaner's attentions. In the air, as well as stale Gauloise smoke, hovered the sickly smell of rotting fruit.

Denis Woodville's awareness of, and embarrassment about, the state of his home suggested he very rarely had visitors. "I'm sorry, bit of a tip," he barked, with an attempt at bluffness. "Fact is, I was never up to much on the domestic front and, since my wife passed away, I . . . Not that I spend any longer here than I have to . . . Busy at the club a lot of the time anyway . . ."

*Escaping* to the club, Jude translated. The squalor of the room brought home to her the emptiness of the old man's life.

"Do take a seat." He gestured vaguely to a selection of subsiding armchairs, none of which looked particularly inviting.

"No, I'm fine. If you could just find that number . . ."

"Yes, yes, of course." Moving aside an ashtray and a couple of smeared beer mugs from a dresser, he riffled through a pile of dusty newspapers and unopened letters. "I've got it here somewhere." He had shown no surprise at being asked for Tanya's number and no curiosity as to why it might be wanted. "Tell the young lady when you do get through to her that, if she's changed her mind, she can have her job back. I haven't found a replacement yet . . . that is, unless of course you were serious about wanting to do it?"

Jude grimaced. "Still finding my feet round here, actually. Bit early for me to commit myself to anything."

"Yes, yes, of course. Damn, it doesn't seem to be here. Maybe it's in this lot." He moved across to attack another pile of detritus on a coffee table.

"Nice-looking dinghy you have in the front there," said Jude, to make conversation.

"Yes, she's a Mirror."

"Ah." This meant nothing to her. "I'm surprised you don't keep it down at the Yacht Club."

"Well, I used to, but, erm . . . well, times change . . ." Jude suddenly understood. Denis Woodville was saying that he could no longer afford to keep his dinghy at the Yacht Club. "I probably won't keep her that much longer. Dinghy like that's a bit of a handful. I'm thinking of selling her . . . and getting something else . . . more suitable for my advanced years," he added, with an unconvincing flourish of bravado.

"Good idea," said Jude, not believing a word of it.

"Damn, it's not here. I know I've got the number down at the club." The very mention of the word seemed to raise his spirits. He looked at his watch. "Should be opening up there soon anyway." The confidence in his voice mounted as the moment of leaving his squalid home drew closer. "Damned place can't function without the Vice-Commodore, you know. If you wouldn't mind coming along with me . . ."

There was a little knot of elderly cronies already waiting for Denis Woodville to unlock the clubhouse. They called out raucous comments about his time-keeping and did not let the fact he had a woman with him pass unremarked. The Vice-Commodore glowed in their attention.

Inside the bar-room, with the lights switched on, he whispered to Jude, "Have to get their drinks sorted out first or I'll never hear the end of it. Can I get you a little something?"

Jude refused, anxious to get away. She had a sense that the pace of the investigation was accelerating.

Denis Woodville lit up another Gauloise and then made a great meal of pouring the drinks, with constant comments about how unsuitable it was for the Vice-Commodore to be involved in such menial tasks. Though it was clear he'd been doing it every night since Tanya left.

None of the others moved to help him. They just sat and pontificated on the appalling state of the world and how much better everything would be if they were in charge. One of them harked back to when he'd been stationed out in Singapore and pretty well ran the show out there. If the half of what these elderly gentlemen said was true, Jude was privileged to be in the company of the finest political and logistical brains in the entire world.

Eventually everyone was supplied with a drink. Denis Woodville took a long swig of his brandy and said, "Now, let's find that phone number for you . . ."

He turned to a neat address book by the telephone. Whatever chaos might reign in his home, here at the Fethering Yacht Club the Vice-Commodore kept everything shipshape. As he picked up the book, he noticed the message light flashing on the answering machine. "Excuse me. Better just check this. Might be the coastguard," he said importantly.

The message wasn't from the coastguard. It was the voice of a bored young woman. "Vice-Commodore, it's Tanya, calling on Monday afternoon. First, I wanted to say thanks for the lunch last week . . ."

Though spoken with total lack of enthusiasm, this still prompted ribald comments from the cronies round the bar.

". . . and the other thing is, could you let me know whether those repairs on the sea-wall have been finished yet? It's just, um . . . well, I was thinking of coming for a walk to Fethering and I didn't want to if the building's still going on, you know . . . Could you call me on . . ."

Jude scribbled the number down on the back of an envelope. "And could I have her address please?"

"How very odd," said the Vice-Commodore, as he passed the address book across. "What on earth does the girl want to know about the sea wall for?"

Jude had a potential answer to that question. An answer that might make a connection she'd been seeking for some time. The girl's reason for wanting the information had been so clumsily fabricated that Jude felt a little charge of excitement.

"It's in code," one of the Fethering Yacht Club members announced. "It all has special meanings for the Vice-Commodore, eh? That's how he and Tanya have managed to keep their affair secret all these years."

The remark was greeted by some token joshing, but soon the old men moved on to more serious matters. When Jude slipped away from the clubroom, Denis Woodville was launching into his views on how the Northern Ireland problem should be solved. His recipe required rather lavish use of a reintroduced death penalty, but "in the long run, it would only be being cruel to be kind . . ."

The Vice-Commodore was in his pomp. Jude felt sure none of his surrounding pontificators had ever seen him in the drabness of his home surroundings.


"Have you talked to Ted Crisp?"

It was the first thing Jude asked when she arrived and Carole was proud to be able to say, "Yes. He's game for a bit of body-hunting . . . round seven."

"Good." Jude pulled out her mobile phone. "I'll see if Tanya's there now."

"You can use my phone."

"Mm?" She was already keying in the numbers. "Oh, it's OK."

"But using a mobile is a lot more expensive."

"Is it?" asked Jude, as though the idea had never occurred to her. "Ah, hello, is that Tanya? My name's Jude. I don't know if you remember, we met in the Crown and Anchor at Fethering on Friday. Yes, that's right. Well, I wanted to talk about a body that got washed up on the beach here last week . . ."

With a rueful expression, Jude turned to Carole. "Maybe the direct approach isn't always the best one. She hung up on me."

"Ah. Still, wouldn't you say that's a sign of guilt or complicity or something? If she had no idea what you were talking about, she'd have said so, not hung up."

"You could be right." Jude looked down at the envelope on which she'd written Tanya's address and phone number. "I think I'd better go and see her."

"In Brighton?"

"Yes. I know she's at home, don't I?-At least at the moment."

"How will you get there? I'd offer to drive you over, but if I'm meeting Ted at seven, I—"

"No, no, don't worry. I'll get a cab."

"A *cab*?" Carole was shocked. "All the way to Brighton?"

"It's not far, is it?"

"It may not be far, but it'll certainly cost you. Depends what kind of budget you're working to, of course."

"Budget?" Jude savoured the unfamiliar word.

"Yes, budget. You know what it means, don't you?"

"I know what it means, of course," said Jude mischievously, "but I've never really come to terms with the *concept.*"

Carole looked blank. But then everyone looks blank when they try to converse with someone who speaks a different language.

Jude raised her mobile phone again. "I'll give her another try. Maybe now Tanya's had time to think, she will want to talk to me."

And so it proved. Guilt, anxiety or maybe simple curiosity had done their work, and Jude set off shortly after in a cab to Brighton.


Carole felt tense, but the anticipation was not unpleasurable. At least something was happening in her life. Searching for dead bodies might not be sensible, but it sure beat the hell out of most other Fethering residents' pastimes.

When the phone rang at twenty-five past six, she felt

a little pang of potential disappointment. It would be Ted Crisp, calling off their seven o'clock tryst.

It wasn't.

"Carole, it's me, Jude. I'd just got to Brighton and paid off the cab when my mobile rang. It was Maggie Kent. Nick's gone missing!"

# 33

"YOU HAVE CALLED the police, have you?"

"Yes." Maggie Kent's voice on the telephone was tight with the effort of controlling her emotion. "At first they weren't that interested. They said lots of kids come home late from school, and it had only been an hour, and Nick was sixteen for goodness' sake, and . . . Then I told them he'd been with Aaron Spalding the night before Aaron died and they began to take me a bit more seriously."

"So they are out looking for him?"

"That's what they say. And I'm sure they are, though at what level of urgency I don't know. But I can't just sit here doing nothing. The thought that Nick's out there somewhere, confused, needing me—perhaps not needing *me*, but needing someone . . . It's so awful, I . . ." The dam on her emotions was cracking. Maggie Kent took a deep breath and evened out her voice as she went on, "I rang your friend Jude, because I thought Nick might have confided something to her when they talked last week."

"And had he?" Had Jude told the mother of her son's presence at the mutilating of a corpse?

"She told me a few bits and pieces I didn't know. But I was really interested in what Nick and Aaron might have said to each other. Nick was in such a dreadful state over the weekend. He hardly slept at all, or ate come to that. There's something really terrible gnawing away at him and I'm scared. I'm scared he'll do what Aaron did."

"You mean kill himself? Has it been confirmed that that's what Aaron did? Because there hasn't been an inquest yet, has there?"

"No, but the police told me. Aaron was seen by a courting couple in a car—they've only just come forward. He was up on the railway bridge over the Fether in the early hours of Tuesday morning. There seems no question he jumped in deliberately.

"And the thought that my Nick might have done the same thing is just too . . ." This time no floodgates would have been adequate to stop the flow of tears.

Carole waited till the note of the sobbing changed and then asked, "So what are you going to do in the short term?"

"I don't know. I'll go mad if I just sit around here. And I feel I should be out by the railway bridge, looking for Nick. But I'm scared, if I go out and join the search, then the phone might ring and I wouldn't be here . . ."

"I'd go out if I were you. Good news'll keep."

"And what about bad news?"

"Generally speaking, that'll keep too," Carole replied grimly.

She had her own ideas of where she'd start looking for the boy. And, with a bit of luck, she'd have Ted Crisp there to help her. Carole Seddon took a large rubber-covered torch out of the cupboard under the stairs, and put on her Burberry.

Tanya lived in a Kemptown bedsit which, because it boasted its own bathroom, the landlord had the nerve to call a studio flat. There was a two-ring gas hob by the sink, but it didn't look as if it got used much. The walls had once been white but were pockmarked with Sello-tape scars and Blu-Tack stains where previous tenants had taken down their posters and other decorations. Tanya seemed to have put up nothing of her own. Double bed, television, video, CD player—that was all she appeared to need to express her identity.

Quite loud in the background, when she let Jude in, was the clinical voice of some pop diva, draining the emotion out of yet another song. Tanya closed the door behind her guest and, with no attempt at social graces, demanded, "What is all this then?"

"I was rather hoping you could tell me that."

"Why should I? Particularly 'cause I don't know what you're talking about."

Perhaps Tanya could on occasion be attractive, but in this aggressive mode she wasn't. She looked massive, stolid and resentful, her face already set into a kind of middle-aged disappointment. As she had been in the Crown and Anchor, she was dressed in black, whether the identical clothes or another similar set Jude couldn't tell. The black laced-up Doc Martens were certainly the same.

Recognizing that there was no chance of being of-fered a chair, Jude plonked herself down into one the landlord must have picked up at a house-clearance dealers. "As I said on the telephone, I'm talking about a body that was washed up on Fethering beach last Tuesday morning. The body of a middle-aged man. We know you saw it."

"How do you know?"

"The usual way. Someone saw you."

"And told you about it?"

"Exactly."

The girl sniffed. Then suddenly she said, "I got to go to the toilet." Pausing only by the CD player to turn up the diva even louder, she crossed the room and disappeared into the bathroom, shutting the door behind her.

Jude wondered whether turning up the music had been a gesture of delicacy, a recognition that embarrassing noises from the lavatory might otherwise be heard in such an enclosed space.

Certainly Tanya seemed to be doing something major in the bathroom. She was in there for a long time. Jude wondered whether the girl was fortifying herself for the interview ahead with a few drugs. The flush on her cheeks when she finally did return would have supported that hypothesis.

The first thing Tanya did after firmly shutting the bathroom door was to flick a switch on the CD and stop the diva in mid-wail. Plumping herself down on the edge of her bed, she began quickly, "All right, about this body . . . Yeah, OK, I was going for a walk on the beach at Fethering and I saw it. And I didn't tell no one, 'cause if you ever been in care, you know that anything where the police is involved is just going to cause you a lot of grief and hassle."

"And did you see anyone else on the beach that morning?"

"No. Oh yes. There was some old girl taking her dog for a walk." Jude wasn't convinced Carole would have liked the description.

"And that was the only person you saw?"

"Yeah."

"But what were you doing on Fethering beach at that time in the morning, anyway?"

"I got a job down there at the Yacht Club."

"No, you haven't. You finished that on the previous Friday. And the Yacht Club isn't open before seven in the morning."

"Well, I, er . . ." Tanya wasn't a very good liar. Lying needs a flicker of brightness, which she didn't have. Caught out in her lies, she turned to anger instead. "Look, why you going on at me? It's my own bloody business where I go and what I do. I'm not in care anymore, you know! I lead my own independent life!" She seemed to be trying to convince herself as much as Jude.

"Yes, of course. Going back to the body . . ."

"What?"

"Did you recognize it?"

"How d'you mean?"

"Had you seen the man before? Either dead or alive?"

"Bloody hell!" She looked deeply affronted. "Seen him dead—what do you take me for? You imagine I'm the sort of person who spends her time with dead bodies?"

"I'm not suggesting that."

"I should bloody hope not. So far as I'm concerned, he's just some poor bugger who fell off a boat or something and got washed up on Fethering beach. Why?" Tanya looked at Jude with a new curiosity and cunning in her eye. "Do you know who he was?"

# 34

THERE WAS NO sign of Ted Crisp by the entrance gate of the Fethering Yacht Club, where they had agreed to meet. Carole looked at her watch and saw with irritation that it was already ten past seven. She had never been late for anything in her life and she couldn't understand why everyone couldn't be like her. There was nothing difficult involved. It was simply a matter of leaving enough time—in fact, a matter of being organized.

Her earlier prejudices about Ted Crisp started bubbling back to the surface. The landlord of the Crown and Anchor certainly wasn't organized. No doubt, over a few drinks with his regulars, he'd completely forgotten the arrangement he'd made to meet Carole. The last thing you could expect from someone with a background as a stand-up comedian was reliability.

Still, she comforted herself, it might be just as well there was only one of them doing the first bit of her search. More than one might attract too much attention. When she fixed to meet Ted Crisp, she had forgotten that at seven o'clock in the evening the Vice-Commodore and his cronies would be setting the world to rights in the Fethering Yacht Club bar. She had once or twice peered covertly upwards and been relieved to see no one actually sitting in the window. Hopefully, on a winter's evening, they'd all be clustered round the bar counter. But there were undoubtedly members up there, and they did represent a security hazard.

Of course, there was nothing to stop her from marching upstairs and telling the Vice-Commodore what she proposed to do. She wasn't planning anything illegal—rather the reverse, it was a very public-spirited act. But such an approach to Denis Woodville would be too public. Carole didn't want to raise a hue and cry. In the unlikely event of her actually finding Nick, she didn't want him to be frightened off by too many people. The boy was in a very fragile emotional state . . . if he was still alive . . . and Carole had to make herself believe that he was still alive.

She lifted the latch on the white gate that led into the Yacht Club's forecourt. It seemed to make a disproportionately loud click in the winter night and an equally loud one when she closed it. The sea was a long way down the beach, its rustling muted. The only sound seemed to be the harsh scrape of Carole's boots on the cement.

She could have found her way to the right boat blindfolded. The events of the previous week, and the images they had spawned, led her inexorably towards *Brigadoon II*. She trembled a little as she approached. The chill she felt had nothing to do with the weather.

Carole stopped, and the whole world seemed very still. She cocked an eye up towards the bar-room's broad window, but her luck held. There was still no outline of anyone observing her.

It was when she took the next step that she heard the noise.

A low keening, like that of some small, injured animal.

And it definitely came from inside *Brigadoon II*.

Carole knew how pivotal her next actions would be. She couldn't be sure what she would find inside the boat, but she had a good idea of what it might be. She must be very cautious.

She remembered exactly how Jude and she had turned the end of the cover over the previous Wednesday. She didn't want to use the torch, but her eyes were becoming accustomed to the gloom. The cut rope had not been repaired. Everything was as it had been.

Carole held the switched-off torch high in her right hand, estimating the direction of its beam. At the moment she flipped back the boat's cover, she pressed the on-button.

Blearily frozen in its beam was Nick's face. He looked about ten years old. Tears coursed down his cheeks and still the low, thin wail poured painfully out of him. He was curled in a foetal position against the fibreglass of the hull. What had been hard ice was now a pool of water which had soaked through his school uniform.

"Nick," said Carole, as gently as she knew how. Jude would be doing this better, her mind kept saying. Jude has a better touch. I'm not good with people.

She forced herself to banish these thoughts. They weren't relevant. Jude might do it better, but Jude wasn't there. Carole Seddon was the one facing the terrified boy. Carole Seddon was the one who would have to cope with the situation. There was no alternative.

"Nick," she murmured again.

The boy squinted into the light. "Who are you?" he sobbed.

"My name's Carole. I'm a friend of Jude, who you talked to last week." He made no response. "Your mother's been terribly worried. She really wants to see you, Nick."

But this was the wrong thing to say. A new tremor of sobbing came over the boy. Through it, Carole could hear him saying, "No, I can't see her. I can't see Mummy. Not after what I've done."

"You haven't done anything so terrible," said Carole, feeling in her words for the soothing timbre she'd heard in Jude's voice. "Nothing that can't be forgiven."

"You don't know what I've done."

"True. All I know is that you need to go home. To see Mummy."

She stretched out her hand over the transom of the boat and, to her huge gratification, saw the boy slowly uncurl himself, rise and step towards her. He put his icy hand in hers. Carole braced herself to take the strain, as Nick stepped on to the back of the boat, preparing to jump down. Maybe I'm not so bad at this people business after all, thought Carole with a little glow of pride.

It happened in a split second. Still in the air between boat and cement, he shook his hand free and landed facing away from her. He hit the ground running and weaved his way through the rows of boats towards the Fether.

"Help!" shouted Carole up towards the clubroom. "Help!" Now she wished she'd brought every member of the Yacht Club with her to trap the boy and seal off his escape.

Dropping her torch in confusion, she ran as fast as she could, but Nick had a start and was a lot faster. She saw him vault over the far fence and rush towards the sea-wall.

By the time Carole, panting with effort, reached the railings, Nick Kent was standing swaying on one of the blue fishermen's chests on the sea wall. Is that coincidence, Carole wondered, or does he know something about the whereabouts of the body?

Such speculation would have to wait. She heard behind her the clatter of feet down wooden steps and men shouting, as she called out, "It's all right, Nick! Don't panic! Everything's all right!"

But the hue and cry she'd feared had started. One of the Yacht Club members had found a powerful spotlight, which he focused on the trembling boy.

That was the final straw. Nick Kent recoiled from the beam, as if the light had the physical power to push him.

Then he turned away and, trailing a thin scream, disappeared over the sea-wall into the Fether.

# 35

"I STILL WANT to know," said Jude calmly, "what you were doing on Fethering beach before seven in the morning."

"And why should I tell you?" Tanya sneered. "You're not police or anything. I don't have to answer your questions."

"No, you don't. On the other hand, you did invite me to come here and the only possible reason for that is because I said I wanted to talk about the body on the beach. But now I'm here, you don't seem to want to talk about it."

"Maybe I've changed my mind."

"You see, I think you do know more about the body than you're saying. The person who saw you on the beach said you had come running down from the direction of the Fethering Yacht Club. I happen to know that the body you found had been stowed there overnight. In a boat called *Brigadoon II*."

There was an involuntary intake of breath from Tanya. Jude knew more details than she was expecting.

"A possible interpretation of your actions would be that you knew the body had been put in the boat, but when you went to the Yacht Club to check on it—or possibly to move it—you found it had gone. That's what made you panic and run off down the beach, where fortunately you found the missing corpse against the breakwater. So maybe then you went off to get help to move it."

"You're talking a load of rubbish." But it was only a token defiance. Jude could see from the sulky set of the girl's chin that at least part of her conjecture had been correct.

"What I still don't know, though, is *how* you came to be involved with the body on the beach. What did it have to do with you, Tanya?"

Carole was well ahead of the others in reaching the sea-wall. As she peered fearfully down over the side, the smell and the realization hit her at the same time. The Fether was at low tide and in the thin evening light the mudflats on either side took on the sheen of rotting meat.

Nick Kent had landed in the mud some feet away from the sea-wall. The impetus of his jump had planted him up to his thighs in the ooze. His thin arms flailed around, like the wings of a moth caught on wet paint, as he tried in vain to get a purchase on the slime around him.

There was the hiss of a large wave washing up the channel from the sea. The level of the Fether was rising fast. And, even as Carole watched, Nick's body seemed to jolt sideways, sinking deeper into the mire.

She didn't think. She acted instinctively. There was

a gleaming new metal ladder against the sea-wall, which had been fixed in place by the workmen doing the repairs during the previous week. Encumbered as she was by her raincoat, Carole swung herself round to take a foothold on the top rung and shinned quickly down.

The ladder stopped about a yard above the mud. "It's all right, Nick. It's me, Carole," she called out to the terrified boy.

In the gloom he seemed aware of her for the first time. "Go away!" he shouted. "I want to die."

"No, you don't. What you've done can't be so terrible."

"You don't know anything about it."

Carole had hooked one arm around a ladder rung and stretched the other out, but was still half a yard short of the boy's hands. She undid the belt of her Burberry, slid it out of the loops and tried to flip it across the void.

Suddenly there was a flood of light from above. The Fethering Yacht Club regulars had arrived at the edge of the sea-wall. "We'll get a rope to him!" shouted Denis Woodville's voice, authoritative and confident. It was in times of crisis that Vice-Commodores came into their own.

But his authority was not unquestioned. There came a rumbling of other elderly voices, offering a wide variety of alternative rescue plans. One of them made comparisons with a similar incident that had happened while he'd been stationed out in Singapore.

Now that she could see where she was aiming, Carole made another throw with her belt. The buckle landed right by Nick Kent's hand. He could easily have taken hold of it and had at least some link to the dry land.

But he didn't. His hands stayed resolutely on the mud.

He meant what he had said. He wasn't going to do anything to help himself. He did want to die.

The metal ladder boomed and shook as someone else came down to join her. "We can get this rope to him," said an elderly male voice she didn't recognize from somewhere above her head.

Carole squinted upwards. "You'll have to lasso it round him. He's not cooperating.

"Damn it," said the voice. "I'll go and get some duckboards. Perhaps we can get across the mud to him." The ladder shuddered again as he clambered back up and started shouting, "Get some duckboards! Bloody kid's on a kamikaze mission! Won't help himself!"

These orders prompted more shouting from other elderly male voices. One advocated ringing the coastguard. One recommended a boathook under the boy's collar. A third said he remembered something similar happening when he'd been stationed out in Singapore. Denis Woodville could be heard saying he'd go to the nearest boat and try saving the boy from the water.

The reasons why managers need to go on management training courses were all too apparent. There was a serious plethora of chiefs, and a serious deficit of Indians.

Carole tried another flick across the void with her Burberry belt. It slipped out of her cold fingers and lay, a dead snake, on the mud between them.

She couldn't see Nick's expression. While the old men above argued about the optimum escape plan, they had forgotten about keeping the light pointing down on to the mud.

But Carole could see less of Nick, there was no question about that. He was now embedded in the ooze up to his chest and had to hold his arms up to keep them free of its embrace. The tide was sending ever stronger waves against the outflow of the Fether, and, with each hissing onrush, the water level crept closer to the stranded boy.

Carole slipped out of her precious Burberry. "Nick!" she called out, as softly as she dared against the rush of the water. "Grab hold of my coat. Then I can hang on until help comes."

She flipped the Burberry out, in the manner patented by Sir Walter Raleigh. It landed, chequered-lining down, flat against the slime. Demonstrating once again that the mind has scant regard for the gravity of situations, Carole found herself thinking of cleaning bills and wondering whether dry-cleaning would remove the waterproof qualities of the material.

The hem of the Burberry was almost touching Nick. He could easily have reached out and grabbed hold, taken a strong purchase on the cloth and given himself a chance.

Still, he did nothing.

"For God's sake, Nick!" Carole shouted in exasperation. "Is this really how you want to die?"

"I don't care how it happens, so long as I die!" came back the petulant reply.

Carole took a deep breath. Once again, the thought came to her that Jude would do this better. But Jude wasn't here. Carole Seddon was the only person who could make the boy change his mind and start participating in his own rescue. And Carole Seddon was bloody well going to do it.

"If you die now, Nick," she began in a firm, no-nonsense way, "what would your father think?"

"Don't talk about my father!" he shrieked.

"Why not? I know he's not around at the moment . . ."

"You can say that again!"

". . . but you used to be close. And if he comes back to find that you gave away your life in such a pathetic way as this, what's he going to think?"

"He's not going to come back! Can't you understand—he'll never come back! He's gone for good!"

Carole changed tack. "All right. Say that's true . . . Say he never does come back . . . That means your mother will have lost one of the two men in her life for ever, and you're about to deprive her of the other. Think of her. Think what this'll do to Mummy."

"It's better than telling her," the boy countered doggedly. "It's better than her finding out what happened."

"For God's sake, Nick, she's your mother! Mothers were put on the earth to forgive their children—whatever they've done."

"Not this."

"Yes, even this, whatever it may be. The one thing a mother won't forgive is herself, if she allows one of her children to take his own life. She'll blame herself for that throughout the rest of her days. Is that the fate you want to condemn your mummy to?" There was silence. "The fate that Aaron Spalding's mother's condemned to?"

Carole knew it had been a risk, and the boy definitely flinched at the name. At the same moment, a rogue wave, a bit ahead of itself, broke noisily behind him. The slap sent up a little column of spray which came down over his head, flattening his hair to a shiny skull-cap.

Whether it was the imminent reality of his demise or Carole's arguments which swayed him, she would never know. All that mattered was that suddenly, convulsively, Nick Kent grabbed hold of the hem of the Burberry. Carole could feel the shock of his weight, the socket-wrenching tug on the arm that grasped the raincoat's collar, and the equally painful strain on the arm that was hooked round the ladder.

"OK, we're coming with the duckboards!" a self-important voice announced from the top of the sea-wall. "Easy does it. We'll just—oh, bugger!"

Carole heard something heavy rushing through the air, then a sound like a small fart as the object flumped into the mud. A slatted rectangle of duckboarding stuck upright at an angle out of the ooze. It was a good three yards away from both the ladder and the sinking boy.

Again, Carole's mind, with its poorly developed sense of occasion, demanded why, in a crisis of this kind, when the best help available was required, the rescue mission seemed to be in the hands of Dad's Army or the Keystone Cops?

From above, she could hear more argument. One pompous elderly voice was saying that duckboards weren't the answer, they should be throwing down a lifebelt. Another argued back that duckboards were the answer, but they needed to be lowered down on ropes. A third announced that a similar thing had happened when he'd been stationed out in Singapore.

"For Christ's sake!" Carole bawled upwards. "Throw down a lifebelt, you stupid old fools!"

This prompted some huffing and puffing of the "Not

very ladylike" variety, but after a few seconds there was a cry of, "Mind your heads!", and a halo of plastic-covered cork whirled down through the air.

With a squelch, the lifebelt came to rest on the mud-flat, between the capsized duckboarding and the stranded boy. Though less than a yard away from him, Nick Kent could no more have reached it than he could have flown. Each inward swirl of water was now lapping over his shoulders.

There was another, "Bugger!" from above, then, "Let's see if we can work it round."

Manipulating the lifebelt with its rope, an attempt was made to flip it nearer to the boy. The ring rose in the air, complaining against the suction of the mud, and then flopped down again, a yard nearer to the sea-wall.

Carole couldn't reach it. Still she clutched desperately at her Burberry, feeling the dead weight at the other end. She longed to change her hold, unhook her other arm from the ladder and get a two-handed grip on the coat, but she didn't dare. There was no hope of pulling him out with the Burberry, but at least they were in contact.

Another bumptious wave came along and broke right over the boy's head. She heard him splutter as he got a mouthful of water. Coughing, he said, "It's not going to work. I'm going to die here."

"No, you're not," said Carole firmly. "Anyway, a few moments ago that's what you said you wanted to happen."

"Not now."

"Good. We'll get you out of this," Carole announced, though she wouldn't have liked to have the provenance of her confidence investigated.

There was another splutter from the boy as a new

wave caught him. Either because of further slippage into the mud or because of the rising water, only his head was now visible, and that got covered by the crest of each incoming wave.

Above them on the sea wall, old men, reliving distantly remembered wartime actions, shouted and countermanded each other's orders. If they ever did get to the point of agreeing a course of action, it would be far too late for Nick Kent.

Carole was aware of the sound of a boat's motor puttputting closer. Craning round from her Burberry tug-of-war posture, she saw a small wooden launch approaching. There were two men in it, though she could not identify them in the gloom.

The boat was certainly aiming for Nick, but looked unlikely to get there in time. The boy's head was now only intermittently visible between the waves. No more sounds of spluttering or protest came from his submerged mouth. Only the continuing tension on the Burberry told Carole he was still alive. But for how much longer?

There was a splash from the approaching boat and she was aware of something moving through the water. It was a man swimming.

Just as the swimmer approached the spot where Nick had been, Carole felt a jolt through her body. The countertension on the Burberry was gone. Nick Kent had let go.

The swimmer was splashing around in the water, fixing something. Then he shouted back to the boat. "All right, he's breathing through the snorkel. Chuck the rope down!"

Carole knew the voice, but in the tension of the moment could not put a name to it.

The man on the launch did as he was told. There was a rattle of anchor cable and the note of the motor changed to idling. The swimmer kept bobbing beneath the surface, near where the boy had last been seen.

"OK," the swimmer called out. "Take the strain!"

It's hopeless, thought Carole. For one thing, the boy's probably already dead. For another, no elderly member of the Fethering Yacht Club is going to be strong enough to pull a body up against the suction of that mud.

But she had reckoned without a winch. As soon as she heard the clank of gearing and the screech of ratchets, she knew there was a chance.

The man on the launch worked the machinery, the swimmer kept the boy's snorkel upright, as he eased the body out of its clammy prison. Winching and manhandling, they flipped the inert mass over the stern of the boat. At that moment there was a cheer from the armchair admirals on top of the sea wall. With remarkable agility, the swimmer then pulled himself up on board as well.

"Is he all right?" Carole called across the void. "Is Nick all right?"

"Will be," called the swimmer's familiar voice. "Just get the water out of his lungs. He'll be fine."

As the tension drained out of her, Carole realized that she had no strength left in her arms. It was all she could do to cling on to the ladder. The challenge of climbing back up it was insuperable.

"Hey!" she shouted. "Could someone give me a hand up the ladder?"

This request seemed set to start a new debate as to

which Fethering Yacht Club member should take on the task, and what would be the best way of approaching it, but fortunately a rough voice cut through the cackle. "I'll get her."

Carole felt the ringing through the tubes of the ladder as a heavy body descended. When she felt his strong arms safely cradling her, she said tartly, "You were supposed to meet me at seven, Ted Crisp."

"Oh, really? I thought you said eight."

"Honestly!"

"Why? Did I miss much?"

There are some questions, Carole thought, that aren't worth answering.

Looking down at the Burberry still gripped firmly in her hand, Ted Crisp said, "Aren't you going to chuck that filthy old thing?"

"Certainly not! Ooh, and could you manage to reach the belt down there?"

By swinging ape-like from the bottom rung and trailing his large foot across the mud, he managed to hook up the belt. He handed it across to her. "There you are, madam. Your natural elegance restored."

"Thank you."

"Though it's about to be shot to pieces again by me giving you a fireman's lift." And he slung her over his shoulder.

Carole got a little cheer from Dad's Navy when she was dumped unceremoniously on top of the sea wall. But her immediate concern was what was happening in the boat below.

One of the Fethering Yacht Club members proved he could do something right by turning the broad beam of his torch down to the little launch.

The bedraggled figure of Nick Kent looked very unsteady, but at least he was upright. He gave Carole a wave and a sheepish little grin.

Standing either side of him were Denis Woodville and, soaked to the skin but triumphant, Bill Chilcott.

# 36

"MY FRIEND CAROLE and I have been working it out, you see," Jude explained. "We've got these two deaths and a disappearance. There's the body you found, Tanya—the one you refuse to tell me more about. There's Aaron Spalding, who committed suicide. And then there's the dentist, Rory Turnbull, who we're meant to think has committed suicide."

The girl had looked frankly bored throughout the speech, but the last words lit a spark of interest. "What do you mean by that?"

"You know Rory Turnbull, don't you, Tanya?"

"Sure." She was about to say more, but changed her mind. Sullenly, she went on, "He was Treasurer down the Yacht Club. I saw him there quite often."

"And he sometimes gave you a lift from Brighton to Fethering for your evening shifts, didn't he?"

She was surprised. "How'd you know that?"

Jude shrugged. "You can find out most things if you ask around enough. Tanya, when did you last see Rory Turnbull?"

The girl coloured. "I don't know. I finished working at the Yacht Club Friday before last . . . Round then, I suppose."

"You're sure you haven't seen him since?"

"No. Where would I have seen him?"

The answers sounded clumsy, but then the girl's normal manner was clumsy. Jude couldn't be absolutely certain that she was lying.

"Anyway," Tanya went on, "I couldn't have seen him the last few days, 'cause he gone missing, hasn't he?"

"How do you know that?"

"It's common knowledge."

"Common knowledge in Fethering. I wouldn't have thought it got talked about much in Brighton."

"I'm still in touch with people from Fethering. Denis Woodville told me."

"I see."

Petulantly, the girl kicked at the carpet with one black-booted foot. "Anyway, what's all this about? Where's it all leading? Is there something you definitely know about this body I saw on the beach?"

"There are two things I definitely know. One is that there is a connection between the body on the beach and Rory Turnbull. And the other is that Rory Turnbull is still alive."

"Well, you're right in at least one of those."

The bathroom door had opened silently and there was a third person in the room.

Rory Turnbull.

# 37

MAGGIE KENT ARRIVED at the sea-wall just after Carole had been deposited there by Ted Crisp. Which was probably just as well. In time she would hear the details of how close her son had come to death, but at least she had not had to witness the agony of the previous half-hour.

Moments later, the three from the motor launch disembarked at the floating jetty a little further upstream and Nick Kent, with a grubby blanket wrapped around him, was led by Denis Woodville and Bill Chilcott towards the waiting group. Carole and Maggie hurried forward to greet him. The mother, oblivious to the filth in which he was covered, threw her arms around her son. Both of them sobbed.

"You two did brilliantly," said Carole to the rescuers. "Amazing bit of cooperation and coordination."

"Only did it because my boat was the closest," said Bill Chilcott gruffly.

The Vice-Commodore's reaction was equally ungracious. "Yes, in an emergency you can't choose the people you have to work with."

There was a silence. A moment of potential rapprochement between the two sides of the feud . . . ?

It seemed not. "I must get this incident entered in the club log." Denis Woodville turned abruptly on his heel and set off towards his cronies.

"And I must get out of these wet clothes." Equally abruptly, Bill Chilcott turned in the opposite direction and strutted off squelching on his way back home.

Carole moved across to the muddy embrace of mother and son. Nick had stopped sobbing, but his breath was coming out in little jerky wheezes. "Should I call an ambulance, Maggie, or get him to a doctor?"

"No, I don't want him to get caught up in hospitals and all that. Nick's freezing cold and he's had a terrible shock. I just want to get him home, get him into a hot bath and clean him up. Then, if there's anything wrong with him, I'll call the GP." Maggie Kent looked dubiously at the crowd of elderly campaigners still clustered by the Yacht Club. "Wish I could smuggle him away without talking to anyone."

"I'll give you a lift," said Carole.

She fixed a meeting point and five minutes later was back in the Renault to pick them up. Carole hadn't even wiped the mud off her own shoes and she made no demur as the slime-covered boy in his filthy blanket was laid across the precious upholstery of her back seat.


Maggie Kent ushered Carole into the bleak front room.

"Would you like a coffee or something? I'd offer you a real drink, but I'm afraid I don't have anything."

"Don't worry. You just go and sort Nick out."

"Yes. He's gone up to start the bath. There's lots of hot water. I'll give him a good scrubbing."

"And, Maggie . . ."

"Yes?"

"It's not my business, but if I were you I wouldn't ask him about what happened. He'll tell you when he wants to."

The mother nodded. "I'd already decided that."

"Good."

"But would you mind staying till I've put him to bed? I'd like to hear your account of what happened."

Carole couldn't say no, could she? "That's fine." She took a look at her watch. "But may I use your telephone?"

It was the moment after Rory Turnbull had appeared from the bathroom, before Jude had had time to recover from her surprise and say anything, that her mobile rang. She snatched the phone immediately out of her pocket. "Hello?"

"Jude, it's Carole. Nick Kent's all right."

"Thank God. Listen, I've found—"

But the mobile was ripped from her hand and switched off. "I don't think you need tell anyone what you've found," Rory Turnbull said coolly.

As someone who'd never possessed a mobile phone, Carole's image of their technology was out of date. They were unreliable machines, prone to constant loss of signal and other breakdowns. So she wasn't that surprised to have been cut off.

She used the last-number radial on Maggie's phone. The ringing went on for some time, then a bloodlessly polite voice informed her that the caller was not responding, but she had the option of leaving a message.

There didn't seem much point. Jude had definitely heard her say that Nick was all right. That was the important news. Anything else would keep.

Odd, though. One moment Jude was answering her phone; a moment later, even though their conversation had been unfinished, she'd switched it off.

Maybe another vagary of mobile-phone technology . . . The explanation gave Carole reassurance. Partial reassurance.

Three-quarters of an hour had elapsed before Maggie Kent came back downstairs. "I've got the worst of it off him. It'll take another few weeks of baths—or possibly a course of sandblasting—to get it all out of his pores, but he's OK."

"You don't need to call the doctor?"

"I think all Nick needs is a lot of sleep. He's tucked up in bed and I've given him one of my sleeping pills. I'll get him a hot-water bottle. But he did want to have a word with you—just to say thank you."

"Fine." Carole rose to her feet, but Maggie still lingered in the doorway, not yet ready to lead her upstairs. "What is it?"

"It's just . . . tell me . . . did Nick really try to kill himself?"

Carole answered with complete honesty. "He thought

that's what he wanted to do, yes. But when he got close to the reality, he changed his mind. He thought of the effect it would have on you and he couldn't allow himself to do it."

"Good." Some of the tension eased from Maggie Kent's shoulders and a warmth came into her tired face. "Let's go up and see him."

The decor of Nick Kent's room was the perfect illustration of a life poised uneasily between the pulls of the child and the adult. A poster of the Manchester United football team on one wall was having a face-off with the pouting images of the latest girl band on the other. A copy of *GFH* lay on top of an *Asterix*. Flashy deodorants and "men's toiletries" stood side by side with Coca-Cola bottles.

Nick was propped up on pillows under a duvet with a Manchester United cover. He looked exhausted but calm. His scrubbed face bore the soft glow of childhood. His eyelids flickered. He would soon be asleep.

"I just wanted to say thank you very much," he slurred. "Wanted to thank you . . . should've thanked the men who pulled me out . . . didn't thank them properly . . ."

"Don't worry. There'll be plenty of time to do that."

There was a shelf of treasures by the boy's bedhead and on it Carole saw something which unleashed a landslide of explanations. Among Subbuteo footballers, swimming certificates and snaps of leering boys from some long-past school trip stood a framed photograph.

It showed a smiling, grey-haired man in his late forties. Undoubtedly the missing Sam Kent.

And also undoubtedly, in spite of the fact that in the photograph he had no tooth missing, the man whose body Carole Seddon had found on Fethering beach.

## 38

"WELL, THANK YOU," said Jude, "for interrupting my phone call."

Rory Turnbull put the turned-off mobile down on a table. "Some people believe it's bad manners to take calls on mobiles in other people's homes."

"Possibly. But that's not why you switched it off, was it?"

"No." He moved to stand, almost protectively, behind Tanya's chair.

Jude took in the pair of them. The dentist looked less rattled than he had when she last saw him in the Crown and Anchor. For the first time, there was some confidence about him, the successful professional in his early fifties. Beside him, the lumpen girl in her crumpled black, surprisingly, did not look out of place.

"So you two are an item," said Jude.

Rory looked as if he might have denied it, but Tanya responded instantly, "Yeah, all right, and what if we are? He's a good man, first man I ever met who actually cares about me, isn't just trying to use me. What's wrong with that?"

"Nothing. There's nothing wrong with love."

"Then why are you here . . . what's your name— Jude?" asked Rory.

"Jude, yes. There could be a lot of answers to why I'm here, but let's start with the fact that everyone who knows you thinks you've committed suicide. You did leave a note to that effect. The police have been searching for you for days."

"I know."

"Well, wouldn't you say that justifies a degree of curiosity? Why does someone want to stage his own death? And what might that deception have to do with the body that was found on Fethering Beach last Tuesday? I assume I don't have to explain to you which body I'm talking about? I'm taking it for granted you were listening from behind the bathroom door?"

"You're right. I encouraged Tanya to get you talking to find out how much you knew."

A couple of details at least were explained—why Tanya had changed her reaction the second time Jude had phoned and the girl's long absence in the bathroom early on in their interview.

"And how much do you reckon I do know?" asked Jude coolly. She recognized that her situation was uncomfortable but was trying to work out whether or not it was dangerous.

"You tell me," Rory replied. "You've clearly made some connections. The fact that you're here and the fact that you're talking about the body demonstrate that. But how much else have you pieced together?"

"Well . . ." She hadn't pieced much together until that

moment, but suddenly certain conclusions became glaringly obvious. "If, on the one hand, you have a middle-aged man who, with maximum publicity, has declared he is about to commit suicide . . . and, on the other hand, you have the body of a second middle-aged man of similar build . . . I might suspect some substitution of bodies was being contemplated."

There was a sharp breath from Tanya, but Rory neither confirmed nor denied the conjecture. He waited to see what else Jude was going to say.

"I don't know how the apparent death would be staged. In a car, I imagine. But not exhaust fumes. No, it has to be a method that would disfigure the corpse sufficiently to make identification difficult. Fire would probably be best. Body wearing Rory Turnbull's clothes found in burnt-out car belonging to Rory Turnbull, body must belong to Rory Turnbull. God knows the poor man had enough reasons to do away with himself. The heroin habit that was ruining him financially, leading him to remortgage his house, put his hand in the till at the Yacht Club, try to cheat the Dental Estimates Board . . . Many men have killed themselves to avoid lesser ruin than that little accumulation. Open and shut case."

Rory Turnbull nodded slowly. "Yes. You have done well, haven't you?"

Tanya had been silent too long. "All right, so what's wrong with all that? It hasn't done anyone any harm, has it?"

"What about Rory's wife, Barbara?"

"That frigid bitch deserves everything that's coming to her! She's never given Rory anything all the time they've been married, just sucked out his lifeblood. And she'll be cushioned by her mother's money, whatever happens. She's not suffering from this."

"All right, Tanya, putting Barbara on one side . . . what about the dead man? The one who would so obligingly pretend to be Rory? Are you telling me he didn't suffer either?"

"Only the suffering he brought on himself," the girl snapped. "He was a waster, out of his head on heroin, who just hung around the beach all the time. And then one day—Monday before last—he took an overdose and Rory just happened to be the one who found the body." She looked at her lover with devout admiration. "At that moment Rory saw a way out of all our troubles. It was then the whole substitution plan came into his mind and he brought the body back here."

"But surely—"

"Tanya!" said Rory firmly. "I think we could do with something to drink."

"There's some white wine in the fridge."

"No. Whiskey." He reached for his wallet and extracted a twenty-pound note. "Could you go down to the off-licence and get a litre of Grouse?"

"But—"

"Now."

She didn't argue anymore, but rose to her feet. Putting his arms gently on her broad shoulders, Rory planted a little kiss on her forehead. "Take care."

"And you."

Tanya flipped her shiny green anorak off a hook on the back of the door and left the bedsitter.

"She's pregnant, isn't she?" said Jude.

"Yes. How did you know?"

"I should have worked it out earlier from the fact that

she'd gone off coffee, but what made me certain was
the way you touched her just then, your concern for her,
as if she was very fragile."

"All right. So she's pregnant. What have you got to
say about that?"

"Nothing. Except I assume that's the reason why you
set this whole thing up?"

"The final reason, yes. The other reasons had been
building for years."

"Rory, men leave their wives for younger women
every day of the week. Very few of them bother to set
up mock-suicides to cover their tracks. Why didn't you
just talk to Barbara, tell her you wanted out?"

"I couldn't do that!" A pallid transformation came
over the dentist's face and Jude realized the extent of
the terror he felt for his wife. "Barbara would never have
let me get away. And if she thought I was still alive,
anywhere in the world, she'd come and find me. No,
I've always known I'd only be safe if she thought I was
dead."

"So you really reckoned you could start over?"

"Not reckon*ed*—reckon. It's still going to happen.
Tanya and I are going to live together in France and
bring up our babies there. I've been salting away the
money for months."

The gleam in Rory's eyes showed Jude how much he
was caught up in his fantasies, how long he'd been nurs-
ing them, and how potent to the middle-aged was the
chimera of one last chance, the opportunity to wipe the
slate clean and make a fresh start. It also showed Jude
that the man she was dealing with was not entirely sane.

"Tanya was meant to come into my life," he went on.
"It's been a long time coming, and there's been a lot of

shit along the way, but she was meant to happen to me. She's wonderful. She's the first woman I've ever known who hasn't expected anything from me. Anything I give her she regards as a bonus. She has no *aspirations* for me."

The fervour with which he said the word bore witness to the agony of the years Barbara and her mother had spent trying to "make something" of Rory Turnbull. Part of Jude could empathize with his need to take action, do anything that would break him out of that straitjacket, out of the suffocating aspirational gentility of the Shore- lands Estate.

"Me and Tanya," Rory Turnbull concluded proudly, "is a love match."

And Jude could see how it was. Two damaged people who had asked for very little and been more abundantly rewarded than they'd ever dared to hope.

Appealing though this image was, it did not change the facts. "I'm sure it is a love match," said Jude, "but does that justify murder?"

He gave her a pained look. "Tanya told you. The man died of an overdose."

"No. Tanya may well believe that, because it doesn't occur to her to question anything you tell her, but it doesn't work for me. The logic isn't there. This whole business has taken months of planning. Your cheating the NHS, your fiddling the Yacht Club accounts, plant- ing the idea of your heroin habit, that's all long-term stuff. I'm afraid I don't believe you set it all up, on the off chance that, when the time came—the Monday be- fore last—you'd stumble across a body the right age and shape who'd just conveniently died of an overdose.

Sorry, call me old-fashioned, but I don't buy that. You'd targeted the man for months."

"All right." He made the confession lightly. "Yes, I saw him first in the summer, down by the pier when I went for a walk one lunchtime. He asked me for money. I gave him some and thought how wretched he was—a man about my age, about my size, and he was reduced to that. And then I thought that, though I'd got all the things he hadn't—the money, the job, the house—I was even more wretched than he was. It was round the time I'd started seeing Tanya. I was still at that stage trying to behave correctly, trying to *do the decent thing*—and it was tearing me apart.

"I saw the man a few times after that—just walked past him, maybe gave him money, maybe didn't—but it was only when I knew Tanya was pregnant that the plan began to form in my mind. And, the more I thought about it, the more it started to obsess me."

Yes, thought Jude, that's the word—obsess.

"And, of course, because Tanya was pregnant, there was a time pressure. There were a lot of time pressures."

"The Dental Estimates Board, the Fethering Yacht Club accountants . . ."

"All that."

"So how did you kill him? Where did you kill him?"

"Here. I'd sent Tanya out to the cinema. She loves movies—particularly weepies. I'd given him the money for a lot of heroin. He'd had a hit. He was feeling good. I smothered him—" he gestured to the bed—"with that pillow." Rory read disapproval in Jude's expression. "Go on, he died happy. Better than the way it would have happened otherwise. Contaminated drugs . . . a fight with another addict . . . an infected needle . . . with someone like that it was only a matter of time. He was already lost."

"No one's lost, Rory. Not even at the very end. Anyway, didn't you think who he was?"

"I didn't know who he was."

"He was a human being."

"He didn't matter."

She was silent for a moment before asking, "And what made you change your plans?"

"Change my plans?"

"Yes. For your plan to work, the suicide in the car had to be staged as soon as possible after the man had died. The longer you left it, the more the body would decay and the more open your deception would be to exposure by forensic examination. Why didn't you do it the night you killed him?"

Rory Turnbull grimaced. "Because of the bloody police."

"What? Surely they didn't know what you were up to?"

"No. The trouble was I wanted to leave it fairly late, so that there wouldn't be many people around. But he'd died about six and—"

"You mean you'd killed him about six."

"Whatever. There's a garage in this block that's hardly used—that's where my car is at the moment, actually. By midnight, which was the time intended to take the body down there, it had started to stiffen up."

"Rigor mortis."

"Yes. I'd meant to put him in the boot, but I didn't want to risk giving the body any unexplained injuries by bending the joints, so I just laid him on the back seat with a coat over him. I left Tanya here, as we'd agreed—

we were going to meet in France a week or so later—and I set off. Just on the outskirts of Fethering, a car came towards me, flashing its lights."

"Bill Chilcott."

"Yes. I thought driving off at speed would draw more attention than stopping, so I stopped. Bill was just being charitable. He told me there were police staking out Seaview Road and stopping every car that came along. Random breath-tests—Sussex Police are very hot on drink-driving. Well, that really got me scared, because there's no other way to the Shorelands Estate except via Seaview Road."

"But why did you have to go home?"

"Because that's how I'd planned it!" he snapped petulantly. "The petrol and the rags and stuff I was going to use were all in the garage at Brigadoon."

"Were you actually planning to stage your suicide in your own home?"

"Yes. On the paved area in front of the house." A vindictive light burned in his eye. "Very fitting—show all the tight-arsed snobs of the Shorelands Estate what Barbara and her bloody mother had driven me to. I thought that'd be very funny. A social indiscretion on that scale . . . they'd really find hard to live down."

No, thought Jude, I am not dealing here with someone who's even mildly sane.

"Anyway, I panicked. I daren't risk the police looking inside the car. I decided I couldn't go through with the plan that night, so—"

"So you hid the body inside your boat at the Fethering Yacht Club."

"Yes, I—How the hell did you know that?"

"Call it educated guesswork. And did you put the life-jacket on it?"

"Yes."

"Why?"

"I don't know. I just thought, if anyone found the body, it might look more like an accident. I wasn't thinking straight."

"You certainly weren't," said Jude coolly. "My next educated guess, incidentally, would be that you went home and the following morning early, terrified that someone might have found the body overnight, rang Tanya and asked her to go to Fethering and check it was where you'd left it."

The dentist looked bewildered. "Did she tell you this?"

"No. I think Tanya looked and the body was missing. But shortly afterwards she found it washed up on the beach. She went to ring you and tell you what had happened. Then two small boys—"

"What?" He turned pale. "How do you know all this stuff? Are you psychic?"

"A bit," said Jude, with a self-effacing grin, "though, as it happens, that's not how I know. So, did Tanya see the boys had put the body back in the boat?"

"Yes."

"Which meant your plan was all set to happen again, a mere twenty-four hours late. Body back in place, no police breathalyzer traps . . . Why didn't you do it on the Tuesday night?"

"Because I was disturbed by somebody. I'd just got the body out of the boat when I heard a noise. There was someone snooping around. A boy."

"Do you think he saw you?"

"Yes. Just as I was lifting the body out of the boat. I was holding it in front of me and I came face to face with the boy. He screamed."

Yes, he would have done, thought Jude. Poor Aaron Spalding, his head filled with half-digested stories of black magic and the Undead. The boy, tortured by guilt, had come back to check the scene of his crime and seen the dead body apparently moving. The Undead had come back to claim its victim. That could easily have been enough to unhinge the terrified Aaron, to make him throw himself into the Fether. Unless, of course . . .

"You didn't harm the boy, did you, Rory?"

"No, of course I didn't! I don't know what happened to him. He ran off along the river bank. He'd got me rattled, though, so I put my plans off for another twenty-four hours."

"But because other people knew the body had been stowed inside *Brigadoon II*, you moved it to another hiding place."

Once again he gave her a look as if she had unnatural powers. "Are you sure Tanya didn't tell you all this?"

"Positive. Don't worry, she'd never betray you."

"More educated guesswork then?"

"If you like. I'd say you put the body inside one of those blue fishermen's boxes near the Yacht Club . . ." A hissed intake of breath told her she'd hit another mark ". . . little knowing that the next morning that whole area would be cordoned off and under the blaze of spotlights while the workmen carried out repairs on the sea wall."

Rory's expression acknowledged the accuracy of this conjecture too.

"So, what with one thing and another," Jude concluded lightly, "it wasn't really that great a plan, was it?"

She'd caught him on the raw. "It was a brilliant plan!" he spat back.

"Oh, I don't think you can use the word 'brilliant' for any plan that has to be aborted."

"This one's not going to be aborted."

"You mean you're still thinking of going ahead with it?"

"Oh yes. I'm going ahead with it. Tonight. Only this time, Jude . . ." He savoured the name as if it had an unfamiliar but not unpleasant taste ". . . you're going to be part of the plan."

# 39

WHEN CAROLE GOT back home from Maggie
Kent's house, she felt quite shaken. Having garaged the
Renault—and not even considered cleaning its interior
until the morning—she found she was shivering as she
walked the short distance to the house. Inside, even before attending to Gulliver's needs, she turned up the central heating and lit the log-effect gas fire. Then, once the
dog was sorted, she poured herself an uncharacteristically large Scotch from the bottle which she kept for
guests and which sometimes went untouched from one
Christmas to the next.

It wasn't only her physical ordeal that had shaken her
up. It was the discovery she had made in Nick Kent's
bedroom. Now she knew the identity of the body she'd
found, she could understand the reasons for the boy's
mental collapse. To have been involved in a black magic
ritual with a corpse was bad enough, but to discover in
the cold light of the following morning that the body
you had seen mutilated was that of your idolized father
would have unhinged the most stable of adults. The ef-

fect it had had on a confused adolescent was all too predictable.

Thank God at least that Nick had held back from wielding the Stanley knife himself.

Carole hadn't said anything to Maggie. The awful truth would have to be faced at some point, but it should wait until the body had once again been found. And then the news should be broken to the unknowing widow by the proper authorities.

Carole was reminded that she had intended to spend that evening with Ted Crisp trying to find the body, but after all she been through another visit to the sea-wall in search of a week-old corpse held little appeal. While the body on the beach remained anonymous, there had been an almost game-like quality to the investigations she and Jude had undertaken. But now the dead man possessed an identity and a family context, the idea of further probing became distasteful.

She decided she'd done quite enough for that evening. Maybe Jude would ring her or call round when she got back from Brighton. In the meantime, however, Carole Seddon was going to have a very long soak in a very hot bath.

Jude lay on the back seat of the BMW, where the body she did not know to be that of Sam Kent had lain a week before.

When Tanya had returned to her bedsitter with the whisky, Rory had got her to help tie Jude up. With soft scarves, over her clothes, so as not to leave any marks on her body.

Then Rory and Tanya had manhandled her down to

the garage and into the BMW. More scarves had been used to tie her wrists and ankles to the armrests, so that she couldn't sit up and attract attention to herself when they were driving. Rory had not bothered to gag her. The car was soundproof.

Jude had been left in the garage for nearly an hour, while the two conspirators presumably went through the final details of their forthcoming elopement, their separate journeys and their blissful reunion in France.

As she lay immobile in the dark, Jude could not feel optimistic. Assessing the feasibility of escape did not take long. Once she'd given up on that, she tried, with limited success, to focus on more spiritual matters. But anger kept getting in the way. This was neither the time nor the manner in which Jude wanted to die.


Bill Chilcott appeared in the Crown and Anchor a little later than usual that evening for his customary half. And, also uncharacteristically, he brought his wife with him. He looked sleekly bathed, the white bits of his turnip head gleaming from a recent shampooing. Sandra was also carefully groomed and both looked smug. They had clearly come to receive the plaudits of a grateful nation.

Over in the Fethering Yacht Club, Ted Crisp reckoned, Denis Woodville would also be reliving his triumphant part in the rescue. And no doubt being upstaged by other ideas of how it should have been done and recollections of similar incidents out in Singapore.

Bill Chilcott was a little miffed to find the Crown and Anchor bar rather empty. And no evidence of anyone who knew about his heroism.

Ted Crisp did his best to make up the deficiency.

"Full marks for what you done out there, Bill. What is it—your 'customary half?' Or will you go mad and make it a pint?"

"Well, as it is a rather special occasion . . ."

"Sure. Have this on me. And what about you, Sandra?"

"Ooh, a dry sherry, please, Ted."

"None the worse for your adventure, Bill?"

"Good heavens, no. Sandra and I do work hard on our fitness. All that regular swimming down at the Leisure Centre has certainly paid off tonight."

"Not to mention our line-dancing."

"No, no, don't let's forget the line-dancing. No, Sandra and I don't give in to *anno domini*. Did you hear how that dreadful man Denis Woodville was wheezing during the rescue? And he didn't swim. He only worked the mechanical winch."

"Well, he smokes like a chimney, doesn't he, Bill?"

"Yes, Sandra, filthy habit. So unhealthy. All his arteries must be totally furred up. If you want my opinion, he'll just keel over one day."

"And good riddance, that's what Bill and I say!"

"Thought you might," Ted Crisp murmured. "But the boy was all right, was he? None the worse for his ordeal?"

"I don't know," Bill Chilcott replied. "He went off with his mother in Carole Seddon's car."

"Oh, is that what happened?" The landlord scratched his chin through the thickets of his beard. "You know, I might just give Carole a call to see that the lad's OK . . ."

    •    •    •    •

When Rory Turnbull finally did return to his prisoner in the car, he seemed blithe, almost euphoric. He was alone. He opened the garage doors, drove the BMW out and closed them again, before setting off at a steady pace west out of Brighton.

At least Jude could speak. She could try to reason for her life. Anything was worth trying. Without much hope, she announced, "It won't work, you know, Rory."

"Oh, it will."

"The body's been dead a week."

"But the weather's been on my side. Below freezing most of the last few days."

"It'll still be obvious he died a week ago. The most basic of post-mortems'll show that—regardless of how much the body's disfigured by the fire."

"I'm sure you're right. No, it wouldn't work . . . if fire was the method I was going to use."

"You're not?"

"No. Change of plan, due to change of circumstances. Always pays to be flexible in one's planning, you know." There was a heady, almost manic, confidence about him now. "By the time the body's found, no-body'll be able to give a precise date of death. All they'll have to identify him by will be the fact he's in my car, he's wearing my clothes . . . and, of course," he concluded smugly, "they'll be able to check his dental work."

"My God! The missing tooth. Did you . . ."

"Oh yes." He was very full of himself now. "I told you, I've been planning this for a long time. I don't know how he'd lost his tooth, but as soon as I noticed it I knew what I had to do."

"You actually took out one of your own teeth?"

"Not difficult for someone of my profession. I made up some story to Barbara about having been in a fight, which fitted in well with the image of general social collapse that I was creating. And then I had a rather distinctive chromium cobalt denture made for me by our usual lab. They always put their own identification mark on all the stuff they make, so there'd be no question it was mine. And the plate also fits into the dead man's mouth well enough."

Remembering something that Holly the hygienist had said in what seemed like a previous incarnation but was in fact only that morning, Jude murmured, "You actually had him in your surgery to check that it fitted?"

"Yes. It was a risk, but I did it after hours. Pretended I was helping him out of charity. He didn't care. So long as I gave him a bit of money to buy heroin, he'd have done anything I wanted, anything. When I offered him money for his passport, he found it and handed it over like a lamb."

"That's how you set up savings accounts, isn't it? In his name. You used the passport for identification."

"Oh yes," he said smugly.

"You've really put a lot of planning into this, haven't you, Rory?"

"I certainly have." Oblivious to her irony, he took it as a straight compliment, and the way he spoke stole away Jude's last shred of hope. Rory Turnbull was impervious to logic. His elaborate scheme would almost definitely not work, his subterfuges would be unmasked by scientific examination, but that didn't matter. He was so caught up in the fantasy of his plan that he was going to go through with it regardless of anything.

"You said," Jude began with trepidation, "you weren't going to use fire . . ."

"No. Not fire. The wreckage'd be found too quickly, which might prove . . . forensically embarrassing. No, I want the car to be discovered in a few weeks' time . . . after the fish have taken some of the flesh off the bodies."

"Bod*ies*?" she echoed softly.

"Yes. I'm afraid, my dear Jude, you know far too much about what I've been up to for me to let you survive. But, fortunately, there has been a rumour around during the last week that I might have had another woman . . ." A rumour that Carole and I helped to foster, thought Jude bitterly, as Rory went on, "Tanya heard about it from old Denis Woodville. And Ted Crisp in the pub suggested last week that you and I might be an item."

"He was joking."

"Many a true word . . . Or at least that's how it'll seem in retrospect. The doomed love affair. The suicide pact. The only way the two of them could be together. Which was, of course, why Rory Turnbull drove himself and his lover to their deaths off the sea-wall at Fethering."

# 40

THE NIGHT WAS still and colder now. A thin moon diffused its watery glow over the snug houses of Fethering, in which, one by one, the lights were being switched off.

The BMW stopped outside the gates that led to the Yacht Club launching ramp and gave access to the seawall. Rory Turnbull calmly got out and opened the lock with his member's key. Back in the car, he said, "I'll close the gates when I leave. On foot. And, I'm sorry to say, alone."

He edged the car forward till it was alongside one of the fishermen's chests. He was eager now and leapt out, leaving the door ajar.

Jude could not see as Rory took out his keys. Nor could she see him insert one into the new padlock he'd substituted for the one sawn off the previous Tuesday night. The padlock opened and he slipped it out of the hasp that held the chest's top down.

As he raised the lid, he caught a foul whiff of decay, but he was too near to his goal to be put off by such a detail. Reaching into the chest, he took a grip on the Fethering Yacht Club life-jacket which was still fixed around the torso of the late Sam Kent.

With sudden strength and in one movement, Rory Turnbull lifted the body out. For a moment he held the putrid flesh against his own body, almost as if it were a lover. Then he laid the body flat on the cement. With both hands, he forced the stiff dead jaws apart. He reached inside his own mouth and removed his dental plate. He fixed it inside the dead man's mouth.

The body had bloated and was bursting out of its clothes, but that did not stop the dentist from starting to remove them. The dead man's clothes would be destroyed and he himself would dress in a spare set he had in the car boot. He had thought it all through. For his plan to work—his precious plan that he had been nurturing for so long—the body when found must be dressed as Rory Turnbull.

"What are you doing, Rory?"

Ted Crisp rose over the side of the sea wall like an avenging fury from the ladder to which he had been clinging. At the same time Carole appeared from the shadows of the Yacht Club. When the landlord had phoned, her curiosity had proved stronger than her exhaustion.

Hearing voices, Jude shouted for help.

"You bastard! I'm not going to be stopped now!"

Rory Turnbull launched himself ferociously at the landlord. The initial impetus caught Ted off balance. For a moment he swayed, about to topple back into the Fether.

But somehow he regained his equilibrium and enfolded the furious dentist in a bear hug. Rory's elbows worked like pistons as he slammed punches into Ted's substantial paunch. The two men weaved around like one crazed four-legged creature on the edge of the sea wall.

Carole meanwhile had freed Jude from the armrests and manoeuvred her out of the BMW to release her other bonds. As soon as her hands were free, Jude threw her arms around her friend. They stood for a moment, instinctively hugging each other. Then Jude reached into the front seat of the car for her mobile phone. "I'm calling the police!" she said.

There was a grunt and the two fighting men were suddenly apart. Rory Turnbull swung a wild haymaker of a punch, which by pure chance caught Ted Crisp on the tip of the chin and sent him flying across the cement.

Freed, the dentist rushed to pick up his precious body. Grasping it under the arms, he dragged it across to the BMW. Carole and Jude watched in amazement as he opened the passenger door and jammed the corpse into its seat. He slammed the door shut and hurried round to the other side.

"You're mad, Rory!" Jude shouted. "You'll never get away with it!"

"Yes, I will!" he shrieked back. "I've got it all planned out! I told you—I've got it all planned out!"

He started the engine and the BMW screeched in reverse back through the Fethering Yacht Club gates. In a howl of tyres he turned it round and shot off fast down the quayside road.

Far too fast. Rory Turnbull misjudged the corner and bounced off a concrete bollard. The BMW spun crazily before smashing into the Second World War mine that was used as a charity collecting box. With the impact, the car burst into flames.

When the wreckage was examined by the police, their first impression was that there were two near-identical bodies in the burnt-out car. In the mouth of one of them was a dental plate which had been specially made for Rory Turnbull.

Detailed post-mortem examination, however, revealed that the body with the dental plate had been dead for at least a week before the crash which killed the dentist.

## 41

"THE IRONICAL THING is," said Ted Crisp, "that because Rory died in a car crash, rather than in an apparent suicide, Barbara will actually benefit from his insurance policies."

"And presumably inherit all that money he'd salted away," said Jude.

"Except," Carole pointed out, "all that money is in accounts that he'd opened using Sam Kent's passport and so probably in Sam Kent's name."

"Does that mean that the Kents'll benefit? That'd be wonderful news. At least they'd get something positive out of the whole ghastly experience."

But Carole threw a wet blanket over Jude's optimism. "No. The accounts would have been set up illegally. I'm sure it'll all go back to Barbara in the end."

Ted Crisp shook his shaggy head. "Whole thing'll take one hell of a lot of sorting out. Still, I should think Barbara and Winnie are ecstatic. They've got shot of Rory and the details of what he was up to will never become public knowledge. Their version of events will become the official version. As Winnie will continue to say to anyone who'll listen, Barbara was just very unlucky in her choice of husband."

Jude picked up the train of thought. "The poor woman worked valiantly to 'make something of him,' but sadly 'you can't make silk purses out of sow's ears.' Barbara and Winnie's image of middle-class gentility will survive untarnished. The high values of the Shorelands Estate will be maintained."

The landlord shuddered. "When I think what that poor bastard Rory must've suffered in that marriage. Being diminished all the time, having every last shred of confidence removed by those two harpies." Another tremor went through him. "Sorry, it's a man thing. You two haven't got the physical equipment to understand what it's like to be systematically emasculated."

"No," Jude agreed softly, "but we can empathize. Anyone who's been in a relationship where one partner blames the other for their own inadequacies knows the kind of pain involved. Strange how it keeps happening. There are enough unpleasant people out there in the world to cut you down to size. What everyone needs at home is someone to support and bolster them."

Carole had got so used to these enigmatic references to Jude's past that she no longer felt a burning urge to ask the instinctive supplementary questions. Well, that is to say, she still felt the urge, but now automatically curbed it.

A week or so had passed since the dramatic events on the sea wall. Carole was wearing her freshly cleaned Burberry. The dry-cleaning, she was delighted to find, had not affected its waterproof qualities at all.

"Have you seen Maggie again, Jude?"

"Yes. I dropped in this afternoon."

"How's she coping?"

Jude grimaced. "It's going to be tough, but she'll come through it."

"Yes."

"And Nick?"

"He's being brilliant, she said. He's a good, bright boy. Whatever else all this has done, it's certainly brought those two closer together."

"Excellent." Carole wondered whether the boy would ever tell his mother the worst part of his nightmare, witnessing the mutilation of what he later found to be his own father's body. Probably not, she thought. But that would be Nick Kent's own decision, and she reckoned that when the time came he'd be mature enough to make it.

Carole considered whether she herself should call on Maggie. No, probably not. Jude was the one with people skills, after all. "And any news been heard of Tanya?"

Jude shook her head. "I haven't heard anything. Ted?"

"Nothing definite. Denis Woodville said he'd tried ringing and got someone else on her number. New tenant. So no idea where she's gone."

They were silent, all wondering whether the poor kid had actually set off to France, to wait for the lover who would never now be coming to join her. They imagined Tanya becoming disillusioned and deciding that no man really cared, whatever they said, whatever they promised, whatever plans they made for you. And then her baby would be bcrn, another child with a single parent, another statistic with limited prospects.

"It'll be tough for Tanya." Jude shook her head sadly. "It's always tough to bring up a kid on your own."

Her sympathy sounded so heartfelt that Carole wondered whether that too came from personal experience. Had Jude been a mother? Carole still knew almost nothing about her neighbor's background. Whenever they got on to personal matters, however much she tried to resist the temptation, Carole always seemed to end up talking about herself.

And there does come a point when you know someone too well to be able to ask about the basic facts of their life. Carole had decided she'd have to set up a dinner party for Jude and a couple of the nosier denizens of Fethering. The village was rich in the expertly curious. Yes, if she invited people who hadn't met the newcomer before, they might be able to winkle out all the details that Carole had so signally failed to uncover. It remained deeply frustrating for her to know so little.

Recognizing that she wasn't going to get any more of Jude's history at that point, Carole moved the conversation on. "What's sad about the whole Rory Turnbull story is that his plan was so preposterous. The chances of it working even first time around were minimal. I'm sure a basic post-mortem would have revealed the burnt-out body wasn't his. And by the time the corpse was a week old, he had no chance of getting away with it."

Jude shook her head grimly. "But by then he was so caught up in his plan that he couldn't let go."

"He'd already committed murder, apart from anything else," said Ted. "He had to go through with it."

"But why go through all that rigmarole? Why on earth didn't he just dump his wife and go off with a younger woman—like thousands of other married men before him?" asked Carole, with the bitterness of experience.

"You underestimate the hold Barbara had on him. I asked him that very question in Tanya's flat and I've never seen a man's face lose colour the way his did. He was literally terrified of his wife."

Another tremor passed through Ted Crisp's body. "Sorry. Man thing again."

They heard the pub door open. Spot on cue, Bill Chilcott appeared. As ever, he was dressed in quasi-nautical style. And there was a smug smile on his root vegetable face. "Evening, mine host."

"Evening, Bill." There was a mumble of greetings from the others. "Your customary half?"

"I thank you kindly. And my customary half-hour away from my other half—from the little woman, that is." Bill Chilcott chuckled, then turned to Jude. "Or is it politically incorrect to make such a remark in the presence of a liberated woman *de nos jours*?"

"I can assure you, it's no more politically incorrect than anything else I've heard you say."

Carole held her breath, but Jude's accompanying sweet smile somehow convinced Bill Chilcott that what she'd said was a compliment. "Oh well, there you go. Of course, I've never spoken a word of criticism of Sandra. She's extremely attractive and highly intelligent—for a woman."

Over Bill's chuckle, Ted passed across the "customary half." "You seem remarkably chipper this evening."

"Yes, well, I do have the satisfaction of having achieved a small victory." He beamed, waiting to be prompted to his revelation.

Carole obliged. "This wouldn't have anything to do

with Denis Woodville, by any chance, would it?"

"As a matter of fact it would. A small matter of trespass. I have warned the old fool often enough. He can't claim to be surprised by what's happened."

"So what did happen?" Carole asked dutifully.

"You know he's had that wretched dinghy cluttering up his front garden for months?"

"Yes."

"Apparently he's trying to sell it now. Fallen on hard times, I'm afraid, our Mr. Woodville. Insufficient pension arrangements." The complacency with which this was said left no doubt that Bill and Sandra Chilcott's pension arrangements were immaculate. "Can't even afford to pay for the boat's space at the Yacht Club. That's rather funny, isn't it? Calls himself Vice-Commodore and puts on airs and excludes perfectly qualified yachtsmen from Fethering Yacht Club membership"—he spluttered at the recollection, but quickly recovered himself—"and yet he can't afford even to keep his own boat there."

"So what happened?" asked Carole, keen to cut through the gloating to the facts.

"Someone came to see the dinghy this afternoon with a view to buying it and, in the course of the potential purchaser's inspection, the boat got moved around a bit." Bill Chilcott snickered in anticipation of his pay-off. "In fact, it was left with six inches of the mast projecting over the hedge into our garden. Which, as I have made clear to Mr. Woodville on numerous occasions, constitutes an act of trespass. Well, you'll never guess what I did . . ."

No one gave him the satisfaction of a response, so he had to deliver his punchline unprompted. "I got a hacksaw . . . and I cut off the offending six inches of mast!" He looked round for response. "Then I threw the offcut into Mr. Woodville's front garden. Result—end of trespass!"

He rubbed his hands together gleefully and burst out laughing at the extent of his own cleverness. As he laughed and laughed, his tuber face took on the aspect of a white-rooted beetroot.

Carole, Jude and Ted Crisp didn't share the joke. They exchanged looks, and all their thoughts went along the front to the Fethering Yacht Club. There they imagined the plotting of revenge by the Vice-Commodore and his band of cronies. Wartime parallels would be being drawn, cunning deeds of sabotage recalled to provide the means for Denis Woodville to get his own back. And no doubt someone would be recalling a similar incident that happened while he was stationed out in Singapore.

The feud between Bill Chilcott and the Vice-Commodore would go on until one or other of them died, and even then the badmouthing would continue until all three—including Sandra—were dead. The two old men's cooperation to save Nick Kent might never have happened.

The old ways of Fethering had reasserted themselves. As they always did. As they always would. Senior citizens would continue to weave their strange square dance around the pillars of Allinstore. Bill Chilcott would appear in the Crown and Anchor at the same moment every evening for his "customary half." And in the Fethering Yacht Club the Vice-Commodore and his cronies would detail how much better a place the world would be if only they were in charge of it.

And Dylan, or someone like him, would be there as

a hazard to the young people of the area. And peer pressure and consumerism would work their evil, and most of the young would survive them, and develop into adults no worse and no better than the current residents of Fethering.

But there'd be a few casualties. Like Aaron Spalding. And Sam Kent.

And Rory Turnbull. A dreamer, consumed—literally—by the fantasy that he could change everything in his life by one final throw of the dice.

For the remainder of his customary half-hour in the Crown and Anchor that evening, Bill Chilcott continued to recapture details of his triumph, unaware of, or unworried by, the lack of response from those around him. Then, having rationed his half-pint by the minutest calibrations of sips, he looked at his watch. "Still, better go back to the little woman. Time, tide and Sandra wait for no man, eh?" He chortled. "So . . . cheerio, ladies. And cheerio, mine host."

"Good night," Ted Crisp called out to the closing door, adding without enthusiasm, "See you tomorrow."

"God," said Carole, "it's so petty. Why don't they just stop the whole feud?"

"Because they enjoy it," replied Jude. "Only thing that keeps them alive—well, together with the line-dancing and the swimming in the Chilcotts' case."

"Yes, you're probably right. Depressing, isn't it?"

A melancholy had settled on them. Ted Crisp tried to break it with forced geniality. "Hold it right there—as the bishop said to the actress. What we all need is another drink. What d'you reckon? Landlord's treat again."

"Really?" Jude grinned. "You know, you always say that as if it's rarer than a total eclipse of the sun. And yet you keep on doing it. You keep on buying us drinks. Your trouble, Ted, is that beneath that gruff exterior, you're a total pussycat."

He looked at her belligerently. "If you wasn't a woman, you wouldn't get away with saying that. Now do you want this bloody drink or not?"

"Oh, certainly. I'll seize the moment while it lasts. Large white wine, please."

"Carole?"

She looked at her watch. "No, thanks, Ted. Better get back. I'm expecting a phone call."

"If you're not there, they'll call back some other time, won't they?" As Carole rose from her seat, Jude grinned one of her big, easy grins.

Carole was torn. There was no phone call she was expecting. All that lay ahead of her was an evening watching television with Gulliver. She knew there'd be nothing much on. Nothing of any interest apart from the news, really. And that was becoming less interesting, as world powers mired themselves ever deeper in crises they did not understand and could not solve.

"Come on, Carole. Like I said, landlord's treat. Large white wine, isn't it?"

"Oh, very well, Ted." She sank back into her seat. "Thank you very much."

Of course, Carole Seddon would never be a natural "pub person," but it didn't do any harm to behave against character . . . just once in a while.